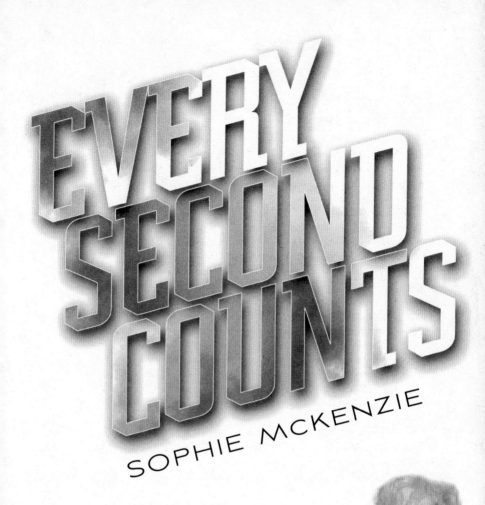

EVERY SECOND COUNTS

SOPHIE MCKENZIE

SIMON & SCHUSTER BFYR

New York   London   Toronto   Sydney   New Delhi

SIMON & SCHUSTER BFYR

An imprint of Simon & Schuster Children's Publishing Division

1230 Avenue of the Americas, New York, New York 10020

Text copyright © 2014 by Rosefire Limited

Jacket photograph of boy and girl copyright © 2016 by Ragnar Schmuck / fstop / Corbis

All other jacket photographs © 2016 by Thinkstock

Originally published in Great Britain in 2014 by Simon and Schuster UK Ltd.

First US edition 2016

For information about special discounts for bulk purchases, please contact Simon & Schuster Special Sales at 1-866-506-1949 or business@simonandschuster.com.

The Simon & Schuster Speakers Bureau can bring authors to your live event. For more information or to book an event, contact the Simon & Schuster Speakers Bureau at 1-866-248-3049 or visit our website at www.simonspeakers.com.

Book design by Tom Daly

Jacket design by Lauren Linn

The text for this book was set in Weiss Std.

Manufactured in the United States of America

10 9 8 7 6 5 4 3 2 1

Library of Congress Cataloging-in-Publication Data

McKenzie, Sophie.

Every second counts / Sophie McKenzie.—First edition.

pages cm

"First published in Great Britain in 2014 by Simon and Schuster UK Ltd."

Sequel to: In a split second.

Summary: Follows two teenagers as they try to bring down the politician who has framed them as terrorists.

ISBN 978-1-4814-3926-8 (hardcover)—ISBN 978-1-4814-3928-2 (eBook)

[1. Terrorism—Fiction. 2. Deception—Fiction. 3. Undercover operations—Fiction. 4. Orphans—Fiction. 5. London (England)—Fiction. 6. England—Fiction.] I. Title.

PZ7.M47867617Ev 2016

[Fic]—dc23

2014029228

For my godchildren: Freddie, Cliona, and Alex

Thank you to Lou Kuenzler, Moira Young, Gaby Halberstam, Melanie Edge, and Julie Mackenzie.

England is in the grip of a recession, and extremist groups are on the rise. After a bomb last year devastated both their families, Charlie and Nat were recruited into the secret English Freedom Army (EFA) as part of an active cell designed to take a stand against terrorism.

Since then they have learned that the EFA is a terrorist organization itself. Secretly led by the charismatic politician Roman Riley, the EFA's real aim is to commit acts of violence and blame others for causing them, thus encouraging the general public to believe the current government is not in control—and to turn to Riley's Future Party for a political solution to the chaos.

Riley—through cell leader Taylor—has recently conned Nat and Charlie into taking part in kidnapping and terrorism, and they are now on the run from both the EFA and the police.

PART ONE

EXCOMMUNICATION
(n. rejection by means of act of
banishing or denouncing someone)

NAT

I held up my hand to show Charlie she needed to wait. She gave me a swift nod. I moved, silently, across the grass. The safe house we were heading for was an apartment in an abandoned building set apart from the rest of the road.

I crossed the wasteland, feeling exposed. It was early evening on a warm spring day and still light. Anyone looking out of the concrete apartment building would have seen me, but as far as I could make out, no one was looking. I reached the cover of a single tree and ducked behind it. I glanced over at where Charlie was waiting a few yards away, on the opposite side of the wasteland. She was dressed, like I was, in jeans and a T-shirt. We'd left our large, bulky packs behind a nearby garbage can and probably looked like a couple of teenagers on their way to meet their friends.

Nothing could be further from the truth.

Charlie met my gaze. Even at this distance I could see the focus and intensity in her dark, slanting eyes. She had cropped her long, curly hair close to her skull, hoping to be less recognizable on the run. It wasn't the prettiest of styles, but it made Charlie's face more beautiful than ever.

At least I thought so.

There was nothing now between me, still hiding behind my tree, and the building over the road. I glanced up and down. Nobody was around. It was time to make our move. I pointed at the first-floor apartment and Charlie gave another nod. She was ready. I ran, reaching the building in three long strides, and ducked down beside the wall. Charlie crouched low on the other side of the front door. She signaled she was going to take a look inside. I nodded, then inched my way to the edge of my own window, ready to risk peering in.

This was the third safe house we'd attempted to access—both the others had been empty. It was also the last on our list. If we didn't find people from the resistance inside, I had no idea what we would do.

I crawled into position, steadying myself, ready to stand up and look in through the window. I was about to move when Charlie let out a muffled squeak. As I spun around, a hand grabbed my arm. I opened my mouth to yell, but a cloth bag was shoved over my head, then pressed tightly over my lips. I gasped for breath, trying to pull my arm free, lashing out at whoever was holding me.

A second later my legs were kicked from under me. I fell to the concrete, yelping with pain.

"Charlie?" I gasped. Fear consumed me. Over the past few weeks our focus had been on survival, not feelings. But mine were still as strong as ever.

"I'm here." Charlie sounded strong. I straightened up. I couldn't tell if she was able to see me or not, but if she was, I didn't want her last memory of me to be me cowering like a baby.

"Keep still and shut up," a voice ordered.

The point of a knife pierced through my T-shirt, a sharp pain against my ribs.

CHARLIE

I tried to punch and kick, but the hands holding me down were too strong. Fury boiled up inside me, but the cloth bag over my head was pressed tightly against my mouth, and all that came out was a muffled yell.

"Calm down," snarled a male voice.

Where was Nat? Was he okay? How could this have happened? Nat and I were always so careful—after a month on the run, we had learned how to slip in and out of the derelict houses where we took shelter without drawing attention to ourselves. And yet we'd been captured approaching this safe house as if we were a couple of idiots with no combat or stealth training whatsoever.

Nat yelled out, a single pain-filled cry. Then silence.

Was he all right? The idea that he might be hurt—or worse—sent ice through my blood. Still pressing the cloth bag against my mouth, the man holding me propelled me inside the house. Our footsteps pattered across the tiled floor. I couldn't hear anyone else. Where was Nat?

Through another door. The air was cooler here. I was shoved into a chair. I tried to get up, but rough hands pushed me down.

"Stay still or I'll cut you," the man hissed.

I froze. A second later my hands were forced together in my lap and bound with tape. I kept very still, trying to conserve my energy and listening hard for signs that Nat was nearby. I could hear nothing. I forced myself to focus. I needed to channel all my efforts into getting Nat and myself free.

"Right." The cloth bag was yanked off my head, and a bright light shone in my eyes.

I blinked, turning my face away from the glare. I was in a small room with twin beds and a chest of drawers.

"Look at me," the man demanded. The light lowered and I looked up. A young guy—not much older than I was—stood in front of me. He had fine, fair hair and delicate features. Despite the hard edge to his voice, I could see in his eyes that he was terrified. I remembered something Taylor, my old EFA trainer, had once said: *A big part of success in any fight lies in the ability to use your opponent's weaknesses against them. Assess, plan, act.*

He might have lied to us and used us, but Taylor had been right about that. The knowledge that my captor was scared gave me a huge advantage. I stared into his eyes, my courage building.

"What are you doing here?" the man snapped, but now that I was watching him, I could hear the slight quiver in his voice. Suddenly, I was certain I could disarm him. I just needed to get rid of the tape around my wrists. Keeping my eyes fixed on his, I felt for the edge of the tape. *There.*

"Answer me." The man held up the knife. But his hands were shaking.

"No." As I spoke, I ripped the tape off my wrists and lunged for his arm. With a single blow, I knocked the knife out of his hand. It clattered to the floor.

I raced over and snatched it up. Then I spun around and held the knife toward him.

The man stared at me, his mouth gaping. I met his gaze.

"Where's the boy I was with?" I demanded. "Is he all right?"

The man held up his hands. I could see in his eyes he believed I would use the knife. "He's fine. He's with Julius."

I pointed to the door. "Take me to him," I demanded. "*Now.*"

NAT

The bag was pulled off my head and I was pushed backward against the sofa behind me. I sat down with a jolt. I was in a living room: sofas, TV, chipped wooden sideboard. The man who had shoved me in here looked nothing like I'd expected. For a start, he was young—but bald and wearing a suit and glasses. His manner was meek, almost apologetic, as he sat down on the couch across from me, his weapon in his hand.

"You're Nat Holloway and the girl is Charlie Stockwell, aren't you?" he asked, laying the blade on the seat beside him. I glanced at it. It wasn't a knife after all—just a vegetable peeler. "What are you doing here? Does Riley know we're here?"

I stared at him. Man, he was scared. *Really* scared.

"Please, Nat," the man went on. "Lennox and I need to know."

"Is Lennox the guy with Charlie?" I demanded, rising to my feet. "Is she okay?"

"She'll be fine," the man said. "Lennox won't hurt her. Uh, I'm Julius Prebert. We just need to know why you're here."

Whoever this guy was, he was definitely no solider. I knew from my training with Taylor that the art of interrogation lay in trying not to give away too much with your questions and that the art of intimidation lay in being hard and unemotional. This man was failing on both counts. Which gave me the edge. I was pretty sure I was physically stronger than him too. But hopefully this wouldn't come to a fight. I headed for the door, determined to find Charlie.

"Wait, Nat."

"You're in the resistance, aren't you?" I asked.

Julius nodded. "Parveen Patel told you about us, didn't she?"

Before I could respond, the door flew open. A second man—Lennox, presumably—stumbled inside, closely followed by Charlie, her eyes blazing. She was wielding a knife. She must have taken it off Lennox.

Julius gasped in horror. He sprang to his feet.

"Are you okay?" Charlie and I spoke together.

"I'm fine," I said.

She gave a swift nod. "Me too."

"Please don't hurt us," Julius stammered.

"Shut up, Julius," Lennox snapped.

I assessed Lennox quickly. He was younger than the bald guy, barely older than Charlie and me, and much tougher-looking. But under the bravado I could see he was trembling too.

I held up my hands. "Nobody's going to get hurt. We just want to talk." I glanced at Charlie. Reluctantly, she lowered the knife. "Julius and Lennox are in the resistance," I said to her. "They're the people we've been looking for—the ones Parveen told us about."

As I said Parveen's name, Julius and Lennox glanced at each

other. Julius had mentioned her earlier too. I frowned. If Par had told them about us, why were they so suspicious?

"Why did you attack us?" Charlie demanded, vocalizing my thoughts. She advanced on Julius. "If you're in the resistance against Riley, why did you put bags over our heads and force us inside?"

"Because we thought you might be Riley's spies," Julius said quickly, his voice quivering.

"They *are* Riley's spies," Lennox snapped. "*She* kidnapped the mayor of London's son. And *he* set off a bomb at the Houses of Parliament. They did that for that scum Riley."

"No," I said. "You've got this all wrong. We were *set up* by Riley. He conned us into joining the English Freedom Army, which he said only existed to stop terrorists, and then he manipulated us into becoming terrorists. I didn't know I was carrying a bomb under Parliament, and Charlie was ordered to kidnap Aaron Latimer."

"That's right," Charlie added. "I thought I was protecting Aaron."

"The bottom line," I said, trying to keep my voice even, "is that Parveen trusted us enough to give us this address, so you should trust us too." I pointed to the window. "We're here alone and unarmed. Is that really how Riley would have dealt with you if he knew you were here?"

Julius nodded. I could see he was persuaded, but Lennox still looked suspicious.

"This could be a double bluff," he argued. "You could both secretly be working for Riley."

"No, don't you get it?" Charlie snapped. "Riley was behind the Canal Street Market bomb that killed my mother." For a split second, her eyes filled with tears. She blinked them away angrily. "The same bomb left Nat's brother in a coma. There's no way we would do *anything* for that man."

"You mentioned Parveen Patel earlier," I said. "She obviously told you about us, just like she told us about you. She gave us the addresses of three safe houses a couple of weeks ago. We've been working our way through them, looking for the resistance, ever since. Surely it isn't a surprise that we're here?"

There was a long pause, and then Julius sighed. "It isn't," he said.

"Then why all the noise?" Charlie demanded.

"Because," Lennox snapped, "Parveen has disappeared."

CHARLIE

Nat and I stared at each other. Parveen had disappeared? *How?* Had Riley captured her? Killed her? I could see the pain in Nat's ice-blue eyes. Even in that terrible moment, I couldn't help but notice how good-looking he was. I loved the strong lines of his face and the way you could never be quite sure what he was thinking, that guarded expression he always wore.

I turned to Julius and Lennox. "So when did you last hear from Parveen?" I asked.

The two men looked at each other. Lennox gave a gruff nod. "Go ahead," he said. "If you really think we can trust them."

"We saw her in London just over two weeks ago. She said you'd contacted her and that she'd given you some safe-house addresses. She hasn't been in touch since. We have a system of checking in for everybody. A weekly signal."

"You mean using the draft e-mail system?" I asked. This was a clever trick we'd learned from the EFA, a way of communicating online without leaving a trail. Basically, you logged on to an e-mail account and left a message in the draft box for the next person to log in and read.

"Yes. Parveen hasn't checked in by draft e-mail since that last message." Julius paused. "You can see why we were suspicious before, can't you?"

"Yes," Nat said.

"Mmm." I pursed my lips, unwilling to forgive them. "There was still no need to threaten us."

"They were just doing what they needed to protect themselves," Nat said.

Feeling disgruntled, I shrugged.

"So how many of you are there in the resistance?" I asked.

Julius frowned. "As far as I know, there are fifteen Resistance Pairs. Parveen was put with the guy from Resistance Two."

"*Pairs?*" Nat frowned.

"Yes. We travel in twos, keeping numbers down for safety," Julius explained. "Lennox and I are Resistance Nine. So far I've met the people in Resistance Four, Six, and Eight, but I know the others only through draft e-mails. We move around using the list of safe houses Parveen sent you. That is, there are more houses, but we don't all have access to all of them. Sometimes we run into other pairs. Most of the time we're on the move, trying to avoid being caught, just like you."

My heart sank. When Parveen had mentioned there being a resistance group in her original message, I'd imagined a real army of people, not a few random pairs scattered across a bunch of run-down safe houses, intent on simply surviving.

If this was all the resistance amounted to, we had no hope of exposing and defeating Riley.

NAT

"So I get the 'pairs' bit," Charlie said dryly. "But where does the 'resistance' come in? It sounds like you just roam about the country, trying to stay out of trouble. How is that going to bring down Roman Riley?"

Julius's face flushed red. "It's hard," he said. "We're operating in total isolation—the police are in Riley's pocket."

"We know. Look, is there any kind of plan?" I asked, trying to sound less scathing than Charlie just had.

"We're doing everything we can," Lennox said defensively. "Mostly we're trying to build up evidence to prove Riley is conning the electorate and that he has some kind of hold over the leaders of the League of Iron so they're prepared to say *they* are the terrorists."

"And how are you doing all that?" Charlie sounded even more contemptuous than before. "Riley has a lot of protection, and he's very smart."

I shot her a warning look, but she avoided my gaze.

"We're working on hacking into his computer network, and we've tried to steal information too." Julius looked away. "We've lost five good people in the past six months, plus whatever's happened to Parveen. It hasn't been easy, but the mayor of London is with us, and however long it takes—"

"Whoa. Back up," Charlie said.

"Yeah." I frowned. "You're saying Mayor Latimer is on our side? Part of the resistance?"

"Yes," Julius said. "Absolutely."

I shook my head. That didn't make sense at all. When Charlie and I had escaped from Riley last month, we had also rescued Mayor Latimer's son, Aaron. And yet, despite this, neither Aaron nor his father had spoken out in our defense afterward, letting the police and the public continue thinking we were dangerous terrorists, even though they both knew Riley had set us up.

"You can't trust Mayor Latimer," Charlie said firmly.

"We're just telling you what we've heard from a couple of the London-based Pairs," Lennox snapped. "They say Latimer has just supplied the resistance with some new gear—tracking and surveillance equipment, a few Tasers."

"Of course, none of it's come our way yet," Julius added. "We don't have any IT, and that"—he pointed to the knife Charlie had taken from Lennox—"that's our only real weapon."

"Right." I nodded. It sounded worse and worse. A known ally of Riley's infiltrating the resistance and no real way of fighting back.

"Well, your setup seems really amateurish to me," Charlie said with a sniff.

I threw her another warning glance. Why did she have to

be so antagonistic? She was right, though. Quite apart from the lack of weapons, it was obvious from the way Julius was talking that neither he nor Lennox had any combat experience, whereas Charlie and I had been trained by one of Riley's best operatives, Taylor, to fight hard, move stealthily—and even handle guns.

"Who's your leader?" I asked.

"We don't have one," Julius admitted. He looked embarrassed. "We're more of a cooperative—sharing information, letting everyone else know we're okay or if there's danger somewhere."

Charlie snorted. Exasperated, I turned on her. "Let's just find out a bit more before we start judging them, okay?"

Charlie shot me a furious look, which faded as I glared at her. After a moment she gave an awkward shrug. "Sorry. I'm just upset that there isn't more of a real organization working against Riley."

"I know." I turned back to Julius. "How come you're both in the resistance?"

"I was a lawyer, in my first job," Julius explained. "Eight months ago I was helping in a case to take Riley to court. My boss died in what was supposedly an accident, and then someone planted evidence that made it look like I'd stolen money from my law firm to give to a woman I'd met precisely once. They made it look like I was bribing her. I said it was all a setup, but the company fired me anyway, so I lost my apartment and my girlfriend." He sighed. "Riley's taken my whole life away."

I turned to Lennox. "What about you?"

"I worked for a car manufacturer, got involved in the trade union there. A friend of mine found out what the English Freedom

Army was really up to. He told the police. They weren't interested. So he told me, and I tried to take it to my union. The next thing I know, my friend's dead and I'm being threatened to keep quiet. So I continue trying to expose the EFA, and all of a sudden there's a warrant out for my arrest for being dangerous—a potential terrorist just like you two."

I nodded, taking this in. "Okay," I said slowly. "Everything you're trying to do is good, but we need to do more and do it faster. We *have* to bring down Riley before the election. That way we all can get our lives back."

"But the election is next week," Julius spluttered.

"Basically, we need to expose him as a murderer," Charlie said. "We need to prove that he set me and Nat up and get evidence on what he's planning next."

Julius and Lennox stared at us, openmouthed.

"Getting proof against him is the only way he'll be forced to resign from power," I added. "We still live in a democracy. If we can convince the public how corrupt he is, they won't vote for him or his party at the election next week."

"That's some time frame," Lennox said with a sneer.

"I know," I said. "But we have to try. The next few days are crucial. I've been looking at the polls. Riley's Future Party is set to do really well in the election—maybe even well enough to form a government. Riley could control the country as early as next week."

"I just don't see what we can do. Riley's set everyone against us," Julius said. "He discredits all his enemies so that people think *we're* the bad guys. Look at that film you and Charlie posted on YouTube and how he twisted everything you said."

This was true. Riley had responded to our attempt to clear our names by saying we were lying and desperate.

"We have to find another way," I insisted. "Talking about him isn't enough. We need to get actual proof and use it."

"We could assassinate him," Lennox suggested. "Get close with a gun or a knife. I'd do it."

I shook my head. "Too risky. You wouldn't get near him."

"Anyway, killing him would make us as bad as he is," Julius added.

I looked over at Charlie. She was still standing a little away from us, arms folded. She rolled her eyes, presumably at Julius's reluctance to take Riley out.

I met her gaze. For all her bravado, Charlie wasn't any more a killer than Julius. Just a few weeks ago she had a gun in her hand and Riley unarmed in her sights and she hadn't taken the shot. Neither had I. I'd told her we'd done the right thing, but Charlie hadn't wanted to talk about it.

A flicker of embarrassment—and vulnerability—showed on her face, then disappeared again. She knew what I was thinking. I raised my eyebrows. "Any suggestions for how we expose Riley?"

Julius and Lennox turned to her. A beat passed. And then Charlie jutted out her chin in that defiant gesture of hers I was beginning to know so well.

"I think it's obvious," she said. "I should join Riley's inner circle, like he wanted me to when we last saw him."

There was a shocked silence.

"You mean pretend to switch sides?" I shook my head.

"Exactly," Charlie said. "I can get close, get evidence of what he's planning, the next bomb or whatever."

"No way." My heart rate quickened. It was true that Riley had claimed to want to bring Charlie into his inner circle, but to me that was obviously a lie, a bold-faced attempt to try to stop her from running away. Anyway, I couldn't begin to imagine the danger Charlie would put herself in if she voluntarily turned up on Riley's doorstep. "Riley's not going to believe you joining him now," I went on. "It's too risky."

"I can make him believe it. Anyway, it's not up to you, Nat." Her fierce dark eyes met mine at last. "It's *my* decision."

CHARLIE

Nat stared at me. I could see the emotions parading across his face: he was annoyed with me for being impatient with Julius and Lennox and angry that I wanted to put myself at risk by going undercover with Riley.

Was that because he was scared I would get hurt? On our first night on the run we'd admitted how much we really liked each other, but since then we had barely spoken about our feelings. There had been so many other things to deal with; life in the past few weeks had been unbelievably stressful: finding food and sleeping rough, always worried that if Riley's English Freedom Army soldiers didn't find us, some random tramp would attack us in our makeshift beds.

The tension in the room grew. Nat and I were still looking at each other. And then Julius coughed. "Um, why does Riley want you to join him?"

"That's my business," I snapped.

I shot Nat a look that meant I seriously wanted him to keep his mouth shut. The truth of it was that Riley had told me my dad—who I thought had died when I was a baby—was in fact alive and a leading figure in the English Freedom Army. I was sure it was a total lie. Well, almost sure. Either way, it was not information I wanted spread about.

Nat gave me a swift nod, then turned to Julius.

"We can talk about this later. Right now we're kind of tired. And very hungry," he said. "Do you have any food?"

"Of course." Julius led us out of the little bedroom and into a small kitchen. He bustled about, fetching us bread and warming some soup while Nat and I retrieved our backpacks from their hiding place and brought them into the house. Lennox sat at the table with us while we ate our soup, and the four of us swapped all the details we knew about Riley. Julius hadn't been exaggerating his lack of knowledge about the other resistance members, but he told us what he could about the people in Resistance Four, Six, and Eight. All of them had been made scapegoats by Riley and many were also wanted by the police.

I could see Nat getting more and more dispirited as we talked. I was sure he had been hoping that if the resistance could operate as a fighting unit, there might be some alternative to my going undercover—and that he would be able to talk me out of my plan. As the light completely faded outside, Lennox disappeared again, returning half an hour later with four bags of fish and chips. I fell on the food, and so did Nat. After we'd eaten, Julius explained that they would have to move on the day after tomorrow, that they never stayed anywhere more than a week so as not to attract attention, and that Nat and I would need to find our own accommodation after that point.

"Four is just too many. People notice a larger group," he said nervously.

"Plus I don't like you," Lennox added rudely. His remark was directed mainly at me, though he glanced in Nat's direction too.

I opened my mouth to tell him I hadn't formed a great opinion of him either, but Nat laid his hand on mine.

"That's fine," he said. "We can sort out the details tomorrow."

I closed my mouth as Julius got up.

"There's only one bedroom here," he said. "I'll bunk in with Lennox for tonight. You two can have the living room, though, um . . . we don't have any spare blankets."

"That's okay." Nat explained that we carried everything we needed in our backpacks.

An hour later we had washed and changed. I felt better than I had for days. It had been great to take a shower, even though the only water in the house was freezing cold. And now we were lying on the sofas in the living area. Ratty and lumpy, they weren't exactly luxurious, but after so many nights sleeping outside, it felt good to be indoors, away from the elements and on something softer than the ground.

Nat hadn't mentioned my plan to infiltrate Riley's group since I'd brought up the idea earlier, but now he said softly, "I don't want you to go undercover. It will be hard enough convincing Riley you want to join him, but even harder getting proof about his plans. You know how careful and how ruthless he is."

I lay back on the sofa. "I'll tell him I need to know about my dad, you know, that I need to find out if he really is alive like he said," I whispered.

There was a pause. Nat's eyes gleamed in the streetlight that shone in through the gap in the curtains.

"You know he isn't alive, don't you, Charlie?" he said softly. "Riley was lying about that."

I turned away. Nat was probably right, but doubt still wriggled away inside me. After my mum died, I'd gone to live with her sister, Karen, but that hadn't worked out, so I'd moved in with my dad's brother, Uncle Brian, his wife, and my cousin, Rosa. I had tried to fit in with them, but they'd never truly felt like family, and I hadn't been surprised when they'd disowned me after I'd been conned into kidnapping Aaron. Apart from Nat, I was alone. Which made it utterly impossible to ignore the idea that my dad might be out there somewhere. The thought of it twisted my stomach into a tight, painful knot. Not that I was going to admit that to Nat.

"The point is that Riley will *believe* I need to know the truth," I whispered.

"And then what?"

"I'll find some way of getting evidence about Riley's next move," I said. "He wants me to join their inner circle, remember?"

"He *says* he does, but it won't be that straightforward," Nat insisted. "They won't trust that you genuinely want to join them. And Riley's not an easy person to lie to."

I said nothing, just stared up at the ceiling.

Nat yawned. "Look, it's late and I'm too tired to deal with you being fixated on this idea right now," he said. "Can we talk about it in the morning?"

"Sure." I pressed my lips together. How dare Nat say I was "fixated?" I turned and glared at him, but he had already closed his eyes.

I watched as he fell asleep. I knew Nat hadn't meant to upset me, but I had just as much right to make a plan to expose Riley as he did. And my plan was certainly a lot better and stronger than anything the so-called resistance had come up with so far.

I sat up, my heart thumping.

I was going to leave now.

No way was I hanging around until morning to have Nat telling me my idea was stupid, Julius muttering nervously that I'd be killed carrying it out, or Lennox saying that he didn't care if I was.

I wriggled out of my sleeping bag and picked up my shoes. I didn't need much, just my share of our money and a few basics.

It was late, but I knew from our experiences over the past few weeks that nighttime offered the most cover for travel. And, anyway, once I'd made up my mind about anything, I hated waiting. I glanced at Nat again. His breath was deep and even. I slid my phone into my pocket. I'd send him a text when I was really on my way.

A minute later I had slipped out the front door and closed it silently behind me. I was going to find Roman Riley and get the proof we needed to bring him down once and for all.

NAT

I woke with a start, my eyes springing open. I blinked into the glare of the bright sunlight streaming in through the narrow gap between the curtains. Too harsh. I shut my eyes again. In the distance I could hear the clink of mugs and plates being set down on a table, a kettle boiling. For a few moments I was back at home with Mum and Dad and Jas and Lucas—back in a time long before I'd ever heard of the English Freedom Army, before the bomb blast that had killed Charlie's mum and left Lucas in a coma, when we were a real family full of joking and teasing and all the normal work and school routines of family life.

A second later reality flooded back. Family life didn't exist anymore. I was an outlaw, unable to return home. Right now, instead of studying for my exams, I was on the run, sleeping rough, hoping to find some way of bringing down Roman Riley through contact with Julius and Lennox, the oddball pairing of Resistance Nine. I had no plan and limited resources.

But I had Charlie. At the thought of her I turned my head and, shielding my eyes from the sharp sunlight, peered at the sofa across from me. There was no sign of her, though her sleeping bag was lying, rumpled, on the sofa. Presumably she was in the kitchen with Julius and Lennox or, possibly, taking a shower. The water here was cold and she had showered only last night, but I knew from our four weeks together on the road that Charlie tended to prioritize washing—whatever the circumstances—in a way that reminded me forcefully of Jas. Was that a girl thing, wanting so badly to be clean all the time? Or was it just the two of them?

I ran my fingers through my hair, smoothing it back, then scrambled out of my sleeping bag. It was a beautiful day outside— a clear blue sky. I checked the time. Nine a.m. Wow. I hadn't slept that late in ages. As I stumbled sleepily toward the kitchen, I could hear Julius and Lennox talking in low voices. The smell of toast wafted toward me. My stomach rumbled; I was starving.

As I walked into the kitchen, Julius turned toward me, a worried frown on his face.

"Morning," he said.

"Yeah." I rubbed my forehead. "Any chance of some toast?"

"Help yourself," Lennox grunted, indicating the toaster.

I wandered over to the counter. The kitchen was pretty basic, but after eating in parks and under bus shelters for much of the past month, it felt luxurious to take a slice of bread and pop it into a toaster.

"Where's Charlie?" I asked, stifling a yawn.

Julius looked up. "Isn't she with you?" he said, a tense edge to his voice.

I spun around, all thoughts of toast forgotten. "What do you mean?"

"She's not in the rest of the apartment." Julius frowned. "I hope she hasn't gone outside. It's risky to wander—"

I didn't hear any more. I was already back in the living room, feeling in my jacket pocket for my phone. I'd switched it to silent last night. My fingers trembled as I pulled it out. If Charlie had gone to the shops or something, she would surely have left a message, wouldn't she?

Yes. Relief swamped me as I opened her text. And then my mouth fell open as I read what it said.

CHARLIE

I stood by the side of the road, waiting for the next car to pass. I had decided to hitch a ride to the nearest city, Manchester, in order to save as much of my money as I could. Despite the dust and the debris from an abandoned construction project, which scattered the asphalt, it felt good to be outside in the sunshine. Good, also, to be traveling light, with just a single change of clothes, my money, and a few toiletries. I was glad not to be weighed down with sweaters and a sleeping bag—and, if I was honest, glad to be free of Nat's attempts to protect me. I knew he only wanted me to be safe, but what I was doing now was the right move.

I was heading for Riley's home in London. I had been there last year when Taylor, our EFA cell leader, had made Nat and me break into the house as a test of our abilities. He had told us the place was owned by a leading League of Iron member and that our mission was to download information from his computer about the League's next planned attack. I still burned with shame and fury when I thought of how we'd been conned into thinking the League was behind all the bombings that Riley had, in fact, organized himself.

My phone rang. *Nat calling.*

I rejected the call. Nat just wanted to try to talk me out of my plan to approach Riley and infiltrate his inner circle, and I didn't want to hear it. I needed all my energy to focus on my mission. Anyway, the less Nat knew about what I was planning, the better. After manipulating us into carrying out his terrorist activities, Riley had tried to kill Nat.

I shivered, thinking how close he had come to losing his life, how close I had come to losing him.

A moment later Nat called again. I shook my head as I rejected this second call. I had been totally right to go off on my own. If Nat couldn't have talked me out of going to find Riley, he would have insisted on coming with me—and Riley would have had no hesitation, I was sure, in trying to murder him again.

My phone beeped. Now Nat had sent a text. It was brief and to the point.

This is crazy, Charlie. Come back.

I switched off my cell phone. There was no point talking. Now was the time for action.

NAT

As the next half hour wore on, I went through every emotion from terror to fury and back again. How could Charlie be so stupid as to race off to Riley without at least talking it through first?

Her text had been sent in the middle of the night, so there was no way I could catch her, even if I'd known what route she was taking to Riley's house in London. She was probably halfway there already. I spent at least fifteen minutes ranting at Julius, explaining what Riley had said about Charlie's father. I knew that was breaking my promise to her, but after she hadn't returned my calls and had switched off her phone, I didn't feel she deserved me keeping my word on that. Julius looked thoughtful as I explained everything.

"What Charlie has been told about her father puts what she's doing in a different light," he said slowly.

"How?"

"Well, it's understandable she'd want to know about her dad. Riley will believe that."

"It's still insanely risky to run off to him without working out exactly what she's doing. Riley's smart—he'll know if she's faking anything. She should have talked it through first."

"Some people prefer to act on instinct and intuition—in the moment, as it were." Julius tilted his head to one side. "Are you sure what you're mad about isn't that Charlie didn't talk her plans through with *you?*"

"No," I snapped. "Of course not." I stood and paced up and down the room.

Julius said nothing further and, a few minutes later, Lennox came in and reminded us that we had to leave here tomorrow and that he and Julius needed to scour the apartment to make sure they weren't leaving any obvious clues to their identities behind.

I rested my head in my hands. Would Charlie manage to convince Riley she genuinely wanted to join him? What would happen if he didn't believe her? Come to that, what would happen if Charlie tried to return to the safe house and found we were no longer here?

She won't come back, I told myself. *She's going to join Riley or die trying. You know how stubborn she is.*

Julius and Lennox started debating which safe house to move on to next. I paid them little attention. I wasn't going to another safe house. I was going to find Charlie and get her away from Riley if it was the last thing I did.

CHARLIE

It took me most of the day to find Riley's house in North West London. The woman who had given me a ride to Manchester had dropped me close to the bus station, and as I scurried along the last few streets, past all the boarded-up stores and houses, I was careful to wear my large, shapeless hoodie and to keep the hood pulled low and my head bent away from all the CCTV cameras. I caught a bus at eleven a.m. and arrived in London just after four in the afternoon. It was strange being back in the city, knowing that Rosa, Jas, Aaron, and my other friends would soon return to school for the summer semester, intent on exams, while Nat and I traveled around the country, intent on clearing our names and exposing Riley.

I checked online and found that the number 16 bus would take me fairly close to Riley's house in Maida Vale. I was lucky it was still running; a lot of bus services had been eliminated in the last few rounds of cuts. London seemed dirtier and shabbier than when I'd left.

I stared at the murals I passed on my bus journey. They showed men in masks with guns and clenched fists—all symbols of armed resistance. They were the work, I knew, of the League of Iron—the right-wing extremist group that had, under pressure from Riley, claimed we were its agents for last month's kidnapping and bombing.

It was clouding over when I reached Maida Vale. Nat and I had been shut in the back of a van when we'd come here the first time, so although I knew I would recognize the house when I saw it, I was relying on what Nat had told me about his second visit to find the way to the correct street. Nat had been taken there by Riley himself, just after the Houses of Parliament explosion. He didn't know the name of the road the house was on, but he'd described what he'd seen on his journey there in Riley's car.

I reached the Maida Vale station, then hopped off the bus. Now I just had to circle the area, checking out each road in turn. Remembering Taylor's training about staying close to walls and walking lightly to make myself seem more invisible, I sped along street after street, past endless derelict buildings and the usual, terrible lines of homeless people slumped in unused doorways. In my head I ran through my plan. I was certain that even if Riley wasn't at home, his guards—soldiers in the EFA—would be. I planned to ask whoever I found to tell Riley that I wanted to see him. I was sure he would meet with me. After all, he'd wanted me to join his core team just a few weeks ago. I couldn't believe he would feel differently now.

Three hours later and I still had not found Riley's house.

I went back to the subway station, where an elderly homeless man with wild, staring eyes started shouting at me. I moved away and thought through what Nat had said again: *After Maida Vale, it wasn't far, maybe just two or three minutes in the car. I was feeling weird from the drug he'd given me, so I can't remember if we went left or right, but there was definitely a pub at some point very near the house.*

I opened the maps app on my phone. I had been using it sparingly, partly to save the battery and partly because I didn't want to see the list of missed calls and texts from Nat that I knew would be there. Sure enough, he'd messaged again. I ignored the text and looked at the map. There were three pubs within two or three minutes' drive from where I stood right now. I had already checked the roads off two of them. This time I headed for the third.

The clouds overhead were darkening in the twilight sky as I stood at the traffic circle and faced the street on my left. The hairs on the back of my neck prickled. This was it. I was sure. I set off, palms sweaty, eyes alert. The houses on this street were all big, just like the one I remembered breaking into with Nat.

Lights were starting to come on in several of the homes. I glanced from left to right. *There.* That was Riley's large brick house, its sweeping drive and neat front yard set behind huge wrought-iron gates. I crept across the road, hiding in the shadows of the hedge that bordered the neighboring house. I reached the edge of the gate and peered in though the bars. The house beyond looked deserted. Despite the fact that it was getting darker outside, not a single light shone from any of the windows and there was no sign of anyone guarding the entrance. I was certain, having met Riley and seen the ops base in Yorkshire, that he would definitely have at least one EFA soldier posted on his doorstep as basic security.

I tugged my hood more fully over my head as a light patter of rain started to fall. I swore under my breath. I knew from sleeping outdoors so much in the past in month that once you got soaked at night, it was almost impossible to get really dry again until the following day. I looked around. There was nowhere to shelter in Riley's front yard, and the hedge in whose shadow I was loitering was both dense and prickly. I glanced along the side of the house. The wooden door at the end must lead to a backyard, which would offer me more shelter—from both the rain and from passersby—than I would find out here.

I would wait for Riley—or one of his guards—to return to the house there. All I had to do was climb the gate and then the yard door. No problem.

Seconds later I had shimmied up the iron railings and, landing lightly on my feet, dropped to the other side. Making as little noise on the gravel as I could, I headed for the side path and the backyard beyond.

NAT

Even allowing for the fact that Charlie had a head start to London, it took me a stupidly long time to get even a very little way. My bus to Manchester broke down twice—unsurprisingly really, considering what an old rust bucket it was—and it was almost dark by the time I reached the Manchester bus station. One of the many downsides of living in a permanent recession was that every company in the world seemed to operate on a shoestring budget, with nothing—from buses to phones—working right anymore.

I headed for the bus station ticket office to buy a ticket for London. I didn't have much money, and this was the cheapest way for me to get to Riley's house. I hurried past several lines of passengers waiting to board other buses. There was no time to lose; Charlie was already hours ahead of me.

I stopped to let a middle-aged lady dragging a suitcase on wheels pass me. She muttered as she was forced to move slightly sideways to avoid my luggage. I was carrying Charlie's sleeping bag and all her spare clothes as well as my own. I didn't want to travel so loaded down, and I'd thought about leaving Charlie's things behind, but Lennox had vowed to destroy anything left in the safe house so there would be no trace of our visit.

When I'd said good-bye to him and Julius, I had gotten the impression they were glad to be rid of me. Understandable, but hardly a show of resistance solidarity. Still, I was used to being alone. It felt like another lifetime since I'd had a real home, before Lucas had gone into his coma and Mum had started spending all her time at his bedside, while Dad buried himself in work. Before then we'd been a real family. But for the past year or so our house had just been the place where my twin sister, Jas, and I looked after ourselves, occasionally passing our parents as they came and went.

Heavy rain started to fall as I passed the next bus for London, a huddle of passengers waiting to get on board. I hurried into the ticket office and joined the short line. My phone rang, suddenly loud over the background chatter.

I yanked it out of my pocket. Was that Charlie? Surely it had to be.

PRIVATE NUMBER flashed on the screen. I hesitated. The phone rang again. The people in the line ahead of me shuffled forward. Absently, I stepped after them, still staring at the screen. My cell rang a third time.

I held it to my ear. Outside the rain streamed down. "Hello?"

"Is that you, Nat?" The voice was male and vaguely familiar.

"Yes," I said suspiciously. Only a very few people had this number. "Who's this?"

"They've taken your sister." The voice was filled with emotion.

"*What?*" My head spun. Last time I'd been in touch—a few

days ago—Jas had been safe at home with our parents. "What do you mean?" The line was moving again, but I was frozen to the spot. "Who's taken her? Who *are* you?"

"It's Aaron Latimer."

I gasped. Aaron was the mayor of London's son. Instantly, my hackles rose. No way could I trust either him or his dad.

"How did you get this number?" I demanded.

"I found it where your parents hide it—the only place it's written down, in your house."

"What?" I asked, bewildered. "How do you know what my par—?"

"They delete the number once they've called you. They don't carry it around with them. They've never even told Jas where they hide it. But Jas once told me where her . . . your . . . mum and dad used to keep a bit of emergency money under a floorboard and I was guessing that's where they put the number and—and it was."

My head spun. "Wait. You're saying you broke into our house and stole—?"

"You're missing the point, Nat." Aaron's voice rose with anxiety. "I did it to reach you, because Riley has taken Jas. His men kidnapped her on her way to my house earlier today."

Suspicion swirled inside me. *Jas kidnapped?* "I don't understand. Why . . . ?"

"It's about as simple as it can be," Aaron went on bitterly. "Roman Riley thinks Jas knows where you and Charlie are, and he's determined to get the information out of her, whatever it takes."

I stared through the ticket office window. The sky outside was growing darker, the rain now pounding down against the glass. I gripped my phone tightly, feeling sick. "Whatever it takes?" I echoed, blood thundering in my ears. No way could Jas stand up to being bullied by Riley's men. "But my sister doesn't *know* where we are."

"I know," Aaron said. "That's what I'm saying. She doesn't know *anything*. That's why we've got to save her before Riley realizes she's useless to him—and kills her."

CHARLIE

The backyard of Riley's house was large and full of bushes, with a fishpond in the middle. I skirted the lawn, keeping close to the bushes to avoid activating the light sensors on the back wall, and took shelter from the rain under a large weeping willow tree. I sat, motionless, watching out for lights to come on in the house. I didn't want to think about what I'd do if Riley didn't come home. I had bought myself a sandwich a few hours ago, but hunger was already gnawing at my stomach. I huddled under the tree, wishing for the first time since I'd left the safe house this morning that I'd brought my sleeping bag with me after all.

An hour passed. The rain grew steadily heavier. I was now cold, and my feet and shoulders felt damp and uncomfortable. Anxious thoughts streamed through my brain: What if Riley was away all night? All week? What if he'd moved? I had enough money for only a few days' worth of food. What on earth would I do after that?

The rain slowed to a faint drizzle. I took out my phone. Maybe I should call Nat after all, tell him where I was. It was sensible to keep in touch. And I *had* run off without saying any-thing, then refused to answer his calls and texts.

Plus I missed him. Badly. We might argue sometimes, but I'd spent the past few weeks entirely in his company, and not having him beside me right now felt like a part of me was missing.

Just as I was about to switch on the cell and make the call, lights blazed from the house. Two downstairs rooms were now lit up. Phone still in my hand, I peered out through the fronds of the willow tree. A figure was walking past the window. It was him: Roman Riley. A moment later the curtains closed.

This was it. I resolved to call Nat later, after I'd spoken to Riley. Nat might not have liked me attempting to make contact with Riley, but maybe he'd change his mind if I was able to report that I was now successfully undercover with the EFA.

I crept out from under my tree. The rain was a light mist on my face. Ignoring it, I sped silently across the grass. No one was looking out from the windows of the house. Long shadows deep-ened the darkness of the yard. I came to the stone paving that sur-rounded the fishpond in the middle of the lawn. A low iron fence had been erected around the water. Crouching down, I followed the fence, heading for the end of the pond and the final stretch of grass before the house.

I reached the last bit of fence. As I stepped out, ready to dart across the lawn, a hand grabbed my arm. I gasped. Something struck me across the back. I stumbled forward. My phone flew out of my hand.

With a splash it landed in the pond. *No.* My arm was twisted up, behind my back. As I yelled out, a hand was clamped over my mouth. My arm was wrenched higher. Pain seared through me. I turned my head. One of Riley's EFA soldiers stood behind me, a beanie pulled low over his head.

"Who are you?" the man ordered. "Why are you here?" He took his hand away from my mouth.

"I'm Charlie Stockwell." I gasped. "I want to see Riley—and I know he'll want to—"

The soldier clamped his hand over my mouth again. "Come on." With a rough tug on the arm still twisted behind my back, he dragged me across the grass toward the house.

I looked over my shoulder at the fishpond. The orange fish swam lazily, their gleaming skin glinting in the faint light from the house. My heart sank like a stone. I might be on my way to see Riley, but my phone was now at the bottom of that pond. It was gone—and with it, so was my only way of directly contacting Nat.

NAT

"Riley's really kidnapped Jas?" People in the ticket office were bustling all around me, but all my focus was on Aaron's voice on the other end of the line.

"Yes. She was on her way over to see me, and they took her. I got a phone call telling me to say nothing to any—"

"Wait. Slow down." An announcement boomed overhead as I tried to process what Aaron was saying. I could understand why Riley might think Jas would know where I was, but why on earth would she have been going to see Aaron in the first place? Jas hardly knew him—though she did know that, despite my rescuing him, Aaron Latimer had done absolutely nothing to clear my name. Okay, so Julius had insisted that Mayor Latimer was only pretending to support Riley, that he was in fact giving the resistance equipment and weapons, but that could easily be a con. And this was *surely* a trick.

"Nat?" Aaron sounded panicky, his voice urgent. "Are you there?"

"Yes," I said. "Does your dad know Riley's taken Jas?"

"No. He's away on some business trip."

"I thought he was supposed to be close to Riley."

"He pretends to support him, yes, but he's not in the inner circle. He doesn't know about this, honestly." Aaron's voice cracked. "I would have told him, but he's on a plane right now, flying back from Singapore. He's been in the air with his phone switched off since it happened."

I said nothing. Aaron had an answer for everything, but then, if Riley had prepped him, that's exactly what I'd expect.

"Nat?"

"So why are you calling me?" I asked.

"Because my dad's not around, my mum would freak if I told her, and we can't trust the police—which means you and I have to go and rescue her." He paused. "Just tell me where you are and I'll come and find you. I've taken money from my mum's account and I can pick you up, wherever you are."

I stiffened. Was this all a trap to trick me into revealing my whereabouts? "Why should I trust you about anything?" I snapped. "You didn't tell anyone Charlie and I rescued you. You let everyone think we are terrorists."

"I know." Aaron blew out his breath. "I know you have no reason to trust me, but I'm telling you the truth. Jas is gone, and I was told to cover up her being missing as long as I could, that if I let anyone know she was kidnapped, they'd kill her."

I leaned my head on the ticket office window. The glass was cool against my skin. "Why would Riley tell *you* about kidnapping my sister? Why not our parents?" On the other side of the window, the bus to London was loading up with passengers.

47

"I don't know," Aaron said. "But . . . but Jas and I have been seeing a lot of each other."

I frowned. Charlie had told me that she'd seen Aaron and Jas together at his party last month, but it hadn't occurred to me that Aaron might have contacted her since. Jas certainly hadn't mentioned it on the few occasions I had talked to her.

"'Seen a lot of her' how?" I demanded. "Are you saying you're her boyfriend?"

There was a pause. "Uh . . . yes."

Again, I had no idea whether or not to believe him.

"Look, your sister and I . . . ," Aaron stammered. "I know Jas hasn't said anything yet, but it's okay. I think she's amazing. Totally cool."

"Too cool for you," I muttered.

"Please, Nat." Aaron hesitated. "I understand why you might think I'm lying to you. But I've realized since I . . . since Riley took me . . . that things aren't what they seem. My dad's filled me in about a lot of things."

In the background, the PA system announced that the next bus to London was about to depart. Outside, the last few passengers were just getting on board.

"What about *my* dad, *my* parents?" I said. "Surely they'd have noticed if Jas wasn't at home by now?" As I said the words, I knew it was, in fact, entirely likely that Mum and Dad would have been far too busy to notice Jas was missing for a few hours. I ground my teeth, a new fury building inside me—this time, at my parents.

"Yeah, right." Aaron snorted. "One of the reasons Jas spends so much time with *my* family is because her own is never around."

Guilt stabbed me like a knife. It wasn't just Mum and Dad. I wasn't around for Jas, either.

"Anyway," Aaron went on, "if your parents think about it at all, they'll probably just assume she's with me, staying over."

"She *stays over?*"

"Look, Nat, I know this is a lot to take in, but we don't have much time. The guy who phoned me said Riley would release Jas so long as I didn't tell anyone she'd been taken, but I can't see that he'll have any reason to keep her alive."

Outside on the concourse, all the passengers were on board the London bus now, the driver just checking over the last pieces of luggage. I clenched my fists, torn between the small part of me that believed Aaron and the larger part that refused to.

"I don't trust you," I hissed. "I think you stole my number and now you're trying to find out where I am so you can tell your dad and he can tell Riley."

"*No,*" Aaron insisted. "My dad is only—"

I ended the call, then immediately scrolled to Jas's name. Blocking my own number, I tried hers. The phone went straight to voice mail.

I hesitated. If Jas had been kidnapped, then Riley would have her phone. Still, if I didn't leave a message, he wouldn't know this call was from me.

I pressed end and raced out of the ticket office toward my bus. Never mind not having a ticket. I'd pay the driver directly.

He was on board now, shucking off his jacket, getting ready to drive.

My phone rang again.

"Nat, don't hang up." It was Aaron again.

I hesitated, my eyes on the bus. The driver was settling into his seat.

"Nat, I swear on my life and my parents' lives and your sister's life that I am telling you the truth." Aaron's voice shook with conviction. "Riley has taken Jas. We have to rescue her."

In front of me, the headlights flashed on as the bus engine growled into action. I stopped moving toward it.

"Think about it," Aaron said. "I've called you on your cell, so I obviously have your number. If me or my dad were going to sell you out to Riley, don't you think I'd have passed your number on already and he'd already have caught you?"

This was a fair point. I hesitated. I still wasn't going to trust Aaron himself, but suppose Jas had been taken, just as he'd described? I had to find out.

"Do you have any idea where Riley's taken Jas?" I asked.

"Yes. I have my dad's tracking equipment on my phone. It's the same as the stuff he's given to the resistance. I got an area trace—for Yorkshire. I reckon it must be that place you rescued me from."

He meant the EFA operations base.

"Right," I said. Up ahead my bus was moving, turning out of its parking space and heading for the bus station exit.

"That's why I need you to help me rescue her," Aaron said.

"You know the place, where it is, how to get inside. You got *me* out of there, so—"

I switched off the call, then my entire phone. There was certainly no way I was going to break into the ops base with Aaron. He had no training for this kind of thing. I hesitated a second, then removed the SIM card from my phone. I'd put it back in if I urgently needed to make a call. I couldn't be 100 percent sure Aaron wouldn't pass my number on to his dad or even to Riley's men, despite what he'd just said.

The London bus disappeared from view. Part of me still wished I was on it. Charlie was in London looking for Riley. I missed her more than I wanted to admit to myself. And I was scared for her too. Still, Charlie had chosen the path she'd taken. Jas was an innocent—and her life was in immediate danger.

I picked up my luggage and headed back into the ticket office to find out the fastest way to the training base.

CHARLIE

Roman Riley stood in the middle of the room, his bright, dark eyes fixed on mine. I glared back as the soldier who'd been holding me let go of my arm.

"She's not armed, sir," he said. "No phone, either."

"Good work, soldier," Riley said, without taking his eyes off me. "Please ask Martina to bring Charlie a blanket. She looks cold. Oh, and some food and water too." He raised his eyebrows. "Or would you prefer a cup of tea, Charlie?"

I said nothing. Why was Riley being so nice? Was this some sort of trick?

Riley nodded as if I'd replied. "Okay, soldier, please see what Martina can rustle up for our guest."

"Yes, sir." The man left.

He shut the door behind him. Riley and I were alone. Riley was still staring at me, searching my face. I looked away, unsure what he was playing at.

Now that I was actually here, I was starting to realize what a huge challenge I faced. This man was responsible for the bomb blast that killed Mum. There was no one in the world I hated more. And yet if I wanted to work undercover, trying to find evidence that Riley's real agenda was to use violence to gain power, I was going to have to convince him that I wanted to join him.

It felt impossible.

Playing for time, I let my eyes wander over the living room. It was simply but elegantly furnished, with leather sofas and a big TV in the corner. Bookshelves ranged across one wall.

"Please sit down, Charlie," Riley said, taking a seat on one of the sofas.

I perched on the sofa facing him and stared down at the rug that lay between us—a soft pattern of reds and golds. It looked—like everything in the room—extremely expensive. Riley leaned forward, his hands clasped together. He said nothing. Was he waiting for me to speak?

I stared mutinously at him, still with no idea what to say.

"Are you all right, Charlie?" His voice expressed concern. Again I wondered why. I had just been caught skulking around in his backyard, yet instead of interrogating me to find out why I was here, he was offering me food and drink and acting like he cared about me. I frowned, and Riley smiled. His features were sharper than they looked on TV and his body slighter, but he was just as charismatic as he always appeared on-screen. It was partly his looks—he was square-jawed and handsome, with dark hair and intelligent eyes that seemed to see right through me—but there was something more than that too. There was a stillness about him, almost as if he carried his own atmosphere wherever he went, like a powerful magnet that pulled everything toward it.

I shook myself. Never mind Riley and why he was being so nice to me, I had to focus on myself, on what I wanted here. Most important, I needed to remember that I must never let my guard down in his presence.

"Charlie?" Riley repeated.

"I'm fine," I said.

There was a knock on the door. A woman came in. She was slender, with long blond hair, and was dressed in elegant gray pants and a black sweater. She crossed the room and laid a blanket and a bottle of water on the sofa beside me.

"Soup and a sandwich okay?" she asked.

"That's great, Martina," Riley said. "Thank you."

Martina leaned over and kissed his cheek. I watched, surprised. I'd only ever seen Riley as a politician, on TV and, of course, as the EFA's secret leader. It had never occurred to me that he might have a personal life. I checked Martina's left hand. No wedding ring.

"Martina is a trained EFA soldier and my girlfriend." Riley sounded amused.

Embarrassed that he'd clearly guessed what I'd been thinking, I looked down at the blanket and the bottle. I wasn't particularly cold now that I was inside, but I was desperately thirsty.

"Go ahead," Martina said. Her voice was crisp but not unfriendly. "It's not poisoned."

I reached out and picked up the bottle. It was sealed. I untwisted it and took a sip. The water felt blissful on my dry throat. I gulped it down greedily, then replaced the cap.

Riley was still watching me, his head tilted to one side.

"So . . . ," he said. "The last time I saw you, you wanted to kill me." He smiled. He had small white teeth. "Why are you here? It's only a guess, of course, but I don't sense this is an assassination attempt gone wrong."

"No. It's not." I fell silent again. Why hadn't I rehearsed what I was going to say? Nat had been totally right. Riley wasn't easy to lie to; how on earth was I going to convince him I genuinely wanted to join his team? I took another swig of water. Perhaps I should avoid that and simply say what *was* true.

I twisted the cap onto my water bottle again, my hands trembling slightly. I knew Riley would have seen. I drew the blanket closer, covering my lap, and then I spoke at last.

"You said, the last time I saw you, that my father was alive," I said quietly. "I need to know if that's true."

Riley sat back, letting his hands rest on the sofa beside him. "Yes, Charlie, it is true. And it's also true that he wants to meet you. Would you like that?"

I looked up. I had the strongest sensation that Riley would see through any lie. Which made it just as well that I didn't need to tell one.

"Yes," I said. "I would."

NAT

It was the middle of the night and raining hard as I jogged along the dark road. I'd had to put the SIM card back in my phone for a few minutes in order to use the GPS function to locate the woods near the ops base, and the skin on the back of my neck prickled as I ran. Was somebody tracking me? I glanced around. Was I being watched? I couldn't see anyone.

My phone beeped several times in quick succession. Hoping the texts were from Charlie, I took a speedy glance, only to find a series of increasingly angry messages from Aaron, sent several hours ago.

Ignoring these, I checked the map one last time. If it was accurate, then the woodland I was looking for should be just around the corner. I switched off my phone and removed the SIM card again so that Aaron couldn't trace me. I didn't have a full address for the operations base—which was basically a derelict farmhouse set in acres of field—but I was certain if I could just find the wooded area that surrounded it, I'd be able to track down the building itself, no problem.

The road was deserted as I ran around the corner. To my great relief, the trees came immediately into view. I darted under the cover of their branches and took stock of where I was—we'd run through these woods several times during our training weekend here months ago. Even though it was dark, I was fairly confident that the farmhouse was through the trees and slightly to the east.

I ran on, ducking under the wet branches, the bushes I passed damp against my legs. It felt different in here. I wasn't spooked by the dark—the moon overhead gave off plenty of light—but the sound of the wind in the branches was like someone whispering the words "leave, leave."

I told myself not to let my imagination get the better of me. But the feeling that someone was watching me persisted, not helped by the memories of the last time I'd run through these woods, trying to escape from Riley and his soldiers, with Charlie and Aaron at my side. The thought of Charlie sent a new anxiety spiraling through me. Where was she? I wondered. Had she reached Riley's house? Was she speaking with him right now? Was she okay?

Of all the people I'd ever met, Charlie was probably the most truly confident. And yet, though she was careful to hide it, I knew she was vulnerable too. All that garbage about her not caring what Riley had said about her dad still being alive. Of *course* she cared. Anyone would.

And I cared about her. More—far more—than I wanted to admit even to myself.

It took about fifteen minutes to reach the edge of the trees. I stopped and peered out across the empty field beyond. Rain pattered loudly on the leaves above my head. The sound was strangely soothing, calming my raw nerves. I could just make out a light in the distance: that had to be coming from the ops base. The two sleeping bags—one tied on either side of the backpack—made my bundle cumbersome. I took my knife, a flashlight, and a length of rope and left everything else in the shelter of a tree. I was on the verge of approaching the farmhouse and finding Jas—and so nervous I felt sick. If Riley's men found me, they would kill me, just as they tried to kill me before.

Part of me wanted to turn around and run away, back through the trees. But Jas was here, my twin sister, to whom I'd been closer, all my life, than anyone else in the world. I would never forgive myself if I didn't at least try to save her.

And then the sound of breaking twigs and rustling leaves filtered toward me. I froze, moving closer to the nearest tree. Was that an animal wandering through the woods? No. Surely no woodland animal could possibly make that much noise. The sounds slowed. The distinct tread of footsteps echoed through the air. It was a person. An EFA soldier? That was most likely, considering how close the ops base was. Except I'd never met a soldier who crashed through the undergrowth so loudly.

Still hiding behind my tree, I peered into the dark woods. A second later he lumbered into view, panting for breath and with a huge scowl on his face.

Aaron. With a gun in his hand.

CHARLIE

It was the middle of the night and I was wide-awake. I got out of bed and checked that the bedroom door was still securely locked. It was, so I crept back into bed and closed my eyes.

Sleep refused to come.

It was surreal—not just being in Riley's house, but being indoors at all. Yesterday evening in the unheated safe house, with its bare lights and cold water, already felt like several years ago. Riley had insisted that I ate, washed, and slept before we talked in the morning. Martina had run me a bath frothing with bubbles and left me shampoo, towels, and a huge bathrobe to put on afterward. I accepted all this hospitality feeling deeply unsettled. Riley seemed to have accepted my curiosity about my father at face value. He had asked no further questions, not about Nat or the resistance—which he surely knew existed—nor what I'd been doing since I last saw him. I didn't get it. Riley must know that I hated him, for goodness' sake. He had told me to my face that he'd organized the Canal Street market bomb that killed Mum. He was too smart to think I'd have forgiven him for that, to trust that my motives were as straightforward as I said they were—and yet here I was, treated like an honored guest.

It had been almost midnight by the time I left the bathroom wrapped in the fluffy bathrobe, my clothes clutched in my hand. Martina appeared as if by magic from a nearby room. She reached out for my jeans and hoodie.

"I'll have them washed and aired by morning," she said in her crisp voice.

I hesitated, then handed the clothes over. I kept hidden the nail scissors I'd found in the bathroom cupboard. They were short-bladed but sharp enough to do some damage if anyone tried to attack me. I followed Martina into a large, elegantly furnished bedroom. I gazed around, taking in the polished wood of the dressing table and the four-poster bed. Thick green and fawn curtains hung at the windows. There were matching cushions on the brown chaise lounge at the end of the bed. My feet sank into the deep beige carpet. It was all so luxurious, especially after my weeks on the run.

"There's a fresh bottle of water by the bed and a bell you can use to call me if you need anything." Martina indicated the wooden cabinet beside the four-poster, above which a long, tasseled cord hung from a brass fitting on the wall. "Okay?"

"Uh, yes, thank you."

"Good night, then." Martina left the room, shutting the door behind her.

I locked it immediately, grateful there was a key, then went over to the bed. A pair of white silk pajamas had been laid out on the pale green duvet. I was guessing they were Martina's. I checked that the door was still locked, then scrambled into the pajamas. They were soft and smelled of laundry detergent. I got into bed and rested my head on the pillow. Now that my hair was cut so short, it dried more or less instantly. I liked the lack of fuss—though, if I was honest, sometimes I missed my long curly hair too. I put the sharp nail scissors in the bedside drawer right beside me, then lay back.

I was still lying there now, hours later, listening for the sound of anyone creeping about outside. The house was silent. I wondered where Nat was. Julius and Lennox had been due to leave the safe house tomorrow. Would Nat go with them? With a pang I wondered how I would get in touch with him. I could have attempted to fish my cell phone out of Riley's pond, but there was no point; it would be damaged beyond repair by now.

I could always use the draft e-mail method to try to reach him, though there was no knowing when he would next have a chance to check for messages. I turned over on my side. There was a tight feeling in my chest. It had been a long time since I'd lain in a comfortable bed. I missed Mum suddenly. There were days now when I went for hours without thinking about her, and then all of a sudden grief would hit me like a wall, taking my breath away with an agonizing smack.

I squeezed my eyes tightly shut. I wanted Nat's arms around me. Until we'd arrived at the safe house yesterday, we'd been close. *Really* close. In fact, despite Nat's reluctance to talk about his feelings, I'd even wondered if we were in love. *In love.* I rolled the words around in my head. We'd admitted that we liked each other, but we hadn't said *those* words. Did Nat feel them? Lying there without him, I knew that I did, though I hated to admit it. A sob rose from my chest, into my throat. I swallowed it down, determined not to cry. Missing Mum and Nat did me no good. I had to focus on Riley and getting evidence against him. I lay, listening to the sound of my own breathing. I was never going to get to sleep tonight.

NAT

There was no time to hide. Aaron had blundered into the small clearing so fast that he saw me right away. It was dark in the depths of the woods, but here on the edge of the trees, the moonlight was bright.

We stared at each other. All the blood felt like it was draining from my face. Aaron was panting, trying to catch his breath. I glanced at the gun in his hand. I could only make out its outline. The detail was hidden by the shadow of his body. But it didn't look anything like the Glock semiautomatics we'd been trained on. In fact, I couldn't place it at all. How on earth had Aaron gotten ahold of it?

I couldn't believe I had walked into his trap. I looked around, expecting to see masked men emerging from behind the trees. But no one came. The only sound was that whisper of the branches in the wind, *leave, leave,* and Aaron's breathing, heavy and labored.

"Man, you have stamina," he said.

"What?"

"Stamina. I've been following you since you reached the

woods. I'm fast, but you were running for nearly half an hour without stopping. I thought I'd lost you twice."

I frowned. What was going on? I looked around again. Still no sign of any EFA soldiers. Was Aaron here on his own? I stared at him.

"How did you know where I was?"

Aaron pointed to my phone. "I knew you'd come to this area, and I'd already gotten the money, so I took a cab."

"All the way here?" I stared at him.

He shrugged. "Your phone gave me your exact location when you switched it on for two minutes. I took my cab to the edge of the woods, then—"

"You tracked my phone?" My voice was an indignant whisper.

"I used my dad's secret GPS stuff. I told you already. He's been giving a whole load of high-tech equipment just like it to the resistance."

"So why are you here?" I demanded.

"Helping you get Jas," Aaron said. "Like I told you I would."

I shook my head. This was a rescue that Aaron was spectacularly untrained and unprepared for.

"I see." I pointed to the gun in his hand, still hidden in the shadow of the nearest tree. "And what about that?"

Aaron grinned, and a dimple appeared in the center of his flushed cheek. "This is just an old toy of mine." He chuckled. "Thought it might come in handy."

For goodness' sake. "This isn't a game, you know," I spat. "The last time I was here, I nearly died."

"I know." The smile fell from Aaron's face. "I know how serious it is. I came all the way here from London. I stole money. My parents will be furious. But I want to help."

"I don't need your help," I said, feeling deeply unnerved. I'd been totally on track before, thinking through how I would sneak into the ops base as I'd done before and search for Jas. Aaron was just getting in the way. "I'll be faster and quieter on my own."

"I can be fast and quiet."

"Really? You sounded like a bear on a ramble just now."

Aaron looked crestfallen.

"And that gun won't help either," I persisted.

"Why not?" Aaron held it up. "It fooled you."

"Only because it was dark. Indoors it won't fool an EFA soldier worth his salt for more than a few seconds."

"A few seconds could make all the difference," Aaron argued.

"Oh yeah?" I said. "Show me how you use it, then."

Aaron obediently held out the gun in front of him like it was a baton. "Hands up!" he said.

"Stop fooling around," I snapped. "Here. If you have to hold it, hold it like this." I rearranged his fingers so that his grip looked more convincing. Then I took the gun off him and shoved it down the back of my pants.

"What are you—?"

"If you want to come with me, you have to do exactly what I say. Deal?"

"Deal." Aaron paused. "Jas said you were grumpy."

"Shut up," I said.

"Okay, boss." Aaron mimed zipping his lips. "What do we do next?"

I peered through the trees again. Desperate though I was to find Jas, it was just too risky to attempt a move on the ops base right now. "We're going to have to wait until daylight, just another couple of hours, then assess how many people are in the house."

"We're going to *wait*?" Aaron sounded seriously disappointed.

"Yes," I said. "I'll work out what to do when we know how many EFA soldiers we're up against."

CHARLIE

I woke with a jolt. It was daylight, with bright sunshine seeping in around the curtains, and someone was knocking on the door. I sat upright, taking a second to remember where I was and why I was here.

"Charlie?" It was Martina, outside the bedroom door. "I have some juice and toast for you. I'll leave it outside."

"Okay, thanks." I got up and padded across the room. I opened the curtains—my room looked over the backyard— then I went to the door and unlocked it. A tray of food and my clothes, clean and neatly folded in a pile, lay on the carpet outside. I brought them inside, ate and drank and dressed, then ventured out onto the landing.

As before, Martina appeared seconds later, emerging from another room across the landing. She looked even more stylish and elegant than she had last night, in a pale pink dress with a thin belt and her blond hair tied off her face in a sleek ponytail. She smiled at me, but it was hard to tell whether it was genuine.

"Roman is waiting for you in the living room downstairs."

She flicked the ponytail off her shoulder. "You can leave the tray."

I set off. After a surprisingly good sleep, I felt more confident than I had last night. Whatever happened regarding my dad, I would surely have time today to start looking for proof I could use against Riley.

Along the landing, I headed for the office Nat and I had broken into last year. We hadn't known it was Riley's office then, of course. Our cell leader, Taylor, had sent us to download information off a computer as a test to see whether we made the grade as trainee EFA agents. I flushed with humiliation as I remembered how easily we had been fooled.

As I approached the office, a masked EFA soldier appeared from around the corner. He spotted me instantly and stood, arms folded. I stopped too. The guy was huge. There was definitely no way past him. The soldier pointed to the stairs. I turned and sped away. Never mind. Hopefully I'd get a chance to check out the office later.

Riley looked up as I walked into the living room. He seemed more distracted than he had been last night, his eyes less intent on me, as if he had other things on his mind.

"I've been in touch with your father," he said immediately. "He is eager to meet you, but he can't come here, so we've decided it's best for you to go to him. Today."

"Oh," I said. "*Today?* Where does he live?"

"I can't tell you, but it'll be a few hours' drive." Riley got up. "Look, I'm sorry I don't have more time to spend with you

before you go. I know your father would have preferred that."
He paused, and it struck me that perhaps all of Riley's hospitality came down to some weird obligation he had to my dad.
He'd described him before as some kind of international leader
of the EFA and other groups. For the first time I wondered
exactly how deep the connection between them went.

"Anyway," Riley went on, "as you know, I'm very busy.
There's the general election at the end of next week, and I'm
speaking at four different rallies today, so I have to leave in a
minute, but Martina will give you anything you need and . . .
and then, like I say, she'll take you to meet your dad."

"Right," I said. My head spun. "Uh . . . so he really is alive?"

Riley stared at me. His expression softened. "Yes, he is." He
walked over to a table in the corner of the room and picked up
a sheet of paper. "I'm sorry, Charlie. I'm forgetting how little
you know. But don't worry. Your father will explain it all to you.
I know how eager he is for you to join him. . . ." He smiled. "To
join *us*."

Was that really the plan? Was Riley seriously prepared to
trust me? Or had he made up the whole thing about my dad in
order to manipulate me, just as he had invented other things to
manipulate me before?

"Can't you tell me anything?" I asked, wondering if Riley
would falter if I pressed him for details. "How come I thought
my father was dead all these years? Are you saying my mum
lied about that? Or Uncle Brian? How come you're so sure this
guy you're in touch with *is* my dad?"

Riley handed me the paper in his hand. "This shows the results of a DNA test. You and your dad."

My mouth gaped. I hadn't been expecting that. "You took my DNA?"

"A swab inside your mouth while you were asleep after a training class earlier this year." Riley shrugged. "I'm sorry, but once your father realized you might be his daughter, we had to act—and there seemed no point telling you anything until we were sure."

"I see." I looked down at the DNA test result, trying to focus on the dense black type.

"Ignore the man's name on the form. It's a false one," Riley said. "Your father lives under a secret identity."

I looked down at the piece of paper. My name was there along with the 99.89 percent probability that I was the offspring of the man named on the form. "But why—?" I started.

Riley cut me off with a wave of his hand. "I really can't tell you more, Charlie. It's up to your dad to fill you in on all the history. But I can say that, to the best of my knowledge, both your mother and your uncle believed your father died when you were a very little girl."

My head spun. Even if all this was true, how on earth was I going to get evidence against Riley now? "Why can't my dad come here?" I asked.

Riley sighed. "Because you're not the only one who thought he was dead. If he were seen in public, if the authorities realized he is still alive, it would be dangerous for him."

"Why?" I asked. "Is he wanted by the police or something? You said before that he was the leader of the EFA, of several groups around Europe. Did he break the law doing that?"

"*Leader* isn't exactly the right word, though in the purest sense it's true." Riley hesitated a moment. "Your father is a freedom fighter and a political philosopher. I already knew what was wrong with our country when I met him. But your father opened my eyes to how exactly it could be put right."

"I see," I said, though I didn't really see at all. I'd been so overwhelmed by the possibility that my dad might be alive that I hadn't given much thought to who he might be as a person. He sounded idealistic, which fit with things Mum had said. Was it possible that he had some beautiful vision for the human race that Riley had twisted to suit his own power-hungry ambitions?

"So my dad isn't the boss of you in a practical sense?" I asked. "But he is, like, an inspiration? For you and other people?"

"Exactly," Riley said. "Now, I really have to go."

And with that he swept out of the room.

I sat back on the sofa, my mind reeling. It sounded like this man who said he was my dad was smart. But was he smart enough to realize what Riley was doing in his name? Sometimes intellectually smart, idealistic people didn't see what was going on under their noses. Maybe I'd be able to show him. Maybe, if he really was as keen to see me as Riley said, he would listen to what I knew. Perhaps once he really understood how evil Riley was—how Mum had died in the marketplace bomb—he would even give me the evidence I needed against Riley.

I really wanted to let Nat know what I'd learned. If I could make it up to Riley's office, I would surely be able find a computer or a smartphone that I could use to leave Nat a draft e-mail, then delete the record from the hard drive—a neat trick Taylor had taught us when we were training. And once I was in the office, I'd be able to search for evidence against Riley, just as I'd hoped to do earlier.

Intent on this new plan, I slipped out of the living room. Before I had taken even a single step across the hall, Martina appeared again.

"Looking for something?" she said sharply. "Because I'd much prefer you to ask and let me fetch it for you."

I stared at her, my heart beating fast. It struck me that under that elegant pink dress, Martina was as strong and muscular as the other female EFA soldiers I'd met.

"Am I a prisoner, then?" I demanded.

"You're a guest," Martina insisted.

I glared at her as Riley emerged from the kitchen, head buried in his phone. He looked deeply troubled, but when he looked up and saw I was standing in the living room doorway, the frown fell from his forehead and an easy smile curved around his lips.

"Was there something else, Charlie?"

I glanced at Martina. She said nothing.

"I just wanted to speak to you again. I mean, you can't expect me to just get in a car with a complete stranger"—I pointed at Martina—"without telling me something about where I'm going."

"Martina and I have been together for the past couple of years," Riley said smoothly. "As I already told you, she's a trained EFA agent, just like you. That's how we met, in fact. She has my complete trust and therefore should have yours." The firm tone with which he spoke made it hard to contradict him, but I was well aware this could all be a trap, that Riley could simply be getting me away from his house—and any connection to him—in order to keep me away from the very evidence I was searching for. And to have me killed.

"Please," I persisted, feeling my face flush, "I mean, I *know* things about my dad. His name was John Stockwell and I've seen pictures. He can't look *that* different now. Can't you show me a picture of him so I can see it's the same man? I mean, that DNA test report could easily have been faked."

Riley studied me for a second. "I don't have any pictures, Charlie. Your father is very careful about that." He hesitated. "There is more I could tell you, but I honestly think it's best if your father explains who he is, what he's done, and all the reasons why you don't know him."

I opened my mouth to argue again, but before I could speak, Riley leaped in again.

"However, although I'm not going to give away his exact

location, I *will* tell you that right now he is in Cornwall. He's staying in my family home."

I frowned. "I thought *this* was your family home," I said.

"It is," Riley said. "That is, this is the home I grew up in. Your father is saying with my son and his mother, my ex. You'll be meeting them all before the end of the day."

NAT

I did a full reconnaissance as soon as it was dawn. I was tired—Aaron and I had taken turns keeping guard, but I didn't really trust him to stay awake, so even the few minutes of sleep I'd snatched had been fitful and disturbed. Aaron, by contrast, appeared to have no trouble sleeping, rolled up in Charlie's sleeping bag and snoring away through his entire rest time.

By seven a.m. I'd skirted the farmhouse, keeping my cover in the woods while looking at the building from every angle. It looked run-down and was made from stone, with two main floors, plus the attic room up top. But I knew from my previous visits here that, though most of the rooms inside were fairly basic, the building also housed a sprawling basement where English Freedom Army operations were coordinated.

Two large cars with darkened windows were parked in front of the farmhouse. My heart sank at the sight of them. Their presence suggested that the place was occupied—and by more soldiers than I could possibly deal with in an unarmed encounter.

On my journey around the edge of the woods I'd seen four separate men and one woman emerge from the house. Even from a distance, they all looked young and fit and muscular— definitely EFA soldiers.

I came back to the little clearing where I'd left Aaron wrapped in his sleeping bag. His head was tipped back against the bark of the tree, his mouth open, and he was making soft, snuffling noises. I nudged his leg with my foot, none too gently. He woke with a start.

"I wasn't asleep," he said quickly.

"'Course you weren't." I squatted down beside him and peered at the farmhouse through the trees again.

My best guess was that Jas was being held in the basement room where Charlie had been kept prisoner just weeks before. For a few moments I imagined her crouching in a dark corner, shaking with fear. My blood boiled as I thought of how terrified she would be, a prisoner, not knowing what would happen to her, unable to answer Riley's questions.

My fists itched to punch him for scaring her. I thought back to the moment when Charlie and I were last here, when both of us had had the chance to take Riley's life. Neither of us had done it. At the time I'd thought this was the right decision, that a cold-blooded murder would have made us as bad as Riley himself—but now I wondered. When *were* you justified in taking someone's life? Once they had done something bad? Or when you knew that if you didn't kill them, they would almost certainly go on and kill others? Or was taking a life never justified under any circumstances?

I honestly wasn't sure anymore.

Riley had taken my sister yesterday afternoon, and it would surely be hours rather than days before he ran out of patience with her and . . . I couldn't bring myself to face what he would do once he realized she didn't know anything.

I forced my focus back to how I could rescue her. The only entry to the basement was through the kitchen. Even if I could somehow sneak in there—and the kitchen window, which I could see from here, was shut and probably locked—I would still have to make it down the narrow cellar steps and past anyone working in the main ops base. If I was going to do it, I needed to move soon—and with as much speed and silence as I could muster.

"Uh, Nat?" Aaron's hair was tousled and his face grimy. As he smiled, his annoying dimple appeared in the middle of his rosy cheeks. "I don't suppose you've got any food with you? I ate all mine on the way here last night."

Shaking my head, I dug my hand into my backpack and pulled out a pack of beef jerky—a dried-food staple that Charlie and I had lived on for weeks. I chucked a strip of the stiff, chewy meat in Aaron's direction. "Here. Have this."

Aaron picked up the jerky and examined it, an expression of disgust on his face. "My mum says stuff like this gives you cancer."

"Well, go home and eat an apple, then." Irritation rose inside me. "I don't suppose Jas has any choice over what she's eating either."

"Oh God." Aaron's face fell. "She doesn't eat enough as it is. I worry that she's too skinny to be healthy, but—"

"Will you shut up?" I snapped, my last ounce of patience finally deserting me. "I need to focus. And fast. If we can't get Jas out soon, Riley will kill her."

Aaron fell silent. He peered past me, through the trees, toward the farmhouse. The beef jerky lay, untouched, on his lap.

An awkward few seconds passed. "You should still eat," I muttered.

Aaron handed the strip of dried meat back to me. "I'll eat when we've gotten Jas." He stood up. "Where do you think they're holding her?"

"Basement, probably." I took a bite of the jerky. It was all very well Aaron being noble about eating, but I was hungry. Taylor's voice from our training classes rang in my ears. *Eat and eat well, whenever you can. Lack of food impairs your brain and your body.*

As I chewed my mouthful, Aaron wandered over to a tree right on the edge of the woods.

"Careful," I warned. "Someone could be looking out."

"Someone is." Aaron leaned forward, as if straining to make out what he was seeing."

"Is it a soldier?" I jumped to my feet, shoving the remaining strip of jerky in my backpack. "Get back. He'll see you."

Aaron turned to face me, his eyes lit up. "It's her," he said. "It's Jas. She's in the attic room right at the top of the house."

"*What?*" I rushed over and peered around the tree next to his.

A pale face was pressed against the attic window. It was, indeed, my sister. She was staring up at the sky.

"Damn," I muttered. "This isn't good."

"What do you mean?" Aaron said. "At least we know where she is."

"Yeah, but the only way to the attic is up two flights of stairs—that's after breaking into the house in the first place. And stairs are a choke point."

"A what?"

"A place where terrain narrows, reducing the combat power of any force passing through it," I said, remembering another of Taylor's lectures.

"Uh, right." Aaron didn't sound like he'd understood. "Well, couldn't we just rush it? If we went really fast, used my gun to keep back any soldiers, we could . . ."

Give me strength. I tried to tune him out, to work out a plan that might conceivably stand some chance of success. It was virtually impossible without knowing exactly how many soldiers were inside. Maybe we should wait a few more hours, see if any of them left the building. Except I couldn't be sure Jas *had* a few more hours.

Aaron's incessant chatter was still a hum in my ear. "So, Nat . . . ?"

I tuned back in. "Yup?"

"Jas says you were doing secret army training for months," Aaron went on, his eyes wide. "What kind of things did they teach you?"

"Among other things, the importance of silence in potentially dangerous situations," I muttered.

"I meant fighting—using weapons," Aaron went on excitedly, clearly not noticing the heavy irony in my voice.

"Guns, knives, hand-to-hand combat, that sort of thing," I said.

"So you really know how to fire a gun?" Aaron asked.

"Yes." I rolled my eyes. "Look, Aaron, I need you to be quiet a minute so I can try to work out how I can get into that farmhouse and up to the attic."

Aaron fell silent at last.

Just getting inside was a big enough problem. There was bound to be someone on duty near the front door, only yards from the bottom of the staircase we needed to climb. I sighed. Whichever way I looked at the problem, I couldn't see a solution.

"What about my gun?" Aaron said stubbornly. "Couldn't we use that to force our way in?"

I kicked at the twigs underfoot. *Honestly.* "I already told you, any half-decent soldier would see it wasn't real in about three seconds. Seriously, that's about all the time that gun buys us."

"Oh." Aaron looked crestfallen.

"Anyway, there is no 'we,'" I went on. "You're not coming with me."

"But I can run really fast," Aaron protested. "In fact, I'm probably stronger and fitter than you are. I was in the CCF at my school. I can climb anything—"

"This isn't a test on monkey nets," I snapped. "Getting into—" I stopped.

Climb anything. Aaron's words echoed in my head. *Climb.*

If I could get up onto the flat roof above the second floor, then somehow scramble up the sloping roof of the attic room, I could break the window and get Jas out that way. Chances were that no one would even hear the glass shatter all the way up there on the top floor.

"I'm going to approach from the roof," I said, checking over the house.

"But it's a sheer wall up to the roof." Aaron frowned. "How will you—?"

"Metal drainpipe." I pointed to the spot I'd just picked out.

"I can climb that," Aaron said eagerly.

"No." I picked up the rope I'd brought with me and slung it over my shoulder. I had that and my knife. I would leave everything else here. "You stay here. I'll come back this way with Jas once I've gotten her out."

"But—"

I didn't wait to hear Aaron's arguments. I was already skirting around the trees, heading to the point nearest the section of farmhouse I wanted to access. I could see most of the front of the building from here. Only one Jeep was parked outside. That was good. Hopefully the three soldiers I'd spotted so far were the only ones present in the house. I dropped to the ground and wriggled, commando-style, across the field. Taylor had taught us how to move like this months ago. There was a real knack to it, involving muscles in my arms and legs I'd never even known I had. But after the past few weeks, I was as fit as I'd ever been. Far fitter than Aaron, I was sure, despite what he'd said. Jeez, the guy was really a bit of a jerk. What on earth did Jas see in him?

I crossed the field in less than a minute. As I reached the slatted wooden fence—rotten and broken and surrounding only part of the farmhouse—I raised my head. No one was anywhere near me. I hadn't been seen. Swiftly, I crawled under the bottom bar of the fence, then clawed as quietly as I could over the gravel to the drainpipe I'd been heading for. I stood up, looking around again. Still no sign of any soldiers.

Hand over hand, I shimmied up the drainpipe, using my feet as leverage against the stone wall. I tested the gutter above the second floor, making sure it would bear my weight, then hauled myself up onto the flat roof above. I lay, catching my breath for a second. The sunlit roof felt warm under my body. It had been less than two minutes since I'd left Aaron. I resisted the temptation to look over in his direction to make sure he wasn't visible and thereby putting both of us in danger. I needed to focus on Jas. Aaron would have to look after himself.

I crawled over to the sloping wall of the attic room. I could just reach the bottom ledge of the window with my fingers. Clutching it tightly, it took all the strength in my arms to haul myself up. I pressed my toes against the wall, trying to get some purchase there. With a low grunt, I hooked my knee over the ledge and peered inside.

Jas was sitting on the bed, her hands—tied at the wrists—in her lap. She looked desperately miserable, her long hair dangling on either side of her face, her skinny legs tucked up underneath her. A surge of fury filled me. How dare Riley put my sister through this?

I gave the glass a light tap. Jas looked up. Saw me. Her eyes widened. She raced over.

"Nat?" she whispered.

"Stand back," I urged. "I'm going to break the glass."

Jas scrambled back onto the bed. Leaning against the wall for balance, I slid off my jacket and rolled it over my hand. With a swift jab, I punched through the window. Glass smashed to the floor beneath. The sound filled the air. I held my breath. Had anyone heard?

But no one came rushing. Still holding my jacket over my hand, I picked out the largest piece of glass and let it slide to the roof below me. Another two quick punches and there was enough space. I eased myself into the room. Once I'd untied the rope around Jas's wrists and helped her through, I could easily haul myself back out again.

I landed lightly on the floor with a sudden and powerful sense of déjà vu. I shivered, remembering how I'd nearly died here just a few weeks ago.

"Oh, Nat . . ." Jas flung herself at me, sobbing.

"No time," I said, disentangling myself from her arms. I sliced through the rope around her wrists. "Come on. I'll give you a leg up."

I bent down, making my hands into a stirrup for her.

And then the door swung open.

Roman Riley stood in the doorway, an amused smile on his face. "Ah, Nat," he said. "I've been expecting you."

I gasped as he raised his arm. I had just enough time to register that he was holding a gun and that the gun was pointing at me. Then a shot fired, pain filled me, and the room spun and turned to black.

CHARLIE

Martina didn't say much during the long journey to Cornwall. I spent most of the time in the car staring out of the window at the countryside flashing past and wondering about my dad. As time passed, my fears that I was simply being taken out of the house to be killed started to fade. In fact, the more I thought about it, the more unlikely it seemed that Riley would go to all the trouble of faking a DNA test and sending me off with his girlfriend on a six-hour drive as part of a hoax. He had said my dad was like an inspiration to him—perhaps that was true. I had certainly gotten the strong sense Riley felt obliged to do what my dad asked.

All of which meant that maybe I really was about to meet John Stockwell. And that maybe he really did want to meet *me*. But what would he be like? I had a few vague memories of a tall man with strong arms and a big smile tossing me into the air above his head, me squealing with delight, but it was hard to know whether those were real memories or simply planted in my head from the videos Mum had played when I was younger—and which I had replayed for myself many times since.

I really knew my dad only from those videos and photos. Back then, when I was a baby, he'd been very good-looking, with golden-brown hair, gray-blue eyes just like Uncle Brian's, and a strong, square jaw. How much would he have changed since that time? He had been twenty-two, like Mum, when I was born—so he'd be in his late thirties now.

Apart from the pictures, all I knew about my dad was that he'd been a soldier, a private. My experience of soldiers through the EFA had led me to think of them as disciplined, serious people. Yet I'd gotten the impression from Mum and Uncle Brian that my dad had been a carefree, even irresponsible, guy. Well, maybe the combination of those qualities tied in with what Riley said about my dad being a philosopher. Perhaps being a soldier had given him life experience, but by nature he was a dreamer. I felt even more hopeful that he didn't really understand the full nature of Riley's crimes and that I would be able to open his eyes.

Having exhausted the little I knew about my dad, I turned my thoughts to Nat. The more I dwelled on it, the weirder it seemed that Riley hadn't tried to get me to talk about Nat or where he was . . . and not understanding made me feel uneasy.

I missed Nat more than I would have thought possible. There hadn't been another chance to find a phone or a computer earlier. Of course, trying to get evidence against Riley was my priority, but I would have liked to be able to send Nat a message too. I hoped he wasn't too angry or worried about me. I imagined him helping Julius and Lennox pack up and head off to their next safe house, and I promised myself that I would take the next chance I got to leave a draft e-mail for him telling him I was okay.

Why not also tell him that you love him? an annoying voice chirped in my head.

No way. I felt vulnerable enough without giving away the depth of my feelings like that. I wished now that I'd pushed Nat to talk more about how he felt about us. But when we'd been on the run, life had been so hard and we'd both been so preoccupied with survival that it had been easy to withdraw from all the emotional stuff. Safer, somehow. Trouble was that now I couldn't be sure that in running off I hadn't just pushed him away altogether. I thought we'd had something powerful between us, but maybe I was wrong. Maybe Nat didn't feel the same about me as I did about him.

I couldn't bear the thought of that. Nat was everything to me. The idea that he might not really like me was too terrible to contemplate.

"Nearly there." Martina's voice brought me out of my reverie.

I followed her pointing finger to the sea, just coming into view across the town laid out to our left. It had been cloudy for most of our journey, but as we passed the town and plunged into the depths of the Cornish countryside, the sun came out, bathing the car in sudden light and warmth.

"How much longer?" I asked.

"Ten minutes, maybe less."

My stomach twisted into a knot as we turned off the main road and traveled through a small village and onto a winding coastal road. The sea was spread out like a sparkling blue sheet beside us. After another half a mile or so, Martina turned up a long drive, lined with tall, thin trees. She reached a set of gates, got out, and pressed the intercom. As she got back in the car, the gates swung open to reveal an old man with a stick at the bend of the drive ahead. A male soldier in a black sweater and combat boots with a machine gun slung across his chest stood beside him.

"Off you go," Martina said gruffly.

My heart thumped loudly in my ears. "Aren't you staying?" The words came out more shakily than I meant.

"Roman's ex and I don't exactly get along." Martina didn't meet my eyes. "You'll be fine," she said. "Don't forget your stuff."

I got out, clutching the small bag she'd given me earlier. It contained the few things I'd brought with me from the safe house, plus the pajamas and toothbrush I'd borrowed at Riley's house last night. As I headed through the gate, Martina turned the car and drove off. I gazed up at the drive. The old man was leaning heavily on his cane. Who the hell was he? I glanced at the soldier beside him. He was probably only a few years older than I was. I summoned up my most recent picture of my dad. Even allowing for the fact that John Stockwell must have aged at least thirteen years since the pictures I had of him, he should still be recognizable—and he definitely wasn't either of the two men I was walking toward. So where was he? Was this all, after all, some elaborate trap?

I walked, dry-mouthed, along the drive. As I got closer, the old man hobbled toward me. He had white hair slicked back off his lined, weather-beaten face. A long scar cut a deep groove along one cheek. How the hell did he fit in to all this?

The soldier kept back, but he was watching me carefully.

I reached the old man. He was tall, over six foot, but he walked awkwardly, hunched over his cane. He held out his left hand, his right still leaning heavily on the stick. I shook, not knowing what else to do.

"Charlie," he said. He had a London accent, a lot less refined than I was expecting. "I can't tell you how much I've longed for this moment."

I stared at his scarred face, my heart thundering as I met his dark, slightly slanting eyes. With a jolt I recognized my own in their shape and color.

"Who are you?" I could feel my face draining of color. This man was surely too old to be my dad.

"A good question," the man said. "One of the big three, in fact."

I stared at him blankly.

"I am known to revolutionary groups around the world as Uchi, which is derived from the Czech for 'teacher.'"

"What?"

Uchi cleared his throat. "Perhaps I should start again. I was born Michael Barnes, the only son of a housekeeper and a council worker. I was brought up in London, went to grammar school, and found my way to Oxford University and then the British army." He paused. "And I am, for better or worse, your father."

PART TWO

EXAMINATION

(n. [1] test; [2] act of inspection, inquiry, investigation;

[3] interrogation)

NAT

I opened my eyes. I was on my side, staring at a patch of wall. Above the wall was a window. My head felt full of fog as I registered the sun outside, high and bright in a clear blue sky.

Where was I? What was happening?

A second later the memory of my attempt to rescue Jas flooded back.

I groaned. It had been a trap. Riley had shot me . . . except—I mentally examined my body—I wasn't in any pain. It didn't make sense. Had he just knocked me out? Drugged me?

I blinked, trying to clear my mind. How long had I been unconscious? And where was Jas? Was she all right?

"Hello, Nat." Riley loomed into view. He squatted next to me.

"Is my brother okay?" That was Jas. She must be on the other side of the room. I tried to turn my head to see, but it felt too heavy to move.

"Nat's fine," Riley said, beckoning Jas over. "See for yourself."

A second later I heard footsteps, and Jas appeared beside him. She looked thin and fragile, her eyes red and sore from crying. Anger rose inside me—and guilt. If I hadn't gotten involved with

Riley's secret English Freedom Army in the first place, trying to be like our older brother, Lucas, Jas wouldn't be in this situation. I was furious with Riley for taking her and for trapping me—and I was even more furious with myself for being so easily fooled.

I tried to reach out and touch Jas's trembling fingers, but the muscles in my hand barely moved.

"Take it easy, Nat," Riley said. "You've been out for hours, but you'll be fine in another ten minutes or so; I only shot you with a tranquilizer."

I lay still, trying to collect my thoughts. What had Riley said before he drugged me? That he'd been *expecting* me? Did that mean this whole operation to rescue Jas had been a trap?

"Where's Aaron?" I whispered, my throat dry.

"Also coming out of his sedation," Riley said briskly. "My soldiers spotted him in the woods; he'll be here soon. I'm very grateful to him for bringing you here."

I frowned. Was he saying Aaron had set me up?

"Aaron wouldn't have led Nat into a trap," Jas said defiantly.

"Not knowingly, no." Riley smiled. "But he did act in a very predictable way once we told him Jas was taken. I'm impressed that he found you so quickly."

"Me?" I stared at him.

"Of course," Riley went on. "I guessed—correctly, as it turned out—that Jas wouldn't know where you were, but also that you wouldn't have left your family with absolutely no way to reach you. All I had to do was lure you here."

My head spun. Was Riley saying that he'd planned this whole

thing using Jas and Aaron in order to get ahold of *me*? As the fog in my brain cleared, it struck me that Riley's only possible motive for entrapping me like this was to kill me—something he had already tried to do twice. So what was I doing still alive?

"Why did you drug us?" I gasped.

Riley ignored my question. He glanced from me to Jas, tilting his face to one side as if considering something. "You know, I see a certain resemblance in your face shape, especially your mouths, but considering you're twins, you two don't look much alike."

I glared at him, flexing my hands. It was easier to move now, though I still felt very weak. "What do you want?"

"Just tying up a few loose ends," he said lightly.

I stared at him. Were *we* the loose ends? What was he going to do with us?

"What about Charlie?" I hesitated, not wanting to give away what I knew about her attempt to join Riley as an undercover resistance agent.

"I saw her earlier," Riley said briskly. "She's not here now."

What did that mean?

"You've seen *Charlie*?" Jas's voice shook. "Is she okay?"

"She's fine." Riley stood up. "On a voyage of discovery, in fact."

So he knew Charlie wanted to find out about her dad. Suddenly I was sure that whole business was a trick too. "You lied to her about that," I hissed. "I *know* you did."

Riley gazed down at me, his face a blank. "I never lied to either of you, Nat. Now, get some rest. Gather your strength."

He turned and walked out, leaving Jas and me alone.

Jas helped me struggle onto my elbows. My head still felt woolly as I took in the room. It was larger than the attic where I'd found Jas, with four mattresses laid out on the floor. I'd been in here before. This was where we'd all slept when Charlie and I had come for our original training weekend—when we'd been put in a cell with Parveen and George, when I'd met Riley for the first time and when I'd been so stupidly impressed with him.

"How long was I out?" I asked.

"I don't know," Jas said. "I don't have my phone or a watch and there's no clock, but it was hours and hours. They took you away and brought me in here. They brought you back about twenty minutes ago." She reached for my hand. "Are you okay?"

I nodded.

"You know he drugged me too when I got here. Once you come around, it's true—you do feel better after a few minutes."

"I'm fine," I said. Humiliation burned inside me. I had been so naive when I first met Riley, thinking that he meant what he said about standing up to extremists, when in reality he was even worse than they were—being both violent and dishonest—all in order to gain power for himself. Jas might be convinced Aaron wouldn't have knowingly led me into a trap, but I wasn't so sure. As far as I was concerned, it was entirely possible that Aaron—and his father—had been in on the whole thing.

I stood up slowly and staggered over to the nearest window. It was set with iron bars, just like the one farther along the wall. Outside, I could see the sun was low over the trees across the field where Aaron and I had hidden earlier. Walking more steadily now, I headed to the door and rattled the handle. If I'd had some kind of flat card with me, I might have been able to force the lock, but as things were, we were stuck. I was sure there'd be a soldier guarding it anyway.

"Nat, I'm scared."

I crossed the room back to Jas. She put her arms around me and started sobbing, her tears seeping into my top.

"What did Riley mean when he said 'tie up loose ends'?" she hiccupped.

I hugged her tighter. I didn't want to think about what Riley meant—or how much danger Jas and I were now in. Anyway, there was no point in alarming her.

"Riley just likes to intimidate people," I murmured, patting her back. "We'll be okay."

Jas looked up into my eyes. "You look terrible," she said. "And what was all that about Charlie? And what about Aaron? Did he really come with you?"

We sat together on one of the thin mattresses. I explained how Aaron had made contact and Jas repeated her insistance that he would never have lied.

"You're my brother, Nat. Aaron respects that. He respects *you*."

I shook my head, unconvinced. Aaron was his father's son, and his father was—at the end of the day—a politician, no more to be trusted than any other politician. I couldn't bring myself to say it to Jas, but it seemed to me highly likely that Aaron had only pretended to be interested in Jas as a way of getting to me.

I steered the topic on to Charlie, explaining—in whispers, in case Riley had the room bugged—that she had gone undercover to get evidence against him. Jas seemed cheered by the news, but I wasn't so optimistic myself. Even if Riley was convinced Charlie wanted to find out about her dad, I couldn't see him believing that she wanted to rejoin the EFA, which would surely make it impossible for her to gather any information we could use against him. Meanwhile, her life was in danger every second she was undercover. Riley had said she wasn't here, but for all I knew, she could be. She might even know *we* were here. It was impossible to be sure.

CHARLIE

The Cornish sun beat down, hot on my cheeks.

"How can *you* be my father?" I glared at the old man, still leaning on his stick. I sounded rude, but I didn't care. "My dad was John Stockwell," I went on, my hands on my hips. "You don't look anything like him. Apart from anything else, you're too old."

There was a pause. The man gazed thoughtfully at me. It was hard to work out how old he actually was. His face was lined and his hair was almost entirely white, but he also exuded energy. It shone through his slightly slanting eyes, their shape and color so similar to my own. I thought of the DNA-test result Riley had shown me, and a chill settled in my chest.

"Okay, let me explain," the man said slowly. "Before my accident I was a soldier in the British army, commanding officer of John Stockwell, your mother's husband. One day seventeen years ago, when we were home on leave, well, John got drunk one night—he often did. He slept it off on the couch and your mother and I"—he sighed—"we got together, just that one time." He looked at me. "You were the result, though I didn't know it at the time."

I stared at him. "You went with my *mum?*" I felt sick to my stomach. It couldn't be true. Mum would surely *never* have been unfaithful.

Uchi sighed. "I'm so sorry, Charlie. All I can say is that your mother was very beautiful and John was a lot of fun, but I'm not sure he really appreciated her. So, in your mum's defense, she was lonely and I was available and, though you might not believe it to look at me now, in my midforties I was still a very handsome man."

Midforties? That meant he must be at least sixty now. I shook my head. Tears pricked at my eyes. If what he was saying was true, Mum hadn't just been unfaithful. She had lied to me . . . lied and lied and lied my whole life.

"I felt very badly about our night together," Uchi went on. "I left the next morning before John woke up. My leave ended a few days later, and I was on another tour of duty before there was an opportunity to meet up again. He sent me a few texts over the next month or so. I replied, but I kept my distance. I was ashamed of what I'd done. I had no idea your mother was pregnant and, even if I had known, I would have assumed the child was John's."

"Did *he* know?" I asked.

"I doubt it," Uchi said. "Let's go up to the house. You must be thirsty after that long drive."

He turned and started walking slowly, leaning heavily on his cane. I followed. It was a beautiful day, the bright sun high in the sky, a warm, salty breeze playing across my face.

"But Mum knew you were my father—and she lied to him and

to me about it." I said the words flatly, trying to let them sink in.

"Don't be too hard on her, Charlie," Uchi said softly. "Your mother was young and naive. She couldn't have known for sure *who* the father was, so she probably decided it was best for everyone if she let herself and everyone else believe it was John."

"It was still wrong," I muttered.

"Anyway, your mum didn't contact me, and then, a few months later, just before you were born, I had my accident." He looked down at his walking stick.

"What happened?" I asked.

"I was paralyzed from the legs down during a training exercise," Uchi said. "I was in the hospital for months, unable to walk. My face was left badly scarred, and as for this"—he pointed to his hair—"I went gray virtually overnight after they told me I had only a 5 percent chance of ever walking again. But I refused to give up, and in the end I got sufficient movement back to hobble along with a stick. I was very angry. Particularly at the paucity of help that was offered once I left the hospital. I alienated my parents, my girlfriend. I went crazy with fury. I didn't give your mother another thought, I'm afraid. Nor John, nor any of my former friends. I became bitter and radicalized against the stupidity of war generally and Western governments in particular. I lost my way in alcohol for a while. Then I traveled: India, Africa, and then, for most of the next ten years, I was in Eastern Europe. I read *everything*. Studied hard. Met some fascinating people . . . and gradually I pieced together my own philosophy."

"Right." We were making very little progress along the asphalt driveway. Uchi moved in what I could only describe as a shuffle, and I was having to work hard to keep my own pace as slow as his. Confused thoughts raced around my head. Alongside the burning humiliation that Mum had lied to me for basically my entire life, I just didn't know how to feel about this man, my *blood* father. Right now it didn't seem real that he was actually my dad. That is, I believed in my head that it was true, but it didn't *feel* true in my bones. Surely you were supposed to experience some kind of connection to your parents. But when I looked at this limping, white-haired old man, I didn't feel he really had anything to do with me. I couldn't make sense of it all. Part of me was curious. Part of me was angry. Part of me just felt overwhelmed.

The strangest thing was having the idea of John Stockwell being my dad taken away—and with it all the stories and pictures I had grown up with. It meant, of course, that most of what Mum had told me about my dad could no longer be true. On the other hand, all the stuff I'd found out from Riley—which Uchi was now confirming—was still relevant, wasn't it? Riley had said that Uchi was a political philosopher, and philosophy was about ideas and ambitions—theories, not practice. Maybe Riley had simply twisted all Uchi's ideas; maybe Uchi didn't know what Riley had really been doing; maybe I would still be able to open his eyes.

"Philosophy's all very well," I said. "But what's happened through Riley and the English Freedom Army isn't just a theory. He's . . . There have been bombs." Mum's disappointed face as we argued in the market just before she died flashed before my eyes. I swallowed, hard. "People have died. *Innocent* people."

Uchi stopped walking. There was a long pause as he looked at me, his brow furrowed, a deeply troubled expression on his face.

"I am very sorry about your mother," he said at last. "I'm sorry about all the innocent lives lost."

So he *did* know. I looked down at the asphalt. Of course he did. I felt myself flushing at my own stupidity.

"I'd like to try to explain it to you," Uchi said.

I met his gaze, my embarrassment giving way to anger. "Explain why my mother had to die?" I snapped. "Yeah, I'd like to hear how you justify that."

As soon as I'd spoken, I inwardly cursed myself. I was supposed to be here to get evidence on Riley. If Uchi knew about everything evil that Riley had done, that could only help me. I needed to keep my feelings out of it. And yet being face-to-face with my biological father brought up a tumult of emotions that made it impossible to focus on what I'd thought would be so straightforward: to get evidence on Riley and expose him. Nat's words about the whole thing being a lot harder than I thought it would be echoed in my head again.

Uchi sighed. "Let's get to the house." He started hobbling along the asphalt again, leaning heavily on his stick. I fell into step beside him, the sun fierce on my face.

Uchi was silent for a moment. Then he cleared his throat. "The first thing you need to understand is that we're engaged in a war."

"*War?*" I frowned. "Against who?"

"Against corrupt democratic governments." Uchi paused.

"And in war, innocent people die. A big part of my philosophy is the necessity for leaders to lead, to make hard decisions, to be ruthless."

Hard decisions meant killing people. My heart thudded against my ribs.

"Before I explain my philosophy, I want you to know that I have inspired quite a following in Eastern Europe," Uchi said proudly. "In fact, that's where I got the name Uchi. Did I explain that? It's from 'ucitel,' the Czech for 'teacher.'"

"I see." How could this man—my own flesh and blood—be talking about theories and teaching in the same breath as bombs and terrorism? Half of me wanted to understand. The other half wanted to yell that he and his views were obscene.

"In my way," Uchi went on with a modest shrug, "I've been as influential as philosophical thinkers such as Gramsci and Locke."

I stared at him blankly. "Who are they?"

He shook his head. "Clearly your education leaves something to be desired. Let me put it in simple terms. . . ." He paused.

Great. Now I felt patronized on top of everything else.

"If I had to sum it up in a sentence, I would say phase one of my revolutionary theory concerns the steps needed to infiltrate, then overthrow corrupt Western democracies."

I stared at him. "You mean like the League of Iron?" I asked, struggling to keep the fury out of my voice. "Using violence to get power and stomping all over people who don't agree with you or who've got the wrong color skin?"

"No. *No*, not at all," Uchi spluttered. "The League of Iron are racist thugs, fascists without a coherent philosophy."

"So you're more like Communists, then?" I asked, remembering my history class last semester.

Uchi shook his head impatiently. "The Marxist-Leninist dialectic is as discredited as the tyrants who abused and oppressed in its name."

I stared at him, not wanting to admit I had no idea what he was talking about.

"My revolution will lead to freedom, not tyranny," Uchi said, his eyes glittering. "Imagine England as a glacier—a river frozen in time by endless laws and small-minded bureaucracy. Once we shine the bright heat of our light on that river, it will melt and flow as nature intended. Take away the state and the people are free to move, to grow, to inspire others in their turn." He turned to me. "All who can make a contribution are welcome. All who wish to build a brave new England will find a role, a place, a home."

"And how do you know that the river-flowing stuff will follow after you've gotten rid of what's here right now?" I asked.

"That's what Riley and the Future Party are for," Uchi explained. "To make sure the country comes with us as we establish a new, libertarian society with basic protections for the vulnerable but everyone able to make their own way, unhampered by the state."

We turned a bend and emerged in front of a square, cream-painted cottage. The pretty green shutters at the window and the flowers that decorated the beds around the house made a sharp contrast with the high-barred gates that ran on either side of the building.

"We can talk more later, but there is one thing I do need you to know right now." Uchi looked troubled. "I had no idea your mother was going to be in that market. And remember, until I read the victim list, I didn't know you existed. Even then I assumed you were John's. It was only several months after you'd joined the EFA and I'd checked your birth date that I realized you might be mine. I asked Riley to get a sample of your DNA. We did the test and—well, the rest you know. I wanted to meet you and have you join us. That's why I asked Riley to bring you to me after the House of Commons explosion."

An explosion in which Nat had been left for dead. I couldn't understand how Uchi could refer so calmly to a bomb blast that had killed and maimed people. I desperately wished Nat were here—he would be as appalled as I was. An image of his handsome, serious face flashed into my head. Where was he right now? Was he busy making plans against Riley? Was he thinking about me?

"What do you say, Charlie?" Uchi stopped as we reached the house. He was panting slightly, presumably from the exertion of walking along the drive. "I know you came here because you were curious about me, but will you stay and let me give you the special treatment and training you deserve?"

"Special training?" I frowned. "For what?"

"Training to be part of the leadership this country will need. For now a part to play at my side. Eventually perhaps a role like

Riley's . . ." He hesitated. "Will you stay here with me?"

A million emotions surged through my head. On the one hand I felt elated. This was *exactly* what I'd hoped for: a chance to be accepted, to find information I could use against Riley and the EFA. And yet I also felt miserable that I was related to Uchi and therefore to all the terrible things he had made happen. Worst of all—and I hated to admit this—a part of me was loving the fact that after all these years I finally had a father, someone who cared about me, who wanted to be with me.

I looked down at the gravel. "I don't know what to say," I mumbled.

"Say yes," Uchi urged. "Apart from anything else, your aunt and uncle have disowned you, so you really have nowhere else to go."

Thanks to you and Riley framing me. I thought the words, but I didn't say them. After the House of Commons blast and my "kidnapping" of Aaron, my aunt and uncle had totally swallowed the police line that I was a dangerous terrorist. I'd seen them say as much in a news interview.

I carried on staring at the gravel, now feeling desperately uncomfortable. I wanted to tell Uchi that I was thrilled to be joining him, but—just as Nat had predicted—it was hard to lie, to cover up my real feelings.

Uchi tilted his head to one side. "I can see you are angry, Charlie. I understand that. But your anger is a positive force and, though you may not believe it right now, everything that has happened in your life so far will serve you well in the future. And you do have a very bright future, Charlie, if you want it. You're part of an elite, even if you haven't yet realized it."

"Right." I sniffed. What a load of nonsense. Parveen and George and Nat were just as smart and strong as I was, but Uchi had been happy to see them all die.

My head cleared at last. I was here to find out what I could about Riley's operations in order to get evidence to expose him as a power-hungry murderer. Uchi clearly worked closely with Riley, so the more time I spent with Uchi, the more likely I was to get proof to use against Riley.

"So where do we begin?" I asked. "More bombs?"

"We have already begun—and yes, bombs are a part of it," Uchi said, looking pleased. "We live in a society where people have been brainwashed into thinking that democracy is the best method of government, that to run a country you need a big state. They're wrong. I believe the state should be scaled back—a few essential services, the army, the police. But aims like that are too radical for the masses, so the masses have to be nudged toward them."

"You 'nudge' them by bombing them?" I asked, genuinely bewildered.

"Yes. We make people realize the state is corrupt and chaotic, and then we step in to clean up the mess."

"But you've created the mess in the first place."

"Well, perhaps in a very narrow sense, but not really if you look at the big picture," Uchi said. "It's like a tornado has already happened and thousands of homes are destroyed. We're just coming along and breaking up a few extra bits of furniture to make the point that everything's gone."

It was on the tip of my tongue to point out that you could hardly compare breaking up some chairs with murdering people in markets, but I held myself back. I needed to convince Uchi that I was at least open to his arguments.

"Actually, there's an important role I'd like you to play in our next operation, if you're willing?" Uchi raised his eyebrows.

The hairs on the back of my neck prickled, despite the sunshine beating down. I hadn't expected *that*. Obviously, an invitation to join the very next job gave me a great opportunity to get proof against Uchi and Riley. And Uchi seemed genuinely delighted to have me with him, but was Riley really prepared to confide in me so quickly?

"Okay," I said, trying to keep the suspicion out of my voice. "What's the 'operation'?"

"I'm not going to give you details right now," Uchi said, "but I will involve you, if you are genuinely prepared to join us. I hear you're a very impressive junior EFA agent already, and I'm looking forward to seeing you in action." He smiled. "But enough of all that for now. Come on. You must be tired after your journey, and I'm certainly tired of standing. Let's go into the house."

I glanced at the cottage again. A second soldier, as young as the guard who had followed us up the path, was standing at the door. I suddenly remembered what Riley had said about this being his family's home, the place where his son and his son's mother lived. Was I going to meet them, too?

"It really is wonderful to be with you at last," Uchi said.

I turned back to him. His dark eyes gleamed with emotion. Instinct told me that whatever terrible atrocities he had planned in the past or was planning for the future, he truly wanted me to join him and to believe in his stupid theories.

"Thank you," I said, forcing a smile to my lips. "It's great to meet you too . . . Dad."

NAT

Jas and I talked for more than an hour while my head cleared from the drug Riley had given me. Our conversation skittered over a whole bunch of stuff, from our concerns over what Riley was doing to smaller, sillier memories from our shared past at home and at school. The only subjects we steered well clear of were Jas's feelings for Aaron and mine for Charlie. I held back mostly from awkwardness. Jas had never really had a boyfriend before, and there had never been anyone serious for me, either. I didn't know how to talk to her about that, and all other topics seemed easier.

"How are Mum and Dad?" I asked.

"Worried about you." Jas sniffed. "Mum's spending even more time at the hospital than ever. Apparently, Lucas opened his eyes or moved his hand or something. Only for a few seconds. The doctors said it was a good sign but didn't necessarily mean anything, but Mum's convinced he's about to come out of his coma."

We fell silent. Mum's obsession with Lucas's recovery had been going on since the bomb that had left him unconscious. I wasn't surprised to hear she was still spending all her time at the hospital, but I couldn't help feeling a twinge of anger. She should have been focused on Jas since I'd been gone, looking after her, not wasting time at Lucas's bedside. No wonder Jas had been spending so much time with Aaron and his family.

"Nat?" Jas tugged at my arm.

"What, sorry?"

"I know I keep asking, but what do you think Riley's done with Aaron?" Color rose in her cheeks. "I'm—"

But before she could finish her sentence, the door swung open and Aaron himself was pushed inside. As he stumbled across the floor, Jas scrambled to her feet and rushed over.

I watched as she flung her arms around him. He held her tightly, then drew back enough to take her face in his hands and kiss her. Jas beamed up at him. Man, she was totally in love.

I looked away. It wasn't just that it felt weird seeing Jas with someone, but couldn't she do better than Aaron? Even if he wasn't secretly working for Riley, he was still—well, he was a bit of a jerk.

The three of us sat on the mattresses, discussing our situation. Aaron—his arm around Jas's shoulders—claimed he'd been drugged and that, like me, he'd had his phone taken from him.

"Riley questioned and questioned me," he whispered. "I told him I was an IT geek, so he'd believe how I tracked your phone. Luckily, he knows I couldn't have said anything to my dad about coming here, so my dad's cover is still intact." He paused. "Which means he won't hurt us."

"It means he won't hurt *you*," I said. "It's your father Riley's best friends with, not ours."

Aaron looked shocked. Jas squeezed his hand, then looked up at me.

"What d'you think they *are* going to do with us?" she asked.

I shook my head, not wanting to speak out loud my belief that the only possible reason Riley could have for keeping me here was to kill me. Jas, too, now that she'd become involved.

"Maybe he's going to try to use Nat to run another mission for him," Aaron suggested.

"I don't think so," I muttered.

Jas gasped. "Suppose Aaron's right? Suppose he wants to use *all* of us for a mission?"

"He won't," I said. Again, I didn't want to say it, but the idea that Riley would want to use either untrained Aaron or anxious Jas on any kind of mission was ridiculous.

"You don't know that for sure," Aaron said, sitting forward. "He might want us to set off a bomb like he got you to do before."

"I didn't *know* it was a bomb," I snapped, irritation rising inside me. "He won't use us if he can't completely trust us, and as he can't—"

"He might force you somehow," Aaron interrupted.

"I'm telling you there's no way I'd do anything for Riley, not even if he says he'll kill me." I stopped at the sight of Jas's horrified expression.

"*Kill* you?" she gasped. "For not doing what he says? Oh, Nat, *no*."

I stared at her helplessly.

"Hey, hey . . . Shh . . ." Aaron hugged Jas to him. "I won't let *anyone* hurt Nat."

"Is that right?" I said, feeling riled. How on earth did Aaron think he was in any position to protect me? Jas sniffed back her tears, then gazed up at him adoringly. Aaron grinned back at her, and a dimple appeared in his cheek.

I rolled my eyes. That smile of his was just about the most annoying thing I'd ever seen. Still, at least Jas had stopped crying. I stood up, walked over to the window, and gazed out through the bars. With both door and window locked, there was no way out of this room. No way to escape what I was more and more sure Riley had planned: our murders.

"I think Nat's a little uncomfortable with us going out together," Aaron said lightly from across the room.

I said nothing.

"No, Aaron. Nat likes you," Jas insisted. She looked up at me. "Don't you, Nat?"

"Mmm . . ." I stared out at the fields below.

An uneasy silence fell. Aaron came over and stood beside me at the window. He took a deep breath.

"Is there a problem?"

I turned to face him. "Jas says you're trustworthy, but I don't know if I can believe you. I think maybe you were in on this whole thing."

"No, Nat," Jas insisted. She was hunched on her mattress, hugging her knees and looking up at us with big eyes.

Aaron spread his hands. "I'm locked up, same as you," he said. "Doesn't that count for anything?"

"Not really." I looked away.

Aaron moved closer, lowering his voice so Jas couldn't hear. "Are you sure this isn't mostly about me being with your sister?" he asked.

"No," I muttered, also keeping my voice low. "But now that you mention it, I'm not sure you two seeing each other is a good thing, your dad being who he is."

Aaron's face darkened.

"What are you two saying?" Jas asked.

"Nat's just asking about my dad," Aaron said. He turned to me and lowered his voice to a whisper again. "And I'm telling him that my dad is trying to expose Riley exactly like he is, none of which has *anything* to do with me and your sister." His cheeks flushed a bright red.

I said nothing, just stared out the window. A few moments passed; the room filled with tension.

Then Aaron folded his arms and leaned over, his mouth by my ear.

"I'm dating your sister, Nat," he hissed. "Get over it."

I shook my head. "Fine," I muttered. "But I have no idea what she sees in you."

Another pause. I kept my gaze on the woods outside, but I could feel my face burning. That had been rude. And stupid. Regardless of whether or not Aaron was a Riley spy, there was no point antagonizing him. And it wasn't fair to Jas, either. I turned to him, ready to apologize, but much to my surprise, Aaron was smiling.

"I have no idea what she sees in me either." He chuckled. "She's way out of my league, but there you go."

I grinned in spite of myself as the tension eased and Aaron moved away, back to Jas. He was still an idiot—and possibly worse. But I decided to give him the benefit of the doubt. For now.

Outside, the sun was getting lower on the horizon, the sky dotted with clouds. Suddenly I missed Charlie with a physical pain.

"Nat?" Jas said, her voice timid.

I turned around.

"We need to find a way out of here," she said.

I nodded. "I know, but the doors and windows are locked, the guards are armed. . . ." I looked at her helplessly. "I don't know what to do."

"Then let us help you *work out* what to do," Aaron said earnestly. "You're the one with the training. Go through the options. Jas and I will help you make a plan. I can run fast and I can fight too. . . ."

I opened my mouth to tell him that fighting would be of no help whatsoever—and then it struck me that, if we were smart about it, fighting our way out of here was our best option.

I frowned as an idea bubbled into my head.

"What?" Aaron asked. "What are you thinking?"

I went over and crouched down beside them. "Listen," I said. Then I drew them close and whispered my plan.

CHARLIE

I followed Uchi into the cottage. In spite of all my anxieties, I was intrigued to meet Riley's son. I was expecting a little boy—after all, Riley was only in his early thirties—so I was taken by complete surprise when a tall, black-haired teenager in black jeans and a gray sweatshirt slouched out of the kitchen, a shorter, dark-skinned woman at his side.

"Gracie and her son, Spider," Uchi said, introducing us.

I shook hands with Gracie. She seemed nice—a lot warmer than Martina and very beautiful, with long, glossy dark hair and clear, tawny skin. Her son looked up. I stared, struck by how good-looking he was: olive-skinned and square-jawed, just like Riley, but with high cheekbones and dark, intense eyes.

He shrugged by way of a greeting. Well, that was fine with me. I wasn't here to make friends. Uchi said he would see me after I'd eaten and asked Spider to show me around.

Spider looked neither pleased nor annoyed by this request. If anything, he seemed bored. He obeyed Uchi in long-suffering silence, showing me around the first floor—a series of rather flouncy, flowery rooms with contrasting patterns on the sofas, curtains, and rugs—then upstairs to the four bedrooms. I was given a small room on the right of the main landing. It was nowhere near as nice as my room in Riley's house, but it looked comfortable enough. A tunic, a sweatshirt, and two pairs of leggings had been laid out on the bed. I picked up the tunic. It wasn't my sort of thing at all, but it would be easy to move in, which, I was guessing, was the point. I wondered how soon my training for the mission Uchi had mentioned would start.

I kept my eyes open for anything I could use to communicate with Nat, but there were no landlines in the house and I was guessing the only computers were kept in the one locked room— off the hall on the first floor—that Spider had merely pointed to in passing, saying it was "Uchi's office." He had a really upper-class accent, very different from both Riley's and Uchi's. That, together with his sneering attitude, was starting to make me think he was a total snob.

After we'd looked around inside, Uchi took me back outside, saying if I didn't need a rest, he was eager to explain a little more about his philosophy to me. It was chilly but beautiful in the backyard. We sat on the patio, looking out at the sea just a hundred yards or so away beyond the grass, which sloped sharply down to where the waves crashed against the rocks. Uchi tucked a blanket over his legs as he spoke. I pulled on my fleece and tried to follow what he was saying, but it was all just so complicated.

"Were you really a soldier?" I asked after ten minutes or so. Apart from anything else, it was hard to imagine someone so old and slow and deliberate in their way of speaking ever having leaped about, firing a gun.

"I was," Uchi said. "Though I don't think I was a very good one: too thoughtful, too independent, too clever."

"And yet you must have killed people," I persisted.

Uchi's dark eyes pierced through me. "Sometimes the means justify the ends," he said.

"And what are 'the ends'?" I asked, determined to make him explain his stupid ideas in language that made sense to me. "What is it exactly you're aiming for? Because I can see that a lot of democratic governments might be a bit useless, but what's the alternative that's so much better?"

Uchi leaned forward. "Let's start with what you just said: 'a bit useless,'" he said. "The truth is that democracy is *extremely* useless. It's entirely half assed. It doesn't get enough done. It's always a compromise. No country can become truly great as a democracy."

I frowned. "What about America? That's a world power."

"Riddled with corruption," Uchi said, waving his hand dismissively. "At any one time at least half the city mayors are taking bribes. Ditto the state governors. And don't get me started on Congress or any of the postwar presidents."

"But—"

"A great country needs a great leader. He—or she—will give the nation hope and prosperity. In return, all the citizens have to give up is the *illusion* of democratic freedom."

"*Illusion?* What do you mean?"

"Well, in a democracy, the majority always wins. So lots

of people—sometimes the most vulnerable—end up ignored. They're not 'free' at all. Meanwhile politicians put all their efforts into winning votes and gaining power rather than doing what's best for the country. And most of the time it leads to chaos. Look at the UK right now. Coalition after coalition government, each reversing the previous government's policies. How can a system like that ever get anything done?"

I stared at him.

"What Uchi's saying is that you think you're free because you have a vote, but actually that vote is bought and sold at levels you're not even aware of," Gracie said softly from the door that led back into the cottage.

I started; I hadn't heard her come outside. Gracie walked over and placed a plate of pastries in front of us.

"Ah, my favorite." Uchi's eyes twinkled as he took one. "Help yourself, Charlie."

I shook my head, unwilling to be deflected from the conversation.

"Well, personally speaking, I don't have a vote yet," I said. "But when I do, what both of you are saying is that I should—everyone should—give my vote to just one person?"

Gracie nodded. "Roman." Her cheeks flushed as she said his name. Was she still in love with him? That would explain why she and Martina didn't get along.

"Yes," Uchi said, apparently oblivious to Gracie's self-consciousness. "Roman offers real hope," he went on, his voice tinged with pride. "That's why the public will elect him and his party in greater numbers than ever next week."

"I see," I said. "And what about once he's elected?"

"Then he and the Future Party will bring in emergency powers and gradually set about dismantling the corrupt democratic system that we currently endure."

I sat back. If the country had any idea what Riley was really like, there was no way they would vote for him. Then he would lose his seat in Parliament and, with it, all hope of gaining real political power.

I *had* to get proof. And before the election next week.

"So Riley's . . ." I paused, searching for the right word. "He's the figurehead for everything."

"Exactly." Uchi looked pleased. "The people wouldn't accept a leader like me, all crippled and scarred. But Riley is young and attractive. He builds up trust among the public with his charm and his emphasis on support for ordinary people, but he is also working secretly through the English Freedom Army."

With its emphasis on bombs and murder.

"I suppose you might say," Uchi mused, clearly unaware of what I was thinking, "that I am the brains behind Riley's charisma."

And behind the bomb that killed Mum.

I took a deep breath. "So what are you planning?"

Uchi chuckled. "Let's not run before we can walk. You might be my daughter, but you know the EFA insists on a cell-based structure in which no single individual knows too much about the overall plan. And Riley will need to be convinced that I have genuinely persuaded you to join us. Anyway, right now I just want to get to know you. We have a lifetime to catch up on." He smiled, then tucked his blanket under his legs and took a large bite out of his pastry.

I stared out to sea, my emotions churning inside me. I was trying hard to tell myself that coming here had been entirely about getting evidence to expose Riley, but it wasn't true. I had thought earlier that Uchi really did care about me. But I was starting to realize that although he said he wanted to get to know me, he hadn't actually asked me a single question about myself. He didn't seem curious in the slightest about my life with either Mum or Aunt Karen or, more recently, with Brian, Gail, and Rosa. He didn't even want to know the superficial kind of things that adults always asked, like whether I had hobbies and which subjects I most liked at school. He hadn't asked me about Nat, or our time on the run, or if I had friends or a boyfriend.

If anyone had asked, I would have said I didn't care, but the truth was that, after so long without a dad and so many years wondering about him, it was hard to come face-to-face with the reality of an actual father and find that he was so wrapped up in himself—not to mention so blinded by his own beliefs that he justified killing innocent people to achieve them. Uchi wasn't a man I could see myself liking or respecting. And that hurt.

"Did you ever get married?" I asked, wondering suddenly if I had a series of half brothers and sisters somewhere.

"No." Uchi sighed. "No wife. No kids. You're my only blood relative, Charlie. Just as I am yours."

I thought of Uncle Brian and how, if his brother wasn't really my dad, then he wasn't really my uncle and Rosa not really my cousin. But there was still Mum's family.

"I have my aunt Karen," I said. "Mum's sister. She's a blood relative."

"Mmmn," Uchi murmured, as if Karen didn't really count. "Ah, yes, of course. I forgot about her."

I gritted my teeth. I was starting to see how Uchi could justify all the deaths he and his stupid theories had caused, including Mum's. It was as if he saw people like chess pieces on a board, there to be moved around for his convenience. Not real.

"What about Spider?" I asked. "Are you close to him?"

"I hardly know the boy," Uchi said. "I've been here myself for only a short while, and Spider was at his school until a week ago. He's been training hard for your mission, though."

"Training?" I gulped. Was Uchi suggesting that this operation he wanted me to be part of would involve the arrogant boy who had shown me around earlier too? "Doesn't Riley mind putting his son in danger?"

"Oh, I think Roman believes that if Spider is to become a man—a soldier—some risks are inevitable, but he's made sure the boy has been well trained."

"By you?" I asked.

"No." Uchi chuckled. "I'm past all that physical stuff now. You know his trainer, I believe. A man called Taylor?"

I froze. Taylor had been the leader of our cell when Nat and I joined the EFA. He had trained us both and, until he betrayed us, I had liked and trusted him. I hadn't seen him since that terrible day, just over a month ago, when he had tricked me into kidnapping Aaron and sent Nat to die in the House of Commons bomb blast. I knew that Riley was ultimately responsible for what the EFA did, but there was no one on earth I hated more than Taylor.

"Is he here?" I asked.

But Uchi was clearly lost in his own thoughts again.

"You know," he mused, "considering how young he was when he became a father, Roman has always made a huge effort to support both Gracie and the boy. I admire him for that."

"What about Taylor?" I persisted.

"He comes every few days. I'm not sure when he's arriving next," Uchi said vaguely. "Not my side of things."

"He'll be here tomorrow," Spider said, loping out onto the patio. With his long, lean arms and legs, his dark, fitted clothes, and his slightly awkward way of moving, he actually looked rather like a spider. "He just contacted me, in fact. Said I needed to get started on your training, Charlie."

I stared at him. *"You're* training *me?"*

"Luckily for you, yes." For the first time since I met him, Spider smiled, revealing a set of perfectly even, white teeth. The smile transformed his face, bringing his good looks to life. For a second I caught a glimpse of his father's charm. Then the sullen expression came back, like a mask. "Come on, then. We've got only a couple of hours now before it gets dark."

As Uchi limped inside, Spider grabbed a pastry and led me down the grass to the sea. The wind whipped up as we walked, and I tugged the fleece more tightly around me. We reached the rocks that led directly to the sea, and there I saw what hadn't been visible from the patio: a large rock pool, roughly thirty yards square, half full with water.

"It comes in from the sea," Spider explained, pointing to the pool. "When the tide comes in, the water level rises."

"Wow." I was genuinely amazed. I'd never seen such a thing before. "It's like your own, natural swimming pool."

"Yeah." Spider looked down his long, elegant nose at me. His voice oozed contempt. "That's what I just said."

What a jerk.

"So where did you get your nickname?" I snapped. "From someone who thought you looked spiky and poisonous?"

"It happened in elementary school," Spider said, again sounding as if the question bored him. "Years ago."

"Where d'you go to school now?"

"Boarding school in the Midlands. When I'm there, no one knows I'm my dad's son. It's like this cool secret. They think my dad's dead—just like you thought yours was."

"You know about Uchi being my dad?"

"'Course," Spider sneered. "You're the only one around here who didn't."

"Right." I said. Did he have a degree in rudeness?

Spider held up the pastry he had brought from the patio. "I'm going to eat this," he said, "while you get changed so we can start training in the pool."

"The pool?"

"That's what I said." He pointed to a pile of black rubber on the far side of a rock I hadn't noticed before. "It's a wet suit."

"Yes. I can see that." I grabbed the suit and went back into the house to change. As I dragged the rubber over my limbs, it occurred to me that being trained so soon after arriving must mean the operation Uchi had talked about was going to happen in the very near future. A shiver crept down my spine as I wondered what it would involve. I couldn't bear the thought of having to go along with a plot in which innocent people might die. I would just have to find out exactly what was planned as fast as possible, then get proof that would show the world how evil Riley and everyone associated with him really were.

By the time I got outside again, the rock pool was full of water and Spider had changed into his own wet suit. It made him look even more like a spider—a dark, malevolent one. I walked down to the rock pool, feeling uncomfortable and self-conscious. Spider's eyes widened as I approached. He stared at me, clearly transfixed, and I felt the heat rise in my cheeks.

A moment later the scowl was back on his face. "Suits you," he sneered.

Sarcastic jerk. "Why are we wearing these anyway?" I asked. I'd expected the mission Uchi and Riley were planning to involve guns and bombs—that maybe I was going to be shown how to arm and set an actual explosive device. I couldn't imagine why I needed a wet suit for anything like that.

Spider glanced at the pool. "What do you think?"

I peered through the water. A row of metal hoops I hadn't

spotted before were fastened to the bottom of the rock. "Are we going to have to swim through those?"

"Yes," Spider said contemptuously. "Why? Can't you swim underwater?"

"I can swim fine." Irritation rose inside me. "Why d'you have to sound so snotty about everything?"

Spider rolled his eyes. "Don't be so emotional. I didn't ask to babysit you."

"*Babysit?*" I glared at him.

Spider pointed to the metal hoops. "There are ten of those, okay? By the end of the class you need to be able to swim through them and back again in one breath. Understand?"

"What are we training for, sports day?" I snapped.

Spider ignored this. He crouched down at the poolside, where two sets of flippers and masks sat in the sun. He handed one set to me. "Put these on."

It wasn't as easy as it looked either to walk in the flippers or adjust the mask correctly over my face so that no water seeped in around the sides, but at last I was in the pool and ready. The water was cold, but the rubber suit kept me surprisingly warm. The flippers, so cumbersome on dry land, made propelling myself through the water light and easy. I swam up and down a few times, enjoying the sense of gliding through the soft waves. Then I dived down and pulled myself through the first hoop. It was too narrow to swim through easily using my arms, but I did a sort of wriggle, which seemed to work. Using a cramped doggy paddle, I made it to the end of the row, then burst back through the water's surface again. I was already out of breath, but I tried to hide it, not wanting Spider to see.

"You need to go faster to do it there and back," Spider said. "Look."

He ducked under the water and swam fast: down and through all ten hoops and back again, far quicker than I had. His movements were relatively uncoordinated on dry land, but underwater he moved like an eel—sleek and smooth. It was mesmerizing to watch.

He knew it too.

"That's how it's done," he said as he reemerged, shaking the water out of his hair.

I stared at him, feeling really annoyed. "Fine." I submerged and swam—faster this time—through the hoops.

We kept going forever, until the sun had almost set and lights glowed from inside the house. Spider showed me how to move my body in a kind of ripple to avoid knocking against the sides of the hoops, which were too narrow to allow for a full arm stroke. It was a tricky technique to master, but after a few tries I got it. Spider acknowledged my progress with a curt "well done," though he still refused to tell me what we were training for.

"Will we need to swim through a tunnel or something?" Despite the improvements I'd made so far, the thought of having to hold my breath while swimming through such a narrow space was really daunting. Not that I had any intention of letting Spider see I was in any way intimidated.

Spider acted as if he hadn't heard me. With his curls dampened and slicked back off his face, his cheekbones were even more noticeable, as were the long dark lashes that framed his eyes. I hated to admit it, but he looked like a model. He took a breath and dived again. This time he swam through the hoops and back in record time, then turned underwater and swam through each one a third time before breaking the surface.

"Did you see that?" he asked, suddenly sounding much younger and nicer than he had before.

"Cool," I acknowledged grudgingly.

Spider's face split with another huge grin.

"You should smile more often," I said dryly before diving under the water and attempting the hoops again.

This time as I emerged into the air, I caught a glimpse of Uchi watching me from the locked downstairs room that Spider had said was his office.

I adjusted my mask and dived, a new plan resolving itself in my head. Apart from Spider, Gracie, and Uchi, I'd seen only two young EFA soldiers since I'd arrived. But Spider had said Taylor was coming tomorrow—and Taylor was both ruthless and very experienced. That meant my best chance for uncovering the details of whatever underwater operation Spider and I were being sent on was tonight.

Later, when everyone had gone to bed, I would sneak into Uchi's office and find out about the mission for myself.

NAT

I paced across the room. Hours had passed since we'd seen
Riley, and our only visitor had been a guard who'd brought
us water and sandwiches, which we'd eaten long ago. It was
already dark. I couldn't see Riley keeping us here much longer.
To be honest, I had no idea why Jas and I weren't already
dead. Whatever the reason, we were going to have to make
our move soon.

Out of the corner of my eye I could see Jas and Aaron watching me from one of the thin mattresses on the floor. I was going
to need both of them to play their parts if my plan was to succeed.

"Could we go over it again, Nat?" Jas said, her anxious voice
quiet in case there were bugs in the room.

I stopped pacing and turned to look at her. My sister's face
was pale and strained. For a moment I had a powerful wish that
she were more like Charlie, trained to fight well and always ready
to kick ass. Then I pushed the thought away. People were who
they were. Jas was gentle and soft. And my job was to protect her.

Play to your strengths. Guard your weaknesses.

This was one of Taylor's maxims from our months of training

for the EFA, and I hoped I had followed it in making my plan for our escape. I crouched down beside Jas and Aaron and went over what they had to do again. Aaron seemed confident about his role, though Jas was still terribly nervous. I had just finished when footsteps sounded outside.

Jas clutched at my arm. "Now?" she whispered.

"Now." I gave her what I hoped was a reassuring nod. We were going to get only one chance at this.

Jas lay back on the mattress. Aaron knelt beside her. I hurried over to the door. As the key turned in the lock, I flattened myself against the wall behind the door so that when it opened, I'd be hidden from view.

Jas let out a tentative groan as the door opened. I chewed on my lip. She was going to need to sound a lot more convincing than that.

"What's the matter?" Aaron bent over her. He, at least, sounded genuinely concerned.

"Aaaah." Jas groaned again, this time with more conviction.

The door opened fully, blocking my view of the others.

"What is it?" The speaker was one of the guards.

I held my breath. Any second he was going to notice I wasn't in view and look around for me. I just needed him to take another step into the room.

"She's in pain." Aaron's voice rose with what sounded like real worry. "I think it's her stomach, but—"

"Where's—?" The guard stepped forward.

Before he could finish his sentence, I rushed him from behind.

My fists drove into his back, one after the other: punch, jab, punch. The guard staggered sideways. I punched him again, this time locking my foot around his ankles, bringing him to the end of Jas's mattress with a dull thud. He lay there, winded, his face screwed up in pain.

Jas scrabbled away across the floor, hands over her mouth. I hurled myself on top of the guard, pinning him down. His legs thrashed on the floor behind him. I knelt on his arms and pressed my hand over his mouth as Aaron sat on the man's legs.

"Cloth," I ordered.

With a shaking hand, Jas passed me one of the strips of torn-off sheet we had tied together earlier. I shoved it into the guard's mouth.

"Again," I ordered.

Jas handed me another strip. Behind me, Aaron was grunting with the effort of tying the guard's ankles together.

"Help me with his arms," I demanded.

Jas crawled over. Aaron, having finished binding the guard's legs, turned toward me. As soon as he got off the man's legs, the guard banged them on the floor.

"Sit on his legs, Jas," I ordered.

She vanished behind me. I felt her back against mine as she sat. The banging stopped. I glanced at the open doorway. Had anyone heard us? All I could see out on the landing were the three bottles of water the guard had been bringing us.

With Aaron's help, I got the next strip of sheet around the guard's wrists and tied it tightly. He was attempting to buck me off him. As soon as Jas and I got up off him, he would kick against the floor and the wall, and the other soldiers in the house would hear. I looked around. We would have to tie him to something solid to prevent him from moving.

Taking another length of sheet, I fastened one end around the guard's bound wrists and told Aaron to tie the other end tightly around the bars on one window. Once this was done, Aaron took another strip and, at my instruction, wound it around the guard's ankles. I ordered Jas to get up, then took the end of the second strip and dragged the guard along the floor until he was stretched out between the two windows. I fastened the end of the second strip to the bars of the second window. Now the guard lay stretched on the floor between the two windows, unable to move at all. He turned his head violently, trying to spit out the cloth I'd wedged down his throat, but it was too far in.

I stepped back and brushed my hair out of my eyes. The guard was secure. It had taken only thirty seconds or so, but we surely had just a couple more minutes before someone realized he was missing. I turned to Aaron and Jas. They were watching me, openmouthed.

"Wow, Nat—," Aaron began.

"Come on!" I raced out the door. There was no sound from the landing. I crept to the top of the stairs. The house was quiet.

I beckoned to Aaron and Jas to follow me down the steps. Sweat trickled down the back of my neck as I reached the hall. I could hear voices coming from a nearby room. I tiptoed over to the front door. Normally there was a guard posted here. Two phones sat on the table by the door, SIM cards resting on top. One was mine. I snatched it up and reached for the front-door handle. Aaron picked up the other phone.

"This is *mine*," he hissed.

"Shh." I turned the doorknob, my heart thumping. Outside, the area was clear. The back of my neck prickled. This was too easy, surely. No guards. Our phones just lying there waiting to be collected.

I slipped outside, turning to make sure Jas and Aaron were right behind me. I took Jas's hand. "Run," I said. "Run hard."

And we set off, over the grass, heading for the trees.

CHARLIE

I waited until the middle of the night to make my move. Breaking into Uchi's office was not going to be easy, but I had get to evidence about what he and Riley were planning. Hopefully, there would be a phone in the office that I could use to tell Nat about the operation. Even if I couldn't supply him with actual proof right now, I should at least be able to give him enough information so that he and the resistance could prevent whatever was planned.

The lock on the office door would be no problem, but the room itself was in the center of the house, across from the kitchen and at right angles to the stairs up to the second floor. I was going to have to be supremely careful not to disturb everyone else. I didn't want to think about the consequences if I was caught.

I checked the time. Almost two a.m. I would wait just two more minutes, and then I'd go. I paced silently across the bedroom in my bare feet, thinking about everything that had happened earlier.

Our swimming training had finally come to an end when Gracie had called us inside to wash for dinner. It had been a surreal moment, as if I were here with Spider on some sort of bizarre teenage playdate. But as I'd headed, shivering, upstairs for a shower, my thoughts had turned to Nat again. I missed him like he was a part of me. Before, I'd known I liked him a lot. But now the strength of how I felt almost scared me. I prayed that wherever he was, he was all right.

I had just showered and dressed when Gracie called up to say dinner was ready. I headed down to the kitchen to find her and Spider already sitting at the wooden table in front of their bowls of pasta. Gracie had evidently made Spider wait until I arrived before beginning, because he scowled at me as he shoveled a huge spoonful of food out of his bowl and into his mouth.

I didn't think I'd be able to eat a thing, but the food—pasta with a sausage and tomato sauce—was delicious and, once I started, I realized that I was starving and ended up wolfing down two portions. Uchi didn't eat with us, though the dark-haired guard I'd seen earlier made a brief appearance. He glanced quickly at me as he picked up the plate Gracie had served for him and took it outside.

Spider and I swapped information on our training. My experience in combat situations and with guns was all that he appeared interested in. At least he was talking enthusiastically now and even smiling from time to time. I hated to admit it, but his smile was dazzling—not that I had any intention of telling him so.

"I can't wait to go on a real mission," Spider said.

I stopped, my fork halfway to my mouth. "Haven't you been on one before?"

Spider stared at me defiantly, his cheeks pinking.

"What actual combat experience do you have?" I persisted.

"I've done loads of simulations," Spider said defensively.

"Great."

"At least I believe in what we're fighting for," he snapped.

"*What?*" I glared at him but bit back the retort that sprang to my lips: that using violence to scare people into electing a would-be dictator was nothing to be proud of. I had to maintain my cover, to keep pretending that I was coming around to supporting Riley's and Uchi's aims. "I believe in what we're fighting for too."

"No, you don't," Spider went on. "You're just here to meet your dad."

"I think that's enough, both of you." Gracie laid a hand on Spider's arm. "Remember that Charlie lost her mother in a bomb blast. This isn't easy for her. Of course part of her reason for being here is to get to know her father, but it's wonderful that she's also open to our cause—and there's a lot of information about all that to process."

She sounded so patronizing I had to dig my fingernails into my palms to stop myself from telling her to get lost. I especially hated hearing her mention Mum. I'd pushed all thoughts of my mother out of my head since hearing about her affair with Uchi seventeen years ago. I couldn't bear the idea that she'd been so irresponsible. Even worse was the knowledge that she'd lied to me about my father. It was like she had left me all over again. Tears pricked at my eyes. I blinked them away angrily. I finished my food, then pretended that I was tired and went up to my room to wait for everyone else to go to bed.

And now it was two a.m. at last. This was it.

I crept to the door, unlocked it, and peered out into the second-floor landing. The house was dark and silent. I already knew Gracie and Spider slept downstairs, at the back of the property. The upstairs rooms were reserved for Uchi and his bodyguard.

I tiptoed onto the landing and looked out the front window. The shadow of a guard—presumably the man I'd seen earlier—was cast across the brick wall. A wisp of smoke from his cigarette trailed up through the air. I knew EFA soldiers were stoic, but when on earth did he sleep?

The stone floor was cold under my feet as I crept downstairs and into the kitchen. I took a short-bladed knife from the block on the counter and headed over to the study door. It was locked, but I'd been expecting that. I slid the knife along the crack in the door, feeling for the catch. I'd been good at this trick when I'd trained for the EFA before and, much to my relief, I hadn't lost my touch.

I found the catch and pressed it back. With a tiny click, it gave way. Wiping away the sweat that beaded on my forehead, I replaced the knife and walked into Uchi's office.

It was smaller than I'd expected. I was guessing it was normally a living room, as a large-screen TV and the two sofas had all been squashed up against one wall, leaving just enough room for a large desk, on which sat two computers. There was a rickety old chair and a wooden bookcase set against the far wall, laden with books on politics and philosophy. There were absolutely no papers or files on either the desk or the shelves. And no phone. I checked the desk drawers. The larger bottom one was locked, while the shallow top drawer merely contained bits of stationery: pencils and pens, a ruler, and a pad of thick, creamy writing paper that looked like it had never been used.

I turned to the two computers. Clearly Uchi kept all important information on these. I switched them both on. As I'd expected, both screens immediately showed a request for a password.

I tried a few obvious passwords—some of the places Uchi had said he had lived, my name and Mum's, a couple of the philosophers he'd mentioned earlier—but nothing worked. Dispirited, I sank down into the chair behind the desk. This was hopeless—as I should have guessed it would be. With its window facing the backyard and its door opening into the main hall, this office was fairly exposed—and Uchi was too smart and too careful to leave any revealing information lying around within easy reach of anyone snooping.

I switched off the computers and rested my head in my hands. Missions and bombing campaigns surely didn't get organized without *something* getting written down.

My gaze settled on the keyboard in front of the nearest computer. It didn't sit right on the desk, as if the slant at which it was naturally set had been artificially raised a fraction. I turned it over. There, wedged under the plastic frame of the keyboard with sticky tape, was a slim, silver key.

I peeled the key off. My fingers trembled as I fit it into the desk drawer lock. It turned with a click. I pulled open the drawer and peered inside. A pile of notebooks met my eyes: Each one was black and bound with leather at the edges. Underneath was a stack of plastic folders. I hauled them all out and started rifling through. The notebooks were crammed with Uchi's sprawling writing, with his name at the top. I couldn't make out much of what was written inside, but it seemed to be a collection of jottings on his political philosophies, the dates going back seventeen years. Well, that made sense. Uchi was old, and older people were often more comfortable writing on paper than electronically. I turned to the plastic folders. Several were empty; others carried names and dates. My eyes flickered over the names:

OPERATION CROSSBOW
OPERATION GUY FAWKES
OPERATION MARKET TRADER

Struck by the title on that last one, I opened the folder. It contained just a few sheets of paper: a typed summary of the Canal Street market bomb and its effects, both immediate—in terms of casualties and press coverage—and long-term—in terms of government response and political capital gained for Roman Riley's Future Party. My mouth gaped as I read:

... the resulting total of four deaths and
seventeen serious injuries was within
acceptable limits for the operation, serving to

strengthen and build on public fears for their
safety and doubts in the efficacy of the police
force. The people's faith in known authority
is measurably eroded. See data below,
compared with that from Op Crossbow for
validation of this assertion.

There followed a chart outlining research findings into public
perceptions of government and police competence.

I closed the folder, feeling sick to my stomach. These cold
statistics made no mention of the real impact of the bombing. It
had killed Mum—the mother of Uchi's only child, *me*—leaving
me all alone. How dare Uchi and Riley write that up as "within
acceptable limits"?

Angrily, I reached for the fattest folder, labeled OPERATION
NEPTUNE.

As I scanned the top page, I realized that *this* mission hadn't
happened yet. That, in fact, the date for it was set just two days
from now. Was this what Spider and I were in training for?

Yes. There was a clear reference to our underwater training,
right here in the first paragraph.

My heart in my mouth, I read on.

NAT

We reached the cover of the trees. No one was following us, but it surely wouldn't be long before someone realized we were missing and raised the alarm. I ran to where Aaron and I had left our bags earlier. Everything was still there. I shoved my cell phone and SIM card inside my backpack and then hauled it onto my back, as Jas and Aaron crashed up alongside me.

"Shh. You two are like a couple of elephants," I hissed. As I spoke, an image of Charlie speeding through these same woods without making a sound flashed into my head.

"Are we safe?" Jas breathed.

"Yes, babe." Aaron pulled her into a hug. "The road's just a few minutes from here."

Babe? Give me strength.

I looked away. We weren't safe by a long shot. If only I had someone from my old cell group with me to help us escape—like Charlie. Or George: a big guy with an easy smile, he had been the rock that our group was built on. And Riley had killed him. Or, more precisely, used him, then had him murdered. He was gone, and Parveen was missing, and Charlie was goodness knows where doing goodness knows what.

A terrible wave of desolation washed over me. The fact that Riley had manipulated us so easily only highlighted just how much more powerful he was than the resistance. In my rush to follow Charlie and then to rescue Jas, I hadn't thought about how weak we really were—and how badly we needed, and lacked, a strong leader to help us make a stand against Riley. Without someone who had the energy and the character to turn the resistance into a force for good, there was little chance we would ever be able to replace Riley and his English Freedom Army with a more honest and democratic party. None of the other existing politicians was anywhere near as charismatic as Riley; most of them were too scared to stand up to him anyway.

I knew that Charlie was driven by revenge for her mum and, though she wouldn't admit it, a desire to find out the truth about her dad, but just getting rid of Riley wasn't enough for me. Mum and Dad were always saying all politicians were useless. I had thought Riley was different, but in fact he was worse.

I shook myself. I didn't have time to think about all this now. Aaron and Jas were waiting for me to tell them what to do next, their expressions anxious and expectant.

"We need to move," I whispered.

"Right." Aaron nodded. "Let's find the nearest road and—"

"No," I said. "That's what Riley will expect us to do; he'll send men to find us. We need to keep to the woods. We head west, then south. Once we're away from here, we'll hitch a ride to London, stay away from the main transportation routes. Come on."

Jas and Aaron hesitated, and then Jas nodded.

"Uh . . . you were great back there, Nat," Aaron gushed.

I shook my head. "Don't congratulate me yet. It's all been too easy so far."

"What do you mean?" Jas frowned. "It didn't seem easy to me."

I opened my mouth to point out that it had been strange that there'd been no guard on the front door, but before I could speak, Aaron took Jas's hand.

"Don't worry, babe," he said. "I told you, we're safe."

Irritation filled me, though whether from Aaron's breezy self-assurance, the hand-holding, or the fact that he had just called my sister "babe" again, I wasn't sure.

"Just try to make as little noise as possible," I muttered.

As I sped off, I went over what we needed to do next. Once we were safely out of these woods, I planned to head for London. I had to bring Jas back to Mum and Dad, get them to take her away. If she was hidden from Riley, then she'd be safe. And if she was apart from Aaron, that wouldn't be a bad thing either.

CHARLIE

The Operation Neptune folder contained notes on its aims and likely impact. The strategy was simple—and very daring: Riley, as leader of the Future Party, was going to host an early-evening cocktail reception at a London hotel and invite members of all the opposition parties. This would be presented as an informal get-together, a way of bringing potential coalition partners into the same room for a drink and a chat. But really the entire thing was a cover that would allow Riley to set off a bomb at the reception and frame the government for the explosion.

Through this single operation, Uchi had written, *leading members of one key opponent are killed, maimed, or reduced in effectiveness while members of another rival become embroiled in scandal and discredited to the public.*

It made sense. A month ago, Riley had pinned everything on the League of Iron. This was just a new scapegoat.

I searched on, trying to find more details. Though I couldn't locate an actual date, the time and place of the bombing were given—seven thirty at the Almeida Hotel—as well as a diagram of the building with an underwater passage from the river into the hotel's basement marked as ENTRY ROUTE. A shiver slid down my spine. This was clearly the route by which the bomb would be smuggled into the building. And the fact that it was under-water suddenly—and horribly—made sense of the training I'd been doing with Spider. Clearly *we* were the ones who were supposed to carry and place the bomb.

I scanned the next sheet of paper, hungry for more informa-tion, including the date of the party and details of who would be attending. But just then a floorboard creaked outside the office. Someone was there. Heart pounding, I jumped up, shoved the papers back in the folder, stuffed everything into the drawer, and locked it.

Footsteps padded across the hall. I held my breath. Whoever it was, was walking away from the study. I heard the kitchen door open and shut. Presumably one of the other people in the house had gone for food or drink. I needed to get out of here before they came back to the hall.

I hurriedly pressed the key back into the sticky tape on the underside of the computer keyboard, checked that both desk and chair were as I'd found them, then sped across to the door and eased it open. Light seeped out from under the kitchen door across the hall. Moving as quietly as I could, I left the office and closed the door silently behind me. I had to press on the catch as it closed, then release. The thud of the lock resetting itself seemed very loud in the still night air. Holding my breath, I raced across the hall and started up the stairs

"What are you doing?"

I jumped. Looked around. Spider was standing in the kitchen doorway, dressed in sweatpants and a T-shirt. His dark eyes glinted in the light that shone from the room behind him.

"I couldn't sleep," I lied. "What are *you* doing? Spying on me?"

Spider glared at me. "Don't make this about me—you're the one sneaking around in the middle of the night." He paused. "Your dad will be interested to know you've been down here."

He walked toward me, his loping frame sinister in the shadowy light. I wanted to back away from him, but instead I made myself step closer, right into his space.

"Don't tell Uchi. *Please.*" I looked up into Spider's dark eyes, sensing that pleading was my best option right now—if nothing else, because he would not be expecting it.

He blinked rapidly, clearly surprised. Even in the soft light I could see his cheeks growing red. Was that because of how close we were standing? I wondered how much time Spider had actually spent with girls. If he was shut up in a boarding school most of the year, maybe he wasn't used to being around them.

Still resisting the impulse to pull away, I bowed my head before him and whispered, "Please, Spider. I wasn't doing anything. I just couldn't sleep."

He hesitated. I was sure he was softening. And then the front door opened. We both turned together. The guard whose shadow I'd glimpsed earlier was still outside. I'd thought it was the guard who'd been in the house earlier, but it wasn't.

It was Taylor.

"Charlie?" he said, his green eyes glinting.

I gulped. The last time I'd seen my former cell leader, he had just tricked me into kidnapping Aaron Latimer, claiming it was for his own safety. It still hurt to think how much I had admired Taylor. He had trained us for several months, teaching Nat, George, Parveen, and me how to fight, to escape, to move undetected, and much else besides.

We had trusted him and he had betrayed us.

"I found her sneaking about, sir," Spider said.

Taylor didn't take his eyes off me. "Go to bed, Spider," he said.

"Yes, sir." Spider slunk off past me up the stairs.

Taylor came over. "Turn out your pockets," he demanded.

I did as he said in silence.

"What were you doing down here?" Taylor asked, patting down my arms and legs. I gritted my teeth and submitted to the brisk search.

"Getting a glass of water." I deliberately didn't say "sir," a term that Taylor used to insist on.

I thought for a second that he was going to call me on it, but instead he just studied my face. I looked back at him, trying to keep my gaze level and cool. Now wasn't the time, but one day I would get my revenge on Taylor for conning us, for leaving Nat to die—and for brave George, who *had* died.

"Right." Taylor sounded skeptical. "Okay. Then get it quickly and go back to your room."

I did as I was told without speaking. Taylor watched me all

the way up the stairs. As I went into my room, I thought back to what I'd discovered about Operation Neptune.

I *had* to contact Nat and tell him what I'd found out. I had memorized his number. All I needed was a phone. There might not be any landlines in the house, but everyone here surely had a cell phone. I just had to work out how to get ahold of one. Fast.

NAT

It took us all of the next day *and* the following night to get to London. I insisted that we hitch rides the whole way: after our recent brush with Riley, I didn't want to risk being spotted on public transportation. If any of us had been traveling alone, we would probably have reached London faster. But I didn't want to leave Jas, and she refused to leave Aaron, so there wasn't much choice.

Our longest hitched ride was down the M1 in the back of a van being used by a young couple who were moving. It wasn't the most comfortable ride I'd ever had, but at least we weren't out in the cold.

The van driver dropped us off at a rest stop near Watford at about three a.m. It was raining, so we darted inside for cover and found a row of seats near the entrance. Jas and I sat down while Aaron went off to the bathroom. After a moment, Jas wrapped herself in Charlie's sleeping bag and then curled up beside me. She looked shattered. Neither she nor Aaron were used to sleeping rough like I was, and though they hadn't complained, it was obvious that being on the run was really getting to them.

Jas had asked—for the tenth time—if she could call Mum and Dad, insisting they would be really worried about her by now. I had said no—also for the tenth time. For a start, I was sure our phones were bugged. It was the only explanation for them having been left out, right by the front door of the ops base. And we couldn't use pay phones to call home, as it was entirely possible both the landline and Mum's and Dad's cell phones had been bugged too.

Aaron had also asked if he could call his dad. I said no to that even more firmly. Quite apart from the fact that Mayor Latimer's phone lines could easily be bugged too, the man hadn't lifted a finger to defend us before and I still didn't trust him.

"But my dad would help," Aaron had insisted. "I know he looks like he supports Riley, but I keep telling you it's just a cover."

"Mmm," I'd said, unconvinced.

"Mr. Latimer's really nice, Nat," Jas had ventured hesitantly. "I mean, I've met him quite a few times now." She smiled shyly at Aaron. "And he's always really sweet to me, you know, putting me at ease, teasing Aaron in a nice, dadish way, like our dad used to with Lucas's girlfriends."

I shook my head. As far as I was concerned, it seemed highly improbable that Latimer was as trustworthy as Jas thought. She tended to see the best in people and was as likely to have been fooled by Aaron's dad as I had been by Roman Riley himself.

"Nat?" Jas's voice brought me back to the present. I looked down at her pale face peeking out from Charlie's sleeping bag. "Please let me give Mum and Dad a call."

"Sorry, but no." I sighed.

Jas looked close to tears.

"We'll go straight home once we reach London," I said, trying to pacify her.

"But we're still on the highway and we don't have our next ride yet," she said, her voice all shaky.

This was true, and I felt bad that Jas was upset, but it was still too big a risk to call our parents.

"Are you hungry?" I asked, hoping to distract her. We hadn't eaten since a truck driver had shared his sandwiches with us at about five o'clock the previous afternoon.

She shook her head. I sighed. Jas had gotten even skinnier since I'd been away from home. She only ever picked at her food at the best of times. I wondered, though I didn't ask, if she'd been eating well at all. Surely Mum would have made sure she was, now that I wasn't around?

"Well, I'm starving," I said. I left Jas on the plastic seat just inside the rest stop entrance and wandered away to the fried food concession next to the mini-arcade. All the games were empty. I took the remaining coins we'd scraped together from our pockets and bought the three of us a burger each. By the time I got back to Jas, Aaron was with her again, his arm around her shoulders. Jas was snuggled in close to him. They looked blissfully happy. I handed them their burgers and then wandered outside, feeling like maybe I was a bit in their way. It was a clear night, and the moon cast a ghostly glow over the deserted parking lot.

I sat on a step and ate my burger. Up until a few months ago, life had made sense. There was family and school and work and friends. Sometimes bad things happened, of course, like Lucas being in his coma, but the world—the background to my life— was a fixed, steady thing that you could be sure of: the police were there to protect you and the vast majority of adults had your best interests at heart. Now I knew that was all an illusion. Now nothing made sense.

Nothing except Charlie. She had seen and experienced the same things as me. She understood.

I missed her so much that it hurt.

I finished my burger and then wandered around the parking lot, licking my fingers. I stayed outside for about thirty minutes. So far I hadn't seen anyone to even ask if they would give us a ride into London, but maybe there'd be more people inside. Perhaps Aaron had even found someone already in the rest stop. I headed back. Aaron and Jas were still sitting where I'd left them, both now huddled under Charlie's sleeping bag. Jas was asleep, her head resting on Aaron's shoulder. He looked up at me as I approached and put his finger to his lips to warn me not to wake her.

I was about to look in the café to see if there was anyone about to leave who might give us a ride when the rest stop door flew open, letting in a gust of cold air. I glanced around.

To my horror, Mayor Latimer was striding inside. His eyes lit on Aaron right away. I froze, watching as Aaron extricated himself from Jas, laid her carefully down on the sleeping bag, and stood up to give his father a hug.

Fury surged inside me. Before I knew what I was doing, I had raced over.

"Hey!" I tugged at Aaron's arm. He stepped back from his dad.

"Nat, this is my father, Jason Latimer."

Latimer held out his hand. His face was familiar from TV and the memorial service for the bomb victims I'd gone to last year.

"Hello." I shook Latimer's hand reluctantly, then turned back to Aaron. "You called your dad? I thought I told you not to make any calls," I snapped.

Aaron's cheeks flushed. "I used the pay phones by the bathroom, not my cell."

"It's fine, Nat," Latimer said quickly. "You're right to be careful, but I have the home phones and our cells checked for bugs every week. And I'm glad Aaron called. His mother's been frantic. And now I can help you. I got back from my trip only a few hours ago. I came straight here as soon as Aaron called, to pick you guys up." He glanced at Jas. "Is she okay? Are you all okay?"

"We're fine, Dad. Thanks for coming." Aaron gave his dad a beaming smile. "Is the car outside?"

"Yes." Latimer turned to me. "I came alone, Nat. I thought it was safer."

"Right." No way was I getting in the man's car. He'd probably take me straight back to Riley.

Aaron turned back to Jas, shaking her gently awake.

"I understand why you're wary of me, Nat," Latimer went on. "I know you must have wondered why I didn't come forward and tell the world that you helped Aaron escape from being kid-napped."

"You did worse than that," I muttered. "You said the League of Iron had done the kidnapping, that Charlie and I must work for them. You backed up all their lies—and because of that, Charlie and I are wanted by the police *and* Riley and can't go home."

"I know." Latimer sighed. "I know it was a terrible choice to make. But it felt like the only way to convince Riley I was—am—on his side."

I stared at him. He certainly seemed sincere. There was an openness in his face that I saw in Aaron too.

"Please come with us, Nat," Latimer said. "I'll take you wher-ever you want to go. I've been wanting to talk to you ever since Aaron told me how you helped him last month. And now you've helped him again—and Jas."

"She's my sister," I snapped. "Of course I helped her."

"Of course," Latimer echoed, his voice soft and soothing. "Look, I don't know what I can say that will convince you I'm working secretly against Riley, but there are plenty in the resis-tance who will tell you that I've helped them over the past few weeks, providing information and equipment."

I stared at him, remembering how Lennox and Julius had indeed told me just that. "So how undercover are you?" I asked. "Do you know what Riley's planning?"

Latimer shook his head. "I'm not in the inner circle, but he thinks I'm loyal."

"But really you just want a chance to get power for yourself."

"No—well, of course I want a chance to make a difference, to have some influence over our country, but not by bombing innocent people, or framing and blackmailing others to take the blame."

I crossed my arms, still unconvinced.

Latimer looked over at where Aaron was helping Jas to her feet. She stumbled as she took a step; her face was drawn, her skin almost gray with exhaustion. "Nat, I know it's hard to trust me, but look at your sister." Latimer lowered his voice. "She can't go on like this. I have to take her to your parents. And if you don't come with us, she'll worry."

I shrugged. I still felt uneasy, but Latimer was right about Jas.

"Okay. . . . We'll come with you—but any sign I get that you're really working for Riley and we're out of here."

"Fair enough," Latimer said with evident relief.

We got into his Bentley. Aaron sat next to Jas in the backseat. She was asleep again within seconds, and Aaron himself started snoring about two minutes later. Latimer drove silently along the highway for a bit, then cleared his throat.

"Is Charlie all right? Did you leave her at the safe house?"

I stared at him suspiciously. Was he fishing for information? Surely if he was in deep with Riley he would already know Charlie was with him. Still, he had said he wasn't in Riley's inner circle.

"Charlie's fine, as far as I know," I said, staring out at the moon overhead.

"Good. That's good." There was a pause, and then Latimer spoke again. "I don't want Riley to get away with what he's done.

And not just because I'm afraid of what he'll do in the future. It's just wrong. Undemocratic."

"And you believe in democracy?"

"It's the least worst system we have," Latimer said.

His words echoed a conversation I'd had with Charlie not so long ago. Where was she? Was she all right? It tore me apart to know that there was nothing I could do for her right now. In a nanosecond I went from feeling useless to feeling angry.

"And I suppose you're selling yourself as the least worst guy?" I snapped.

Latimer chuckled. "If you like," he said. "I've been called worse. . . . Uh, where do you want me to take you?"

"Home first," I said. "You're right that Jas should be with Mum and Dad. I want them to take her away somewhere she'll be safe."

"What about *you*?"

"I'm going to stop Riley," I said. "I want to get proof that he's used and murdered people just to get power."

"Me too," Latimer said.

I didn't sleep as we drove home. I still half-expected Latimer to head toward Riley's house. But he didn't, and by six thirty a.m. we were parked at the end of my road. I had worried that Riley might have spies watching out for our return, but there was no one in sight. I left Jas asleep in the car with Aaron and let myself in, using the spare key from under the loose paving stone out front.

No one was home. I looked around, from room to room. It was weird seeing all the familiar things in the house—little details like the photos in the living room, the piano Jas used to play, and her room—full of dressmaking fabric—and mine, which I'd once shared with Lucas. I felt completely disconnected from everything I saw, as if they belonged to another person and another life.

I didn't want to linger, so after a couple of minutes I let myself out and headed back to Latimer's car. "Mum and Dad aren't there," I said.

"So where now?" Latimer asked. "Your dad's workplace?"

I glanced at Jas.

"We should try the hospital," she said. "Mum often takes Dad to visit at this time."

I nodded. "Riley will think of that too, so we need to be careful."

The hospital was fairly busy, though the visitors' parking lot was barely a third full. I spotted Mum and Dad's car right away. So they *were* here. I asked Latimer to drop me and Jas, then leave.

"What about Aaron?" asked Jas.

"Yeah, I'm not leaving Jas," Aaron added.

"Jas needs to hide, and your house is too obvious, Aaron." I turned to Jas. "Mum and Dad will find somewhere safe; it's the best thing."

Jas's lips trembled, but she nodded.

"But how will I know where she is?" Aaron protested, his voice swelling with emotion. "I need to be able to contact her, to know she's okay." He pulled Jas toward him. "I don't like this. I mean, how long d'you think we'll have to be apart?"

Two fat tears trickled down Jas's face. "Oh, Aaron." Her voice broke over the words.

For goodness' sake. Couldn't Aaron see he wasn't helping? "Please don't make this harder than it needs to be," I said.

Aaron hugged Jas tightly. "Oh, babe, I don't want you to go," he said.

"I know," Jas wept, clinging to him as if her life depended on it. "I'll miss you so, so much."

I stared helplessly at Latimer.

"Nat's right, Aaron," Latimer said firmly. "Best Jas goes—and safer for her if we don't know where right now."

"I'll call you when I'm settled." Jas disentangled herself, tears still streaming down her face.

Aaron looked close to tears himself, but he nodded. Latimer cleared his throat. He looked from Jas to me. "Please don't either of you forget I'm here if you need anything."

"Thank you," Jas said.

"I'll be fine," I said.

"Okay." Latimer hesitated. "Look, Nat, I'll give you my number. You can call me later for news about the resistance. I'm expecting a call from the guy in Resistance Pair Eight later. There's supposed to be a meeting today. I don't know where yet. I'll be told at the last minute. I'd be happy to bring you along, if you like."

"I can figure it out on my own," I said. "Thanks."

"Right, but if you don't manage to connect with them, please call me. I can get you supplies, food, shelter—whatever you need." He reached into the bag at his feet and handed me a box containing a brand-new, sealed burner phone. Just one glance at the brand name showed me it was a high-quality cell phone. Ten crisp fifty-pound notes lay on top, plus a business card with the mayor's cell number. "Take this. It might help."

I stared at the money. I didn't want to take anything Latimer was offering, but it was stupid to refuse money and a phone. I took the box, the business card, and two of the notes, then pushed the rest of the cash back to Latimer. "I'll pay you back," I said.

"No need."

I scrambled out of the car. Jas gave Aaron a final hug, then got out too, wiping her face. Aaron looked devastated. "See you soon, right? And call me—it's a new phone, a new number, remember, so no bugs. Okay?" Jas nodded, her lips trembling again.

"Come on." I took her arm before she could burst into tears again and led her across the hospital parking lot. I knew there would be CCTV cameras here, so I told Jas to pull up her hood and did the same with mine. Jas and I made our way swiftly through the hospital hallways toward the ward where Lucas had lain since the bomb left him in a coma. As we walked, I took the number of the phone Latimer had just given me and made Jas memorize it so she could call later.

"But not until it's safe, understand?"

"Yes. . . . Um, Nat?" Jas said timidly as we entered the elevator to the third floor. "Um . . . do you like Aaron?"

I stared at my shoes, feeling awkward. "He's okay, I guess." I hesitated. "But it's what you think of him that counts, isn't it?"

There was a silence. The elevator doors opened. As we stepped out, Jas said quietly, "I love him."

"Right." Now I felt really embarrassed. I didn't know how to tell her that I thought Aaron was a bit of an idiot and not anywhere near good enough for her. "Okay."

Jas glanced at me nervously, like she wanted to say more. Luckily, a few moments later we reached Lucas's room.

I peered in through the window. Mum and Dad were sitting on either side of his bed. Mum was holding Lucas's hand. She looked even more exhausted than when I'd last seen her five weeks ago. And surely Dad's face hadn't been that lined when I'd left. I glanced at Lucas, at the pale, smooth skin of his face, at his closed eyes and at all the tubes and wires running in and out of his body. He—on the other hand—looked exactly the same as when I'd last been here.

As Jas opened the door, Mum and Dad looked up. They saw her, then me right behind. Dad's jaw dropped. Mum gasped. For a second we stood, staring at one another. Then Jas was across the room and hurling herself into Dad's arms. He hugged her, but his eyes were on me.

"Oh, Nat . . ." Mum stood up. All the color had drained from her face.

"What are you doing here, Nat? Are you sure it's safe?" Dad asked.

"How did Jas find you? Are you both okay? Jas, where've you been? Did you stay at Aaron's? I was worried when you didn't call. Oh, but, Nat, you look so thin." The words tumbled out of Mum in a sob.

The three of them walked over, and for a moment we huddled together, our arms entwined. I was the first to pull away. Good though it was to see my parents, something felt different about them. I couldn't put my finger on what it was, but it was definitely there.

"Jas didn't find me, Mum," I explained. "I found *her*."

"What?" Dad frowned. "We thought she was with Aar—"

"She was kidnapped," I interrupted.

Mum gasped again. "No, please God, *no*."

Jas quickly explained how she'd been taken by Riley's men. I took over the story, describing how Aaron had called me and I'd gone to rescue her.

"But why didn't you call *us*?" Dad asked.

I looked at him. With a jolt I realized I was actually an inch or so taller than him now. When had *that* happened? I'd been taller than Mum for a long time now, but not Dad. I remembered Lucas—who, of course, had shot past Dad soon after he turned fourteen—teasing me about my height, or lack of it, when I was a kid.

"Nat, why didn't you tell us what was going on?" Dad insisted.

"Nat didn't want you to worry," Jas offered timidly.

"But—," Dad started.

"There's no time to talk," I said flatly. "Jas and Aaron and I got away, but Riley wants us dead. He was using Jas to get to me, but now she's a witness to what he's done. She's in as much danger as I am. You need to take her away somewhere and keep her safe while I get it sorted out."

"Get it *sorted out?*" Dad echoed, his forehead etched with a frown. "How can you get Roman Riley *sorted out?* What can you do alone?"

"I'm *not* alone," I said. "There's a resistance. Aaron's dad is part of it." I stopped. The truth was that the resistance was weak and disorganized—and I still couldn't really be sure of Latimer. I knew I could trust Parveen, but I had no idea what had happened to her. Which left just me and Charlie—and what could two teenagers do against the cleverest, most ruthless politician in the country? "That doesn't matter right now," I went on. "What counts is you protecting Jas. You *have* to take her away somewhere safe."

Dad nodded. But Mum looked horrified. She indicated the hospital bed behind us, where Lucas lay, pale and still as ever.

"What about him?" she said. "The doctors say he's been show-ing signs of altered consciousness, that his condition is changing."

"Doesn't mean he's going to wake up, love," Dad said wearily, and I sensed this was a conversation my parents had had more than once in the past few weeks.

Mum looked at him, then at Jas and me. "I can't leave your brother," she said, her mouth trembling. "He needs me."

There was a silence.

Dad and Jas looked down at the floor. Fury filled me. I glared at Mum.

"*Jas* needs you," I snapped. "Lucas is in a coma. You need to get it together, Mum, because Jas is here and *really* needs your help, while Lucas isn't truly here at all—and you can't help him anyway. Stop putting him first. Stop putting your own need to be here first."

Mum's eyes filled with tears. I could feel the shock radiating off Jas and Dad. For a moment I felt a wave of guilt wash over me. I gritted my teeth. My feelings weren't relevant. I had to be strong for Jas's sake.

"Nat, there's no need to talk to your mother like—," Dad started.

"And you're just as bad," I said, turning on him. "Spending all your time at work so you don't have to deal with the mess this family has become."

Dad's jaw dropped. I took a step back, away from both of them. "Okay, now listen. You have to leave. *Now*. Take Jas and go. It doesn't matter where, but it needs to be somewhere Riley won't find you."

"Nat, please . . ." Tears streamed down Mum's face.

"There's no time to talk any more," I said, steeling myself. I looked from her to Dad. "This nonsense over Lucas ends here. Start doing your freakin' job as parents and look after your daughter."

And with that I turned on my heel and walked out.

I sped along the hallway and down the stairs, all the way to the first floor. I broke into a run as I turned onto the pavement. I hated how harsh I had been. I just hoped I'd said enough to make Mum and Dad act. My nose and throat tingled, and tears pricked at my eyes. I forced them back. My job now was to find a way to help Charlie expose Riley. It was the only way to keep my family safe.

I pulled the phone Latimer had given me out of my pocket,

determined to try to call her again. The screen swam blurrily in front of my eyes. I wiped my face angrily. This was no time for tears.

Charlie's number was now out of service. I didn't know who else to try, so I called Julius to see if Resistance Nine had heard from her. As the phone rang, I wondered uneasily if Riley's men were still trying to find us.

The cell phone rang a second time. And a third. But Julius didn't answer. I didn't want to leave a message, so when the call went to voice mail I just said, "Call me," and hung up.

A few moments later, as I rounded the next corner, my phone rang. An unknown number showed on the screen. Could that be Charlie? If she'd lost her own cell phone, she might have had to borrow—or even steal—another to contact me.

It was a risk, but one I was prepared to take. Glancing around, I lifted the phone to my ear.

"Hello?"

"Nat?" It was a girl. Was it *her?*

"Charlie?" I could hear the desperation in my voice.

"Nah—and charming message you left for Julius just now, by the way."

I gasped. "Parveen? Are you okay?"

"Never better." There was a dry chuckle on the other end of the line. "But you sound like crap."

CHARLIE

The entire day and another whole night had passed and I still hadn't managed to get ahold of a phone—or a computer—in order to warn Nat and the resistance about Operation Neptune. If Gracie and Spider had cell phones, they must keep them well hidden. As for computers or other gadgets, the only ones I had seen were the password-protected machines in Uchi's locked office.

Anyway, since Spider had caught me outside Uchi's office, Taylor had barely let me out of his sight. He had come up to me the very next morning and in a low, menacing voice said, "Your father might have bought into your sudden conversion to our cause, but not me. And not Riley."

I looked up into his mean green eyes. Once I had thought Taylor was a hero. Now I loathed him for betraying us. I couldn't hide how I felt. Taylor would see through any attempt at pretense anyway. No, my best bet was to admit my feelings toward him.

In any deception, use as much of the truth as you can.

This was one of Taylor's own maxims—and it would surely help me now.

"Just because I hate you doesn't mean I don't believe in what Uchi is trying to achieve. I understand that sometimes people's lives have to be sacrificed—and I'm up for this mission we're training for," I said, keeping my gaze level. "I just think you should have trusted me and the others, not used us. You should have cared whether we lived or died."

A shadow passed across Taylor's face. For a moment he looked taken aback. Then his expression hardened again.

"I *did* care, Charlie. I care about what we're trying to achieve. Just remember *that's* what's important here. Not you. Not me. Not any individual."

"I know that," I said.

Taylor drew himself up. I could see he didn't believe me. "I know that, *what?*"

I took a deep breath. One day I would get my revenge on Taylor. But now was not the time.

"I know that, *sir,*" I said.

Taylor kept Spider and me busy with our underwater training for the rest of the day. As ever, his training was clear, focused, and effective. Each time we swam, we tried to extend the length of time we could stay underwater and the number of hoops we were able to swim through. By the end of the afternoon we were both able to do the full circuit—there and back—three times without taking a breath. And Spider himself was growing on me. I could see that his arrogant airs and graces were really just a defense mechanism, that under the surface he was actually a bit lonely. I caught him looking at me several times and though he made a face on each occasion, asking haughtily what I wanted, I sensed he would have liked to get to know me better, that all he was waiting for was a little encouragement.

It was flattering that someone so good-looking was interested, but Nat still filled my mind: Nat and me together, the way that felt—not just the touch of his fingers on my skin, but how I felt whole when he was with me. Spider might have model-style good looks, but the way I felt about Nat went far beyond superficial stuff like cheekbones and curly hair. Still, if Spider liked me, maybe I should use that to get him talking. Perhaps I could even talk him out of the bomb plot. Spider was still young and, though Riley and his mum had clearly completely indoctrinated him, maybe with a bit more time I'd be able to show him that blowing people up could never be justified, especially if the aim behind killing them was to help put Roman Riley in charge of the country.

It was a different story with Uchi. There was no way he was ever going to change his mind about what the EFA were doing. And though I could see he liked the idea that he'd found his long-lost daughter, he didn't quite know what to do with the reality of an actual person. He'd seemed surprised when I'd asked why, if he was so delighted to have me in his life, he was prepared to let me take on such a risky mission. "Because you're an elite soldier, Charlie," he'd said, as if this were obvious. "You're trained, you're smart, and you're naturally cool under pressure. It's your destiny to be involved." I wasn't sure how to take any of that, though I couldn't deny that I had liked hearing his praise.

Not wanting to think about Uchi—or the fact that my own father was behind Riley's evil—I focused on our training. At least I was able to keep up with Spider now when we swam, and I clung to the slim chance that I'd be able to find some way of disabling the bomb before it went off. Or, maybe more realistically, at least an opportunity to warn the people at the party. I was also determined to get my revenge on Taylor. Riley and Uchi might have masterminded the blast that killed Mum, but it was Taylor who had actually sent the bomb into the marketplace.

These thoughts and emotions crowded my head throughout my second day, and I slept fitfully that night, finally falling asleep just before dawn, then waking late.

I splashed some water on my face and hurried downstairs, determined today to find a way of contacting Nat, whatever it took.

But as I reached the bottom of the stairs, Gracie was bustling about. The front door was open, and from the looks of the large car being loaded up outside, the entire household was on the move.

"Ah, good. You're up," Gracie said.

"What's going on?"

"Everyone's leaving," she said breathlessly. "You and Spider. The mission is tonight." She disappeared into the kitchen.

Tonight?

My heart skipped a beat. So it was starting already. Now I really was running out of time. Perhaps I'd be able to use someone's phone while they were all distracted, getting ready to leave.

I ventured outside. Uchi and Spider were already out there, standing in a patch of bright sunlight.

"Please get your things together, Charlie," Uchi said as I appeared. "We are heading out in fifteen minutes."

Spider raised his eyebrows, his eyes sparkling with excitement. I went inside, packed up my few changes of clothes and the small items I'd brought with me, and hurried back outside. We got into the car right away: Uchi and Taylor up front where the windows were darkened, Spider and me in the back.

Spider was quiet for most of the journey. I imagined he was worrying about our mission. Well, let him. I barely thought about the underwater swim that lay ahead. I was totally preoccupied with how on earth I was going to get a warning to Nat.

After about an hour and a half, the van stopped behind an abandoned rest stop on a busy road. The brick wall where we parked was crumbling and stained, the windows all boarded up. Both the back and side doors were hanging off their hinges. The side door was sprayed with graffiti and labeled RESTROOM. The air was hot and humid. Even from here I could smell the stench of rot and drains.

"Where are we?" I asked.

No one replied.

"Over there! That's got to be Dad." Spider pointed to a black car turning in to the back of the rest stop.

"Good," Uchi said. He hobbled toward the car, which had slowed to a stop.

I watched as Roman Riley got out.

"Uchi." He threw his arms around the older man, ruffled Spider's hair, then turned to me with a smile. "Charlie, how are you?"

I shrugged. I knew that I should try to make more of an effort to convince Riley I was under his spell, but it was hard. I suddenly remembered the moment months ago when he'd stood in front of me, unarmed, and I'd held a gun in my hands. I hadn't shot him. If I had, Riley would be dead now and none of this would be happening.

I still didn't know if that had been the right choice or not. Nat had said that it was good I wasn't capable of killing anyone. But surely Riley deserved to die. I shook myself, unable to work it out, as Riley turned back to Uchi.

"Come on," he said, pointing to the building. "We can talk in there. I can give you ten minutes."

"All right, Mr. Important," Uchi grunted. "Just remember I knew you when you were a question without an answer."

Riley chuckled. "Hurry up, old man," he said. "I've got a rally to get to."

As they disappeared inside the shabby building, Martina emerged from the car. She was wearing a fitted green suit and looked as pretty and elegant as ever. She waved at me, nodded at Spider, then went over to Taylor. The two of them bent their heads over a smartphone, discussing what they were looking at in a low mumble.

I fantasized for a second about wrenching the phone from them and using it to call Nat, then forced myself back to reality.

I wandered along the side of the rest stop toward the bathrooms. The air was still and heavy. Behind me, Martina and Taylor were still deep in conversation; Spider was lounging against the side of the car, gazing up at the clear blue sky.

No one was watching me. The chances were high that there

was an interior door from the bathroom into the station where there could be a pay phone. I called out to Taylor. "I need to pee, sir," I said.

He waved his permission, and I headed for the bathroom. Inside, I spotted the interior door straightaway and raced over. It was locked. I was just about to try to prize the lock open when I heard Riley and Uchi talking just yards away on the other side.

I froze, then eased myself closer to the door.

"In the car, all on schedule." That was Riley.

Uchi said something I couldn't make out. I pressed my ear against the door, its wood warm on my skin, straining to hear.

"That's not realistic, Uchi." Riley sighed. "Not in that time frame, but Charlie will be fine. Just like Spider. And the casualties will be extreme."

My stomach screwed into a tight knot. *Extreme?* What kind of bomb were we planting?

Uchi said something I couldn't catch. And then the door to the outside opened. Taylor appeared behind me.

"I thought you were using the bathroom." He raised his eyebrows.

"Keep your hair on, *sir*." I followed him back to the car, still feeling shaken. Up until this point, I'd thought only in terms of trying to protect the people at the party—but suppose the bomb Spider and I were carrying was more powerful than the one that had exploded at the market. Even the four deaths inflicted there were four too many, of course, but what if London itself was the target?

How many people was Riley planning to kill this time?

NAT

I stopped in my tracks. Above me, the sun burned high in the sky. Around me, traffic hummed and late commuters hurried to the subway station. My phone, pressed to my ear, felt hot against my skin.

"Parveen?" Her voice had shocked the tears right out of my eyes. "Where are you? Are you all right?"

"Never better," she said breezily. "If you don't count being pursued by Roman Riley, just about getting away with my life, and spending the past three weeks lying low in the middle of nowhere with no access to the Internet."

"Riley came after you?" I asked, my head spinning. "How did he know where you were?"

"It was a mess," Parveen said crisply. "I was with the guy from Resistance Two. His girlfriend was killed in one of Riley's bombs—an early bomb, before the one that left your brother in a coma. The guy from Two has been working against Riley for nearly a year. Anyway, you know how the League of Iron said *they* did the House of Commons bombing but only 'cause Riley made them?"

"Yes," I said. "What's that got—?"

"Listen. I'm telling you. The guy from Two thought he knew where the League of Iron leader—you know, Saxon66—was hiding out. The resistance had heard Saxon wanted to join us, so they went to make contact and I got caught up in—"

"The League of Iron leader wants to join the resistance?" I asked, shocked.

"Yes. In fact, as of last night he *has* joined. *And* that heinous Goth woman he hangs out with, WhiteRaven. If you ask me, she's even worse than he is."

"But we can't let them be part of the resistance. They're as bad as Riley."

"I know." Parveen sighed. "It sucks. But the point is that while trying to find them, I almost got captured by Riley. That's why I've been out of contact. Nightmare." Parveen paused. "Hey, Nat, you sound weird. Have you been *crying?*"

"No. 'Course not." I sniffed, rubbing my face with the back of my sleeve.

"Good," she went on, "because yesterday I finally made it to the main London safe house, and everyone's there."

"Including Saxon 66 and WhiteRaven?" I said, still unable to believe that two such violent racists had been allowed to join the resistance.

"Yeah. We're all just one big happy family at resistance HQ," Parveen said dryly. "Apart from the League of Iron couple—who are now Resistance Pair Seventeen, by the way—there's me and the guy from Two and the people from Six, Eight, and Ten, plus

Julius and Lennox in Nine, who you met the other day. We're having a meeting later. Apparently, the mayor of London's coming along. He's been supplying the guys in London with all sorts of tech and a few Tasers. We're hoping he'll be able to give us some muscle, maybe even real weapons, as well."

"Really?" This lined up with what Latimer himself had told me earlier. I felt some of the tension inside me ease. I was starting to believe that perhaps he really was on our side.

"Julius and Lennox have news about Charlie, by the way," Parveen added.

My heart leaped. "Really? Is she okay? Where is she?"

Parveen chuckled. "Ah, I heard you guys were an item. About time."

"What's that supposed to mean?"

"Nothing. It was just obvious between the two of you, though both of you were too pigheaded to see it."

"What's the *news*, Par?" I asked pointedly. A gaggle of schoolkids headed past. They were laughing, not a care in the world. I had been like that once, a million years ago. Avoiding the group, I headed for the shelter of a boarded-up store doorway. The street was full of them. When Lucas had first been brought to this hospital, the street had been thriving and busy. Now hardly any of the stores were even occupied.

"She's with Riley. Successfully undercover," Parveen said, suddenly sounding very businesslike.

"How do you know? Did she get a message out?"

"Nah. The guy from Resistance Ten managed to hack an

e-mail Riley was sent from a guy called Uchi. It was encrypted, but we've got this new software, thanks to Latimer, so—"

"What did the e-mail say?"

"I'm getting to that." Parveen tutted at my impatience. "It was basically an update on how Charlie is training for a mission. Something called Operation Neptune. There's a film of her actually in training."

"Can I see it?"

"It's in the draft e-mail box," Parveen said. "We got it this morning and we've been trying to work out what it means, what kind of mission they're planning."

"I see." I leaned against the boarded-up door. The wood felt cold against my back. "But Charlie hasn't been in touch herself?"

"No." Parveen hesitated. "But from the e-mail, it looks like the guy who sent it—Uchi—is her dad, so she's obviously found him. That's all we know."

"I'll take a look at the film," I said.

"Good," Parveen said. "The safe house address is there with it. Come here as soon as you can."

She hung up. Filled with a new purpose, I opened the browser on the smartphone Latimer had given me. I logged on to the resistance e-mail address and checked the draft e-mail box. I found Parveen's message easily enough. It was brief and to the point, simply giving me the South London address of the safe house where she and the other Resistance Pairs had gathered.

The video attachment was a grainy color film. It looked, as Parveen had said, as if it had been taken on a cell phone, and it showed the back of a house, a patio, and a swimming pool, its waters disturbed. I peered closer. Two smudged figures in wet suits were visible, slipping through a series of narrow hoops set to the bottom of the pool. I couldn't be 100 percent certain, but one of the figures looked a lot like Charlie. The other was definitely a boy.

Was that the training class Parveen had referred to? I frowned. EFA training normally involved guns and bombs, not underwater party tricks. I watched the two people swimming. After a couple of minutes they got out. I stared, transfixed, as Charlie removed her mask. She looked amazing in that skintight suit. She said something to the boy with her. He was about our age: tall and slim, with a shock of curly black hair.

As I watched, the boy's face broke into a huge smile. Man, he was *really* good-looking. I felt a stab of jealousy as the two of them walked around the pool. The boy was standing too close to her. He pointed to something in the water and touched her shoulder.

"Get off her," I found myself growling under my breath.

Who was that guy? The film ended as abruptly as it had begun. I played it again. Swimming through hoops? What was that about? It didn't make sense. I closed my browser and headed to the station. I knew, as I got on to my train and headed to meet Parveen, that whatever Riley was planning must be going to happen soon, that with the election just four days away, everything was coming to a head, but as I headed toward South London, all I could think about was the guy with the black hair putting his arm around Charlie and how jealous it had made me feel.

CHARLIE

The streets of London gleamed from the rain as the large car glided silently along the busy road. I peered through the window, wondering where on earth we were going. We had been driving for hours since the meeting with Riley, who had sped off in his own car with Martina after just a few minutes.

It struck me that apart from a quick "hello" and "good-bye," Riley hadn't spoken to his son at all. Maybe I could use the fact that he paid Spider so little attention to help make Spider question his views and his plans.

Up front, Uchi and Taylor were talking in low voices. I leaned across the backseat and tapped Spider's arm.

He looked up.

"So, do you see much of your dad?" I asked quietly.

"Not really." A self-conscious flush spread over Spider's cheeks. "He's so busy. Plus, he doesn't want people to know about me, says they'll just come snooping around. He wants to protect my mum from all that too."

I said nothing. Privately, I suspected that Riley was more

concerned with protecting his privacy than his family, but I didn't want to antagonize Spider.

"That must be hard," I said. "It's a shame you don't see more of him."

Spider scowled. "It's fine," he said. "Dad's busy with important stuff. It's all cool." He turned away and looked pointedly out the window.

I sighed inwardly. I was useless at this kind of thing, trying to talk to people about their feelings. Jas would have managed to get Spider to open up with her gentle, friendly warmth. And Nat would have found a way too.

Nat . . . I'd have given anything for the chance to hear his voice, to find out if he was all right, to tell him I was sorry for running off and not contacting him right away. Tears pricked at my eyes. I forced them back angrily. This was so *not* the time to get mushy. I was still no closer to warning the resistance about tonight's bomb than I had been two days ago. And time was running out fast.

I sat back in silence, trying to work out how I could make a call. . . .

About half an hour later Taylor pulled up outside a grungy-looking concrete block in Hackney. He got out, looked around, then pronounced that it was safe for us to leave the car. We headed straight into the basement apartment. It was, like most of the EFA bases I'd been to, a mix of high-tech equipment and shabby décor. The paint was peeling from the walls, but the living room was set up with an entire bank of screens showing CCTV shots from around the capital. Three EFA soldiers, all with masks and guns, were hunched over a group of photos pinned to the far wall. I tried to take a closer look, but Uchi hurried Spider and me through to the kitchen—another run-down room with rusting appliances and a chipped countertop. He left us sitting at the table in the center of the room while a masked soldier made coffee, announced there wasn't any milk, then went back to the living room. We stared at each other.

"What's going on?" I asked.

"The operation is a bomb," Spider said. "Taylor said I could tell you now. It's tonight. We're taking it somewhere—I don't know where yet—and setting it to go off at seven thirty."

This was confirmation of Operation Neptune. My heart lurched into my throat.

"A *bomb*?" I said, trying to look like I had no idea about what was planned. "What else do you know?"

"Nothing." Spider gave a rueful shrug. "Sorry. I'd tell you if I did."

I stared at him. I was certain he was telling the truth. That was always how the EFA acted—no single individual in possession of too much information.

"Okay, thanks," I said. I looked around. There was no landline in the kitchen—and concertina shutters on both the windows and the back door. Even though it was two o'clock in the afternoon and a bright spring day outside, it was gloomy in here. The dark dampness of the place was like a physical presence, weighing down on me.

A phone in one of the other rooms rang, then stopped. A few moments later, Uchi hobbled to the kitchen door and peered around. "Spider, it's your mother," he said, holding out the handset. "You can take it in the coat closet if you want privacy."

Spider got up without looking at me and took the phone. He vanished, and Uchi gave me a gruff smile, then pulled the door closed behind him.

I sat back in my chair. I could hear everyone bustling about next door, but in here it was quiet. Spider had left his sweatshirt on the counter. As I glanced at it, I noticed the edge of his cell phone peeking out from underneath the hood.

I stared at it, my chest tightening. This was it, the opportunity I'd been waiting for. I grabbed the phone and swiped the screen, praying the phone wasn't set to request a password.

It wasn't. My heartbeat quickened as I checked the door. It was still shut. I punched Nat's number into the handset and held it to my ear. A continuous tone sounded. *Number unobtainable.* What did that mean? That Nat had lost his phone? Had it forcibly taken from him? Or dumped it because it had been compromised?

Footsteps sounded along the hallway. I had just enough time to shove the phone behind my back before the door opened. Taylor peered into the room.

"Just checking you're okay," he said. His green eyes pierced through me.

"I'm fine." The phone felt clammy in my palm.

Taylor gave me a curious look. Then he nodded and withdrew.

Hands shaking, I peered at the phone again. I had only one more opportunity to make a call.

The emergency services were out—thanks to Riley's ability to control the police—and aside from Nat's, the only other useful number I could remember was Parveen's. We'd swapped them via the draft e-mail system weeks ago, though agreed to use them only in absolute emergencies. It was probably hopeless; after all, the last I'd heard, she'd gone off the radar. She was most likely a prisoner, or even dead. Still, it was my only remaining chance. I pressed the numbers in quickly.

The phone rang. And rang.

"Hello?" Parveen's voice brought back a million sudden memories—of our training; of big, affable George; of Parveen's wicked laugh; of Nat's kiss.

"Par, it's me, Charlie," I whispered.

"Charlie?" She actually gasped. "Where—?"

"Is that her?" Nat's voice sounded in the background. My stomach somersaulted. "Give me that."

Parveen was complaining, but Nat clearly snatched the phone from her because the next thing I knew his voice was in my ear.

"Charlie, are you okay?"

Tears sprang to my eyes. It was just so good to hear him. For a second I forgot where I was and everything that had happened since we parted.

"I'm sorry I ran off," I whispered.

"It's okay." Nat lowered his voice. "Where are you?"

I tried to pull myself together. "London. Riley's planning an attack at his own party—a cocktail reception—it's tonight."

"Tonight?" Nat let his breath out in a hiss. "Any details of what's involved?"

I told Nat what I'd seen in Uchi's file. "It's a bomb. Almeida Hotel basement. There's an underwater route into the hotel. Spider—that's Riley's son—he and I are supposed to be bringing the bomb in through an underwater tunnel or pipes or something."

"Yeah, the resistance got ahold of some footage of you swimming," Nat said. "Operation Neptune, right?"

"Yes."

"Was that Spider you were swimming with?" His voice tensed as he spoke.

"Yes. Look, Nat, the bomb's planned to go off at seven thirty this evening. Can you get to the hotel, warn the staff? Get the party called off?"

"I'll talk to the others. But if Riley's son is involved, this is a great opportunity to let the mission play out, then capture him *with* the bomb *in* the hotel. It will connect Riley to the bomb like nothing else. He won't be able to disown his own kid. Mayor Latimer—you know, Aaron's dad—he's coming here this afternoon in person and—"

"The mayor of London?" I hissed. "But you can't believe anything—"

"We can trust Latimer," Nat interrupted. "Seriously. I didn't believe it at first either, but it's true."

I said nothing. No way was I trusting Latimer.

"Anyway, we need him." Nat lowered his voice. "Everyone's doing their best, but the people here are untrained." He paused. "There's no one here as good as you."

I felt myself glow with pride.

"Charming," I could hear Parveen saying in the background.

I glanced at the door. Footsteps sounded in the hallway again. I didn't have long. "I miss you." The whisper slid out of me unexpectedly.

"Me too," Nat said. "Charlie, get out of there, *now*. You've given us enough info to go on. I don't like you being caught up in this. Let Spider—or whatever his stupid name is—take the bomb in by himself."

"No," I whispered. The footsteps were getting closer. "I've got to be part of it. It'll look too suspicious if I run off at this point. Anyway, if I'm there, I can help you guys stop and capture Spider—he won't be expecting me to turn on him."

"But you're in danger. You could be—"

The door started to open. I switched off the call and shoved the phone behind my back as Spider slouched in. He went straight to the sink and reached for a glass. Heart racing, I shoved the phone back underneath Spider's sweatshirt and went over to the window. There hadn't been time to delete the call. I just had to hope that Spider wouldn't check his call log.

"Apparently, we're leaving in one hour for a venue nearer the location where the bomb's got to be planted," Spider said, holding his glass under the tap and filling it with water.

"Can you tell me anything more?" I asked.

"You'll be carrying a bomb into a building underwater." That was Taylor. He was standing in the doorway. "That's all you need to know right now."

"Yes, sir." I met his gaze, the desire for revenge surging through me again.

Taylor's eyes were like lasers. There was no remorse and no doubt in his expression. "You need to focus on the mission, Charlie," he said. "This is a big deal with big consequences, a chance for you to show how committed to the cause you are. The EFA is counting on you both to deliver."

PART THREE

EXUVIATION

(v. to shed or cast off, as in a covering no longer needed)

NAT

I sat in the kitchen of the resistance safe house and took the mug of milky tea that was handed to me. It was a long time since I'd been in a room and listened to so many people all talking at once, and the whole thing was starting to freak me out. Part of me wished I hadn't come. But that, of course, was stupid. Working with the other resistance members was the only way to defeat Riley and, for the first time since I'd realized just how evil and powerful he was, that now seemed possible. This was mostly thanks to all the high-tech equipment Mayor Latimer had supplied, which ranged from computers to surveillance trackers and even a handful of electronic shock guns, or Tasers.

The sight of all the hardware the mayor had smuggled in to the resistance had finally convinced me that the man, as I'd said to Charlie, must genuinely be on our side. The others spoke about him enthusiastically too, especially those from Six and Ten, who had actually met him.

"He's taking a big risk making out like he's a Riley supporter and secretly helping us," one of the guys had pointed out. "Most people who know what Riley is really up to are going along with him in the hope that he'll reward them if they do. I'm not saying the mayor isn't ambitious, but at least he believes in democracy."

Maybe this was true. Maybe it wasn't. But I couldn't see any reason why Latimer would pretend to support us for more than the time it took to kill every resistance member.

The other people in the resistance weren't quite so impressive: mostly a bunch of misfits as unsuited to life on the run as Aaron and Jas. Although they were clever, thoughtful people, I felt far more experienced when it came to understanding the practicalities of dealing with Riley.

There was no one here who wanted to take charge and lead an organized campaign against him. No one, that is, except the League of Iron leader, Saxon66, whose presence I was doing my best to ignore.

Right now we were all eating sandwiches in the kitchen of the safe house—another shabby building with no hot water—and waiting for Latimer himself to arrive. I still hadn't heard from Jas or Mum and Dad, but as I'd warned them not to call until they had new phones, that wasn't surprising.

I was worried about them, of course—and about the bomb and about Charlie—but right now I was mostly preoccupied with the fact that of all the loud, angry voices in the room, by far the loudest and angriest was that of Saxon66.

"Riley forced our hand, didn't he?" he said, turning to the woman with long black hair who sat beside him.

WhiteRaven nodded, her forehead screwed into a frown. She

glanced around the table. I noticed, a hot fury building in my guts, that she avoided all eye contact with Parveen and her Resistance Pair in Two, a friendly black guy called Dwayne. I had seen for myself, at close hand, just how foul Saxon and WhiteRaven were. As far as they were concerned, England would be better off if everyone with a different-color skin left the country. I couldn't understand why the other resistance members had allowed them to join. I certainly wasn't prepared to share what Charlie had told me while they were here. Parveen had just made a face when I'd pushed her to explain how it had happened, saying that she and a couple of others had objected but that they'd been overruled.

"We need everyone to work together, whatever their respective views," Julius had argued when I'd gone to him in protest. "It was a majority decision. There's strength in numbers, Nat, and we need to be as strong as possible to deal with Riley."

"Riley manipulated us," Saxon66 was now saying. "He *made* us claim responsibility for the bombs. There wasn't anything we could do."

"That's ridiculous," I said, speaking for the first time.

Twelve pairs of eyes turned to look at me. The vein in Saxon's temple bulged as he glared at me.

"Ridiculous?" he growled.

"Yeah," I said, setting down my mug of tea. "At least it is as far as the House of Commons bomb was concerned. Riley was able to manipulate you only because he knew you'd been fiddling your accounts and you'd have gone to jail for tax evasion if he'd shown the authorities the evidence."

Saxon66 curled his lip. "And how do you know that?"

"Because I stole the accounts for him," I said.

A collective gasp ran around the room. WhiteRaven swore under her breath. Saxon clenched his fists. "You're wrong. You don't know what you're talking about."

"Are you seriously telling me Riley didn't use those accounts?" I interrupted. "Come on. He's always managed to have something over you, to make you do what he says. And you've always let him get away with it instead of standing up and telling the world that he's trying to blackmail you. Instead of doing the *right* thing."

A tense silence fell in the room. Everyone was still staring at me. I caught Parveen's eye. She gave me a swift nod.

"I agree with Nat," she said.

"Oh, you would, you Paki tart," WhiteRaven sneered.

A gasp of horror flew around the room. Parveen stood up. So did Dwayne and two other men, including Lennox. Fists clenched, they all started shouting at WhiteRaven and Saxon66.

I sat back. Across the table WhiteRaven had leaped to her feet and was shrieking that the resistance was full of bullies and cowards. Saxon66 sat, hunched and glowering, next to her.

"Please, please, this isn't helping." Julius stood up, wringing his hands.

The shouting continued. At least Saxon didn't look like he wanted things to get physical. Much to my surprise, he was neither speaking himself, nor squaring up for a fight. A moment later, WhiteRaven slumped into her seat next to him. She still looked furious but was no longer shrieking.

As a result, the shouting eventually died away.

I spoke into the lull.

"I don't think Saxon and WhiteRaven should be part of this group," I said, keeping my voice carefully calm and even. "Their views and what they've done in the past make them as bad as Riley."

Parveen, Dwayne, and Lennox nodded. Most of the other people around the table looked uncomfortable, as if they knew this was the truth but didn't want to face it.

"We're a small group," one girl said with a frown. "We need all the people we can get."

"But we can't trust them. We don't even know their real names," Dwayne pointed out angrily.

Saxon66 cleared his throat. "My name is Gavin Shields and she's Pam Gerritson," he said, glancing at WhiteRaven. "And all that matters right now is stopping Riley."

I stared at him, surprised both by the ordinariness of his name and his reasonable tone.

"Exactly," Julius said with relief.

There was a low murmur of assent around the table. I shook my head. "This is wrong," I persisted. "If we join forces with people who are as bad as Riley, how can we justify trying to defeat him?"

"Looks like you've been overruled on that," Saxon said. His voice was light, but this time I could hear the threatening undertones. They sent a shiver down my spine. However reasonable Saxon appeared to be, it was an act. He was still a thug, and I didn't want to have anything to do with him.

"Nat's right."

Every head turned. Jason Latimer stood, unsmiling, in the doorway of the kitchen's safe house. The girl from Six who must have let him into the house hovered at his side. Two large, muscular men were visible over his shoulders. With his suit and tie and his brisk, businesslike air, Latimer looked totally out of place. Yet he gazed around the room with complete confidence.

Saxon66 stood up. "You don't even know what we're talking about."

"Oh, I know exactly what *you're* talking about." Latimer leveled his gaze at Saxon. "You let Riley use you for the sake of avoiding a tax fine and in the hope of future rewards. Now that you've realized Riley won't touch you with a six-foot pole, you're out to get him by any means necessary."

"We're *all* out to get him," Julius said, his tone pacifying.

"That's not the point," Mayor Latimer went on, "Like Nat just said, if we don't behave better than Riley, then we're just as bad as he is."

At this several people nodded. I stared around the table feeling incredulous, then glanced at Parveen. She rolled her eyes. We had made exactly the same arguments the mayor had made and had been ignored.

"It's very simple," Latimer said. "We can't allow people whose methods are antidemocratic to help bring down Riley. We can't kill people or torture them or operate outside the law for exactly the same reason."

"What about guns?" Lennox asked hopefully.

Latimer shook his head. "We have a few Tasers, but using guns would be morally bankrupt. And think about the impact on the public. Even if we expose Riley, they won't trust us unless we give them something better to believe in."

"Well, when you put it like that . . . ," Julius said.

Several of the women nodded. Parveen stuck her nose in the air.

"You mean when a middle-aged white man puts it like that," she said contemptuously.

I turned to Saxon66. "You need to leave," I said.

"Absolutely," Dwayne added, his voice thick with fake politeness. "And I'm more than happy to show you to the door."

Saxon looked around the room. "Fine," he said. "You don't have the guts to do what's needed anyway."

"Suits me." WhiteRaven stood up beside him.

Together, in silence, they walked out. As the front door shut behind them, the girl from Six gave a nervous cough.

"Is it safe to let them go?" she asked. "Won't they go straight to Riley?"

"I doubt that," Latimer said. "They don't want him in power any more than we do."

"They don't know that I know what he's planning anyway," I said.

Every head swiveled to look at me. I kept my gaze on Latimer, who raised his eyebrows. "What do you know, Nat?" he asked. "What is Riley planning?"

I quickly explained what Charlie had told me. Latimer and the others were surprised—but not shocked—that Riley was planning to set off a bomb at his own cocktail reception. As I'd hoped, everyone agreed that catching Riley's son in the act of planting the bomb was our best chance for exposing Riley himself.

Latimer himself was already invited to the party and was able to give us some useful details. He produced his invitation, which showed that the reception venue was the hotel's Churchill Room and that it was due to take place between six thirty and eight thirty p.m.

"It's supposed to be this informal thing," he said, while the guy from Ten surfed the Internet and found a floor plan of the hotel's first floor and basement. "A social occasion for partners and kids." He grimaced. "At least if I'm there I can keep an eye on Riley, make sure he's occupied while you guys lie in wait for Spider and Charlie and the bomb."

I nodded. A few moments later the guy from Ten printed out the hotel floor plan, on which both the Churchill Room and the basement underneath were clearly marked.

I pored over the plans. "We need two teams, each taking a different route to the basement," I said. "There are two ways down: one at the front, here." I moved my finger across the blueprints. "One at the back, there. As soon as the teams find the bomb, they let you know. You send the press down."

"Yes." Parveen's eyes sparkled. "As soon as the press realizes Spider is Riley's son, they'll make the connection and Riley will be exposed."

I looked around the room. Everyone was looking at me. "We

have to make this work," I said. "If the public doesn't see proof of what a murdering fraud Riley is, they will vote for him and his party at the election in a few days and he'll end up having real political power. He won't *need* bombs after that. He'll say the country's unstable and the government has to introduce emergency powers or something and he'll be able to do what he likes."

"Agreed," the mayor said.

"What about the bomb?" Julius asked. "We still have to stop that from going off."

"Charlie said the bomb wouldn't be primed until they were inside. Spider's job is to set the timer," I explained. "I'm sure that's right. Riley isn't going to risk his son carrying a bomb that could go off any second."

"May I suggest each team includes one of my men?" Latimer pointed to the two beefy bodyguards, still waiting by the door. "They're not trained, but they are strong."

"Sounds good," Parveen said. "I'll take one of them. Nat can take the other."

I nodded. Latimer frowned. " No," he said. "This isn't a job for chil—" He stopped himself. "What I mean is, it's wrong to put so much responsibility on your shoulders."

"But we're trained for this," Parveen argued.

"And we know Charlie," I added. "She'll react quicker if she sees us. If it's a bunch of strangers, she won't know that she can trust them."

"True," Parveen said. "Plus, Charlie's trained like we are, so she'll get what we're trying to do right away."

"Trained for what, exactly?" Latimer asked, still looking skeptical.

"Combat, stealth . . . ," Parveen said.

"Exit strategies," I added.

Latimer raised his eyebrows.

"That's getting out of places," I explained. "Charlie was always the best at opening locked doors with a credit card and—"

"Come on, Nat. Being able to open a locked door won't help Charlie or any of you if you're up against men with guns."

I exchanged a look with Parveen.

"We know how to use guns," I said. "Riley trained us in that, too."

Latimer looked shocked.

"It's true," Parveen said. "He trained us so he could use us. Then he tried to throw us away."

Latimer blew out his breath. There was a tense silence.

"None of us want to put them at risk," Julius ventured timidly. "But Nat and Parveen aren't exactly ordinary teenagers, are they?"

"No." Latimer looked tight-lipped. "Well, perhaps if the teams going into the hotel are bigger, that will offer you more protection?"

"No," I said firmly. "If we go in too heavy, we'll be stopped by hotel security. If anyone thinks we look suspicious, the whole thing will fall apart. I say we sneak in through front and back entrances—two pairs. And it really has to be only people with stealth training"—I glanced at the two bodyguards—"or brute strength. We don't want to be thrown out before we've even found the bomb. And we don't want anyone at the hotel tipping off Riley so he can abort the mission at the last minute. He's got spies everywhere."

"But won't you need more than four people to overpower whoever's bringing in the bomb?" Latimer persisted.

"It's just Riley's son, Spider, and Charlie," I persisted. "Charlie said so. And remember she'll be there to help us too."

Latimer fell silent.

"That's the one bit of Riley's plan I don't understand," Julius said quietly. "I mean, I get him sending kids through the pipes— adults would be too big—so I can see why he's using his son. But why Charlie? He can't really trust her after everything she's done, despite her wanting to know about her dad."

"What's her dad got to do with it?" Parveen asked. "I thought he was dead."

I explained reluctantly about Riley telling Charlie her father was still alive. I felt bad doing so. I knew Charlie would hate everyone finding out. But Julius already knew, and anyway, there wasn't much choice. Despite the circumstances, it was good to know I would see her in just a few hours' time.

"How are you going to get past hotel security and down to the basement?" Latimer asked, a worried frown creasing his forehead.

"I don't know," I said. I checked the time. "But it's four thirty, which gives us three hours to work it out before the bomb goes off."

CHARLIE

It was finally happening. I still hadn't seen the bomb itself, but Spider and I were all set to plant it in the hotel basement. I didn't know much more than I had before, though from various hints Taylor had dropped, it was obvious the pipes we would be swimming through were narrow—which was why Spider and I had been picked for the mission. We were slimmer than any of the older EFA soldiers.

Taylor had assured us that the route through the pipes was straightforward and that, though there wasn't room for breathing equipment, we would have to hold our breath underwater for only just over a minute. I was a lot more worried about how I was going to stop the bomb than I was about the swim into the building. I just had to trust that once I was alone with Spider, I would find a way.

Right now the three of us—and Uchi—were waiting for the go-ahead in an apartment near the docks just a couple streets away from the hotel. Everyone was tense with anticipation. My mind kept flickering back to Nat. Was he here somewhere? Was the rest of the resistance? Did they have a plan of their own for sabotaging Riley's attack? Taylor slipped outside, leaving Spider at one end of the room watching TV and me curled up on a sofa at the other end. Uchi turned away from the window where he'd been standing and limped across the room leaning heavily on his stick. He reached me and bent down so that he could speak in a whisper.

"Please be careful on this mission, Charlie," he said, his voice low and gruff. "Now that I've found you, I don't want to lose you again."

I stared up at him, surprised. There was real emotion in his eyes. Something twisted uncomfortably in my guts. In spite of my hatred of everything Uchi stood for, he was still my father. I sighed. Why did it all have to be so complicated? I sat back, wondering just for a moment if it might be possible to change the way Uchi saw things so that the two of us could somehow end up on the same side, against Riley. He patted my arm, then hobbled off again.

Who was I kidding? Uchi would never change his views. And I would never support Riley. We might be father and daughter but on this our attitudes were polar opposites.

I checked the time on the waterproof watch Taylor had just given me. Spider had one the same. Both watches were set with the exact time and synchronized with Taylor's own watch, so that we could all operate as one unit. It was six thirty p.m. I hadn't been left alone for a second since I'd made my phone call to Nat. Spider had given no indication that he'd seen I'd used his cell phone. I was sure that he had been too busy receiving Taylor's last-minute instructions to check his call log. I tried to focus on how I could get the bomb away from him once we were under-way. He might be slim, but he was wiry and muscular too. At least he didn't seem to be armed, as far as I could tell.

Riley's words about the effects of the bomb being "extreme" echoed through my head. What did "extreme" mean? How many people was Riley hoping would die? I shivered. Nat had said he and Parveen were with the resistance, which was good, except that I had little faith the resistance would really be able to make a stand against Riley. There was Mayor Latimer, of course; Nat had seemed convinced that Aaron's dad was genuinely on our side. At the time I'd been skeptical, but Nat wasn't stupid. Maybe if he trusted Latimer, I should too.

At that moment Taylor came back into the room, two tote bags in his hand. "It's time," he said. He dropped one of the bags next to Spider, then crossed the room and handed me the other. "Spider will change in this room," he said. "You can use the bath-room next door."

"Sure." I took the bag and went into the bathroom. This was it. I squatted down and unzipped the bag. I'd expected to find a wet suit and a mask inside, but instead I found myself pulling out a summery, strappy green dress; a gray silk cardigan; and a pair of gray pumps. I stared at each one in turn.

Why the hell did Taylor want me to wear these?

NAT

We traveled in the back of a van to the road nearest the hotel. I had to admit that Latimer's contribution of both men and technology had made a massive difference. The two men he'd sent over—Sean and Simon—were fit, muscular, and definitely up for a fight, and we were all outfitted with tiny earpieces and microphones so we could keep in touch with one another.

Latimer had gone home to get changed for the party. He'd told us that he would see us there and that Aaron would be with him.

"I'd rather he wasn't, but I just called to tell him he should stay home, and he's insisting that if he doesn't come along, it will look suspicious," Latimer had confided shortly before leaving the safe house. "I don't want Aaron anywhere near a bomb, but he wants to help. And he'll be useful—he can keep an eye out for you while I'm busy."

"If you're sure," I'd said, privately hoping Aaron wasn't going to get in our way.

And then the mayor had paused and said something

extraordinary. "To be honest, once I told him you'd be there, Nat, wild horses weren't going to keep him away. He thinks you're about the bravest, coolest person he's ever met, a real hero."

"That's stupid," I said, feeling my cheeks burn.

Latimer raised his eyebrows. "Actually, I think the same thing."

I turned away, covered in embarrassment.

"I'm not perfect, Nat," Latimer went on, lowering his voice so none of the other resistance members could hear. "I'm ambitious and I've embellished and fudged and spun like all politicians do, but I believe in democracy. And when I look at someone like you, fighting back in spite of all you've been through, I believe in this country's future, too."

The van stopped with a jolt, bringing me back to the present moment. Aaron and his dad were both wrong. I was no hero. Even now, armed with a Taser, I was scared witless.

The others looked over. I checked the time. It was a quarter to seven.

"Time to go," I said to Parveen.

She nodded, her face serious and determined. Outside the van, she set off with Simon toward the back of the hotel. I headed to the front entrance with Sean. Cars were already pulling up outside the hotel, depositing a series of leading politicians. After a few minutes, Riley and a woman with long blond hair emerged from a black Lexus. Riley turned and waved to the small crowd that had gathered. He was laughing, looking like he didn't have a care in the world. As I watched, Riley put his arm around the woman's shoulders and ushered her into the hotel.

"We've just seen Riley," I whispered into my mike. "No sign of Latimer. Maybe he's inside already. We're heading in now."

Static fizzed in my earpiece. "Hearing you loud and clear. We're already past the fire exit and hotel rear security, heading down to the basement." That was Parveen.

"Well done," I whispered into my mouthpiece. "Over."

Sean and I followed the crowd of politicians to the hotel's main entrance—just past the door shrouded by the canopy—and slipped inside, our baseball caps pulled low over our faces. I looked around. A trickle of guests were coming through. No one I recognized, but it was obvious they were all following the same sign:

FUTURE PARTY RECEPTION
CHURCHILL ROOM

Sean and I headed along the hallway. As we drew close to the Churchill Room, a line of people were waiting to have their bags searched. The mayor and Aaron were at the head of the line, intent on the first security guard as he explained something I couldn't hear. Riley and the blond woman were just behind them, talking with the second security guard. I grimaced. Riley was unbelievable: smiling like that when all the while he knew a bomb was going off here in just over half an hour. Some of the kids here were really little, dressed up in fancy shirts and dresses, clutching their parents' hands.

I glanced at Sean. It was time to find a route down into the basement. Presumably, the bomb was going to be set to go off immediately under this room.

"How are you doing, Par?" I whispered. "We've found the venue."

I listened attentively.

There was no reply. I gulped. Perhaps now that she was in the basement, Parveen was out of range. Or perhaps the ear-pieces didn't work as well as they were supposed to. I hesitated. "Parveen, come in," I hissed. "Simon?"

Sean and I exchanged anxious glances. Then Sean also spoke into his mike.

Nothing.

It was eight minutes to seven. Most of the guests must be here by now. Blood thundered in my ears. Sean made a circular motion with his finger—the sign to continue moving. He was right. There wasn't time to worry about Parveen and Simon right now. We needed to keep going.

I glanced at the security line again. The Latimers and Riley and his girlfriend had disappeared. The party must surely be well under way by now. I crept along the hallway, searching for the stairs I knew led down to the basement. Sean sped silently alongside me. As we turned the corner, I checked the time again: 18:54. My heart thudded. I had to make every second that followed count.

Sean nudged me. He pointed to a door up ahead marked CHURCHILL ROOM. The stairs down to the basement were across the hall from it. Sean headed toward them. I was about to follow when I noticed that the door into the Churchill Room was ajar. No guard stood outside. That was odd, wasn't it? Riley posted security guards everywhere. And he certainly didn't leave vulnerable entry points unlocked.

I turned to call Sean back, but he had already disappeared down the stairs. Heart thudding against my ribs, I pressed my ear against the door. No sound came from the other side. Surely a room full of people would make more noise? I eased the door open and peered inside.

The room was empty—just a few tables and chairs stacked in the corner and a sideboard along the nearest wall. The door across the room, which led to the hallway where the security guards had been checking bags, was open.

I stood, bewildered, looking around the room. There was only one other way out, an open fire exit, which led directly outside the building.

I frowned. This didn't make sense. There was no sign that anyone had ever been here, and yet I'd seen crowds of people—including Riley and Latimer—heading this way just a few minutes ago.

So where had everyone gone?

CHARLIE

The dress and the shoes fit perfectly. I picked up the handbag and the cardigan and went back to Uchi, Taylor, and Spider— who was now dressed sharply himself, in a skinny-fit gray suit.

"Why am I wearing this?" I demanded. "Where's the wet suit?"

"One step at a time," Taylor said, his face impassive. "Let's go." He opened the door that led to the street.

"Good luck, Charlie," Uchi said.

I glared at him, then followed Taylor, Spider at my side.

We walked along the street, past one of the huge political murals that littered the capital—this one showed a pair of crossed-over machine guns. Taylor handed Spider a small leather backpack, which Spider arranged carefully over his shoulder.

"What's in that?" I demanded. "Is it the bomb?"

Taylor said nothing.

I tugged at Spider's arm. "Tell me what's going on. Why are we dressed up?"

Spider ignored me. We turned onto the dock. A marina was spread out in front of us, hotels on either side. Was one of these the Almeida? Yes. Except for some reason instead of going *into* it, people were coming *outside*, then walking over to the boat across the way. My heart pounded. All this time I'd been seeking to expose Riley I'd assumed that, once I was actually on the mission with Spider, I'd be able to do something about the bomb. But now, as we headed along the dock, I had to face the fact that time was seriously running out and I had absolutely no idea what was really planned, only that it was due to take place in just over thirty minutes—and that it would cause "extreme casualties."

I pushed past Taylor and stopped, blocking his way. "I'm not going any farther until you tell me what's going on," I said.

"It's a mission, Charlie," Taylor said impatiently. "That's all you need to know."

"But what about the swimming? I can't do that in this dress. How are we taking the bomb in? And why are all those people leaving the hotel?"

"No more questions." Taylor seized my arm. "And just so you know, Nat and Parveen can't help you."

I stared at him. How did Taylor know that Nat and Parveen were even aware of the mission? "What do you mean?"

Taylor narrowed his eyes. "We know you've been in touch with them, Charlie."

My breath caught in my throat. I opened my mouth to deny what Taylor said, but he was already speaking again.

"We know Nat and Parveen and probably others from the resistance are coming here today to try to stop the bomb. And we have a team in place to prevent that from happening." Taylor glanced at the thick black watch that he had synchronized with mine and Spider's earlier. "In fact, I'm expecting confirmation they have both been captured."

I stared at him, horrified. Was he saying that Nat and Parveen were being watched? That they were in danger?

Taylor sighed. "You didn't really think we were just going to let you back into the EFA that easily, did you? I told you before: Uchi might trust you, but Riley and I were never going to buy a miraculous conversion. Come on, Charlie. Whatever you think of me, you know how smart Riley is."

Panic filled me. All my efforts to pretend to be open-minded about Riley and his ambitions had been utterly pointless. Riley had seen through me right from the start.

"We need to get going." Taylor's eyes glinted. "And I strongly suggest that if you want to see Nat ever again, you'll continue with the mission. Don't try to run off. And no attempts to raise an alarm."

I stumbled numbly on as the horrific truth settled inside me. Far from helping the resistance to undermine an EFA bomb plot and expose Roman Riley, all I had done was lead them into a trap.

NAT

I glanced at the time as 18:55 ticked on to 18:56. There was still no sign of anyone in the room, which, according to everything we'd been told, was supposed to be hosting a large cocktail party. Something had gone terribly wrong.

"Parveen? Simon?" I hissed into my mouthpiece.

Still no reply.

"Sean?"

Silence.

My guts twisted. Now Sean had vanished too. What was happening?

The security guard I'd seen Riley laughing and joking with just a minute or two before was walking over. "Hello there," he said.

I glanced over my shoulder, looking toward the stairs that led down to the basement where I'd last seen Sean. There was definitely no sign of him.

"Hello?" The guard frowned as he reached me. "Can I help you?"

"Yes," I said. "The, uh, the party, the cocktail reception. Where are all the people, the politicians, everyone who came in here?"

The guard stared at me, as if considering whether or not to tell me. His eyes flickered over the dark chinos and thin cotton top I was wearing under my jacket, deliberately chosen by the resistance as simultaneously sharp enough for the party but also loose enough to move in easily.

"Please," I said, thinking fast, "I'm looking for my dad. We got separated."

The guard nodded. "Party venue shifted to a boat. Last-minute security change."

I stared at him. Had Riley somehow known we were coming? And then it hit me. Latimer must have told him.

A blinding fury filled me from head to toe. The man had seemed so sincere, I could barely believe it. But there was no other logical explanation.

"What boat?" I demanded, clenching my fists. "Where is it?"

The guard pointed to the fire exit. "It's called the *Kimberley Jack*, moored behind the hotel. But you're probably too late, and I'll need to check your bag if—"

I raced across the room, through the fire exit, and onto the marina. A boat with a blue hull was chugging away from its mooring. The name *Kimberley Jack* was clearly written along the side.

I stared at the boat in horror. It was still close enough for me to make out Latimer and Riley at one end of the deck, deep in conversation. I scanned along the railings. *No.* There was Charlie. She was facing away from me, but it was unmistakably her. She was wearing a green dress, the skirt flapping around her legs. The dark-haired boy from the video and Taylor stood on either side of her. I watched them, bewildered. Charlie had said she and Riley's son, Spider, were swimming into the venue underwater. Had she been conned? Had the whole thing been some elaborate trap?

"Parveen? Simon? Sean?" I listened intently, but there was still no reply. They were gone. And so the truth dawned: Latimer had betrayed us to Riley. Riley had decided to abandon his bomb plot and—instead—use the occasion to entrap the resistance. Parveen and the others were either captured or killed.

I could barely take it in. Terror gripped me. I ducked behind the nearest boat and glanced around. Was anyone after me? It didn't look like it. The marina was virtually empty.

I told myself to run, to hide. I could take stock, then attempt to contact the resistance later. Except—if Latimer had told Riley about our plan to foil the bomb plot, then Riley must also know that Charlie was secretly working for us.

I had to warn her, to save her, but the boat was already a couple of yards away from the dock, chugging steadily past the other boats, heading toward the open river.

No, no, no.

A sick feeling settled in my stomach. I was, surely, too late.

Latimer had betrayed us.

Riley had won.

And Charlie was going to die.

CHARLIE

Taylor led Spider and me off the open deck and into the main cabin. It was a large, square, brightly lit room with striped streamers over the portholes. I stared at the streamers as they fluttered in the light. They were lilac and white—the Future Party's signature colors. Uchi had told me the other day the colors stood for hope and peace.

What a con.

We stood in silence, surrounded by politicians talking, kids squealing, and waiters offering colored drinks from silver trays. Lilac and white balloons hung from the walls.

My head spun. I still couldn't believe that Riley knew I was working with the resistance and that Nat and the others were here, right now, trying to stop the bomb plot. Taylor had said he was waiting for confirmation they'd been taken. He'd meant Nat specifically. And Parveen. Were they okay?

And what about the bomb? Were we still going ahead with Operation Neptune? Taylor had certainly given the security guard who checked Spider's backpack a very meaningful glance. The guard had nodded at him, given the backpack a cursory look, then waved us on. The bomb was still, obviously, in the bag, and the guard was, equally obviously, in on the whole thing. I looked around as two children in orange life jackets ran past and clocked two other security guards in their navy uniforms. Did they know about the bomb as well? It was Riley's party, so presumably everyone who worked for him was in some way involved.

I gazed past the guards, searching desperately for someone who *wasn't* on Riley's side. Someone I could warn. Someone who might be able to help Nat and the others. Across the room, Mayor Latimer was talking with Riley. Nat had said that, for all his professed support for Riley, Latimer was secretly in league with the resistance. Was that really true? If it was, why hadn't Latimer warned anyone that the venue for the bomb plot had been changed? Or had he been kept in the dark until the last minute, just like I had?

I spotted a politician I recognized from TV. I'd seen him arguing once with Riley. He definitely wasn't on the same side politically. And as far as I could remember, he was quite a senior figure in his own party. I took a step away from Taylor and Spider.

Taylor caught my arm. "Don't even think about it," he hissed, steering me into an alcove. He eyed me warily. "I've got confirmation that some of the resistance has already been captured. Look." Leaning over me, so that no one else could see, he shoved his phone under my nose. The screen showed Parveen, bound and gagged, her eyes wild with fury. Two men I didn't recognize sat beside her, similarly trussed up.

"They are prisoners and Nat soon will be," Taylor went on.

"We have eyes on him right now. Remember, Charlie, if you attempt to draw attention to our mission in any way, Nat and the others will die—and we'll set the bomb off anyway."

I looked up. Taylor's mouth was set in a grim line. Spider hovered beside him, his dark eyes darting everywhere but my face. Despair filled me. "But . . . but . . . ," I stammered. The inside of my mouth felt like ashes.

"Get ahold of yourself," Taylor snapped.

"When did you find out?" I whispered.

"I suspected you knew about Operation Neptune back in Cornwall," Taylor said. "And, unlike your father, neither Riley nor I believed in your sudden conversion to our cause. So we set a trap to see if you would 'borrow' Spider's phone and reveal our plans to Nat, which, of course, you did." Taylor narrowed his eyes. "You know as well as I do, Charlie. Riley has ears *everywhere*. And you also know that trained EFA agents do not leave their cell phones lying around unguarded."

He shot a look at Spider, who was still refusing to meet my eyes.

I gulped. So it was *my* fault that the resistance plan had been exposed.

"Did you hear the whole conversation?" I asked.

"Just your side of it," Taylor said. "Enough to tell you were speaking with Nat." He shook his head. "Never let your emotions cloud your judgment, Charlie. You stayed on that call far too long."

A terrible chill settled around my heart. "So you're going ahead with the bomb?"

"Of course," Taylor said. "It's going to happen at seven thirty, just as we planned."

I closed my eyes, the full horror of the situation settling inside me. I leaned back against the cabin wall, feeling the *chug-chug* of the boat's engine throb through my dress. And then a new thought occurred. I snapped my eyes open. "Wait a sec," I blurted out. "We're on a boat on the river. How will Riley get away from the bomb? What about the guards? Spider's his son. How is Riley going to save him? Or you? Or—?"

"It's all arranged, Charlie," Taylor said. "You and I and the rest of the EFA will be quite safe."

I felt sick. Taylor steered me out of the alcove. We seemed to be waiting for something. Across the room, Riley and Martina were still deep in conversation with Latimer and Aaron. I stared past them, unseeing, at a lilac rosette pinned to a large vase of white roses on the sideboard. Hot fury raged inside me. I had let Riley—and Taylor—trick me *again*. I gritted my teeth. I would stop this bomb and get my revenge on them both, if it was the last thing I did.

A man dressed as a clown, with oversized red shoes and a big red smile painted on his face, was ushering a group of small children toward the door at the end of the cabin. The children were laughing and chattering at the tops of their voices. As I watched them leave the cabin, I remembered what I'd overheard Riley say about the "extreme" effect of the bomb. Had he meant "extreme" in the sense of many innocent lives being lost? All those kids?

Beside me, Spider straightened up. I followed his gaze. Riley had left Martina and the Latimers and was walking across the room to the makeshift stage, where a microphone stood ready for him. A woman I didn't recognize was calling for quiet. As she started to introduce Riley, the room fell silent.

Taylor touched my arm. This was obviously our cue.

"This way," he said curtly.

Gripping my arm, he ushered me out of the cabin and down a set of stairs. Spider followed right behind me. The boat felt deserted. Clearly almost everyone was in the main cabin, listening to Riley. I checked the time on my synchronized plastic watch: 19:03. Taylor had said the bomb was still planned for 19:30.

Which meant that I had less than thirty minutes to try to stop it.

NAT

I stared after the *Kimberley Jack* as it chugged past the other boats along the marina. It was about fifteen yards long, the deck running on either side of a central cabin festooned with lilac and white balloons and streamers.

Latimer, Riley, Charlie, and most of the people on deck had disappeared into the main cabin, leaving just a small group near the front and a couple of security guards watching them. No one was looking in my direction.

How *dare* Riley and Latimer play games like this with people's lives? Blood thundered in my ears as the boat moved slowly past the jetty. It was only halfway along the marina, still close to the other boats. Maybe there was a chance I could catch it before it reached deeper water. If I could just get on board, I could find Charlie, warn her that Riley knew she was a spy, and somehow save her.

And if I got a chance to push Riley and Latimer overboard, so much the better.

I raced along the boards, swerving onto the next jetty.

"Parveen?" I gasped into my mike, hoping against hope that this time she might answer. "Sean?"

Silence. They were definitely gone, probably captured. I was on my own.

I reached the end point of the jetty as the *Kimberley Jack* began to turn away from the marina. It was still only a few yards away and moving slowly. But it was bound to pick up speed soon.

I tore off my shoes and jacket; shoved my phone, the earpiece, and the mike underneath them; and dived into the water. The cold made me gasp. I swam hard, pulling against the clammy drag of my clothes. My Taser was in my pants pocket, but it would be no use to me once it was wet.

Never mind. I would just have to do this without a weapon.

I kept my eyes on the security guard watching the group in the bow. I couldn't let him spot me. I glanced toward the back of the boat. There was a set of iron rungs attached to the hull near the stern. If I didn't let my pace slacken, I had a good chance of reaching those. I took a deep breath and dived under the water. It was hard to see, but I forced myself to keep going. Stroke after stroke after stroke. The pressure on my chest was huge, but I kept going. After another ten seconds, my lungs were desperate for breath. I dragged myself on, knowing in a few more moments I would have to surface for air.

One more pull.

One more.

One.

CHARLIE

Belowdecks the boat was a lot less festive than up in the main cabin. The walls were painted a grayish white and the floor laid with some sort of grimy-looking plastic. Taylor led Spider and me along a hallway to where a thickset security guard stood beside a door marked PRIVATE. Taylor made the sign of the EFA—an open hand followed by a fist.

"Evening, sir," the guard said quietly. He opened the door beside him and stood back to let us pass.

The door opened on to a small cabin with two sleeping berths on either side of the door and a sink. As soon as we were all inside, Spider bent down, brought a screwdriver out of his backpack, and began unscrewing the large metal grille at the bottom of the wall.

"Okay, remember the package is all ready. You just have to set the timer, like you've been shown," Taylor said calmly. I stood beside him, my heart thudding. Clearly he was planning on keeping me where he could see me the entire time.

"Yes, sir." Spider carefully removed the grille and laid it on the floor.

"Through there," Taylor ordered. "I'll replace the grille when you're in."

Spider crouched down and eased his way into the tunnel behind in the wall.

It was some kind of air duct, and it looked tiny. No way would Taylor himself have fit inside. Spider disappeared from view.

"Now you, Charlie," Taylor commanded.

I stared at him. "*Me?*"

Taylor nodded. I bent down and peered into the tunnel. I could just make out Spider's feet a yard or so along the vent. Was Taylor seriously going to let me go with him to set the timer on the bomb? That didn't make any sense. Taylor and Riley *knew* that I had passed information to the resistance. Why on earth would they trust me to help carry out this mission?

"Go on," Taylor urged. "You have to use the air duct or you'll be caught on the boat's CCTV. Don't let Spider get too far ahead."

I crawled into the tunnel, my heart beating fast. I had no idea what was going on, but maybe—just maybe—this turn of events would give me a chance to overpower Spider and take the bomb off him, or, at the very least, sound a warning to everyone else on the boat.

NAT

My clothes weighed me down as I pulled myself through the cold water. It was Charlie who'd been training for an underwater swim, not me. I'd never been the strongest of swimmers.

Faster. *Faster.* The pressure on my chest grew heavier and heavier.

At last my fingertips felt the side of the *Kimberley Jack.* I slid up the hull, my head breaking the water, my lungs bursting.

I gasped for air, trying to make as little sound as possible. Above me chatter and clinking glass from the main cabin filled the air. The iron rungs I'd spotted before were just a yard away. Half a yard. About to pass. As they reached me, I caught ahold and swung myself up and out of the water. I crawled to the top, suddenly cold in the brisk air. I peered over the side of the deck. There were still five or six people—plus the security guard—at the front of the boat. Any one of them could have seen me if they'd looked up, but no one did.

Water poured off me as I swung myself over onto the deck. Then, crouching low so I couldn't be seen through the portholes of the main cabin, I raced to the back of the boat. I straightened up under the awning that hung over the end of the main cabin. I shook the worst of the water out of my hair and wiped my face. Shivering, I crept back around the deck and peered into the first porthole I came to. Inside the cabin people were talking and drinking. The room was decorated with bunches of lilac and white balloons, matching the streamers that fluttered over the portholes.

I heard footsteps behind me and spun around.

"Nat?"

It was Aaron, his mouth gaping. For a split second I reeled back, shocked. I'd completely forgotten Latimer had said Aaron would be at the party, watching out for me. And then all my fury gathered in my fist. If Latimer knew this was a trap, his son must have known as well.

I lunged forward, gripping Aaron around the throat, pushing him to the back of the cabin and pinning him against the wall, out of sight of everyone else.

"How could you?" I demanded. "After everything you said to Jas, after all the help we gave you!"

Aaron's eyes widened. "Wh-what are you talking about?" he gasped.

"Your dad told Riley the resistance was coming to stop the bomb from going off, so he changed the venue to this boat and . . . and neither of you even tried to warn us." I tightened my grip. "Your dad set us up. He sold us out to Riley, and now Riley's got Par and—"

"No." Aaron's voice was a hoarse whisper, his face reddening above my hand around his neck. "*No*. Dad had no idea Riley changed the venue till we got here a few minutes ago. We've been trying to get a message to you, but Riley's kept us talking the whole time. I managed to slip away only because he's making a speech."

I stared at him. There was no guile in his eyes. I thought back to the eager way he had followed me to the ops base and the adoration in his eyes when he looked at Jas.

Whatever Latimer had done, I was certain Aaron hadn't been any part of it. I released my grip around his throat.

"I need to find Charlie," I said. "If someone from the resistance has told Riley we're trying to stop the bomb, they'll also have told him that Charlie isn't really on his side. She's in danger."

"At least there *isn't* a bomb," Aaron said, feeling the skin where I had held him. "I mean, Riley can't set one off on board. He'd be killed himself."

"That doesn't help Charlie." I shivered as a gust of wind whipped my cold, wet clothes around me. "So have you seen her?"

Aaron nodded. "Yeah, in the main cabin a few minutes ago, just before I came on deck to try to call you. She was with Riley's son and that guy who works for him—Tyson, is it?"

"Taylor." I spat out his name, then turned toward the main cabin. Never mind that I was dripping with water and unarmed. I would just rush inside and grab Charlie before anyone could stop us. The marina was still well within swimming distance. We could dive overboard. Get away.

"Wait, Nat." Aaron pulled me back to face him, his expressive face contorted in a frown. "Let me fetch Dad, tell him you're here. He'll be—"

"No," I said, glaring at him. "Even if *you* didn't know about it, your dad must have told Riley we were coming after him."

"That's not true. I—"

"Well, *someone* did." I shivered. "Your dad knew what we were planning. He—"

"So did everyone else in the resistance," Aaron insisted. "It's not fair to blame my dad. It could have been *anyone*. Or . . . or maybe Riley just overheard Charlie when she called you to warn you about the bomb?"

I stared at him in horror. It hadn't occurred to me until he said it, but it was indeed entirely—and terrifyingly—possible that Charlie's phone call to me had been bugged or eavesdropped upon. All of which left her in more danger than ever.

"I *promise* you my dad wants rid of Riley as much as you do," Aaron went on.

"I don't care," I said, unsure now what to think. "It doesn't matter right now anyway. All that matters is that I *have* to find Charlie."

"Okay. Okay. I hear you." Aaron pointed along the side wall of the cabin, past a row of portholes. "There's a door just around the corner."

"Thanks." I took a step away from him. I would search the entire boat if I had to, though how I was going to get Charlie away from Taylor and Riley's son without a weapon, I had no idea.

"Uh, wait."

I turned back impatiently to see Aaron peeling off the sweater he wore over his white shirt. He handed it to me. "Wear this." He glanced down at my lower half. "Man, you are soaked, but I'm not giving you my pants."

In spite of the tension, I grinned. "I wouldn't wear your pants if you paid me." I tugged off my own top and slipped on the sweater. Immediately I felt better.

"Let's go," Aaron said.

I frowned. I knew I could creep through the main cabin without drawing attention to myself. But Aaron had no such skill. I'd be seen by the security guards immediately if he was with me.

"Maybe you could *find* me something better to wear?" I suggested.

"Sure." Aaron nodded eagerly. "There's probably stuff belowdeck."

"Thank you." With a grin, Aaron disappeared, and I sped away to find the door that would take me into the main cabin and to Charlie.

CHARLIE

I followed Spider through the air duct. It was hot and narrow. My elbows and knees were soon sore, rubbing against the metal. Agonizing thoughts crowded my head. Riley was planning a despicable attack on this boat in order to kill one group of politicians—and many of their families—and frame a bunch of others for the explosion. His aim was to shine through the chaos and win the general election in just four days' time. And I was the only thing standing in his way. Somehow, I had to find a way to keep the bomb from going off.

But why were Riley and Taylor letting me anywhere near it in the first place?

"Will I have to do anything when you set the timer on the bomb?" I asked as we crawled on.

"No." Spider's voice echoed down the air duct toward me.

"Then what am I doing here?"

"Ask my dad," Spider said dismissively. "Ask *yours*. They're the ones who told me you had to be here."

I fell silent. Was it possible that this entire mission was—at least partly—an elaborate trap designed to kill me? I shivered, suddenly terrified. Would Riley really go that far? No. It didn't make sense—there were surely easier ways of getting rid of me.

My mind raced over what I'd learned in the past half hour. The truth was that there were lots of things about this mission that didn't make sense: Why, for instance, was Riley was putting his own son in danger by having him set the timer? In fact, why use an inexperienced teenager at all? The EFA was an extremely powerful organization containing scores of highly trained soldiers. Even if Spider had been shown how to operate the bomb, there must be other people who could do it more efficiently.

Even more bizarre was the fact that only a maniac would set a bomb off on a boat and expect to survive it. And Riley was no maniac. Taylor had said it was all figured out, but how on earth were they planning to get themselves and all the people working for them off the boat without either being hurt in the blast or looking, at the very least, suspiciously well informed if they left just before the explosion? It was Riley's party, for goodness' sake.

Another minute passed. Then I heard Spider pushing at the air duct grille up ahead. It clattered to the ground. We clambered out into what looked like a boiler room. It was completely empty, but the sound of an engine nearby filled the space with a low hum, making everything around us vibrate slightly.

I stared at the backpack over Spider's shoulder. Should I make a move to grab it now? I inched forward as Spider crouched down to replace the grille. As he turned, I caught the metallic glint of a gun inside his jacket.

I froze. "Where did you get that?" I gasped.

Spider ignored me, just headed past a bank of machines toward the far end of the room. I mentally assessed my chances of overpowering him. Spider was taller than me and wiry. Even if I could catch him off guard, it wouldn't be easy to wrestle the gun off him.

Maybe my best chance was to try *persuading* him not to set off the bomb.

"Spider . . ." I hurried after him.

"What?" Spider turned to me. His hand rested on the gun. Did he really know how to use it? Taylor had trained him personally, which meant he almost certainly did.

"Please, Spider," I said, wringing my hands together. "What we're doing is wrong. Killing all these people."

Spider hesitated. For a moment I thought maybe he would listen. His expression softened a fraction.

"Please," I went on, "we don't have to do this. We can choose *not* to."

"Shut up." Spider's eyes grew cold. "I'm not listening to this. I have to set the timer. There's only twenty minutes left."

"No," I said. "I'm not letting you kill everyone."

Spider hesitated. His hand hovered over his gun. I sensed his reluctance. He didn't want to threaten me, let alone shoot me. That gave me a chance. Maybe I couldn't overpower him and keep him from setting the timer, but I could still run and yell a warning to get everyone off the boat.

I turned and bolted away. Hurtling through the only door, I

found myself in another hallway. The door across the way said STOREROOM. I hesitated, unsure whether to turn left or right to look for the stairs back up to the main cabin. I was determined to find the other passengers, to start shouting that there was a bomb. Once the news was public, Riley would have no choice but to take the boat back to shore. As I turned to the right, Aaron raced around the corner. His eyes widened as he saw me.

"Charlie!" he gasped. He ran up to me, stopping in front of the storeroom. "I just saw Nat. He's looking for—"

"Bomb." I grabbed his arm, my stomach flipping over at the thought that Nat was here, in danger along with everyone else. "There's a bomb. The timer's being set now. You have to help me warn—"

But before I could finish my sentence, a dark blur raced past me. Spider punched Aaron, the full force of his fist ramming into Aaron's face.

Aaron spun, then crumpled to the floor, clutching his head.

"Don't move." Holding his gun in one hand, Spider gripped Aaron's arm with the other and started dragging him into the storeroom. In seconds he had shoved Aaron inside and turned the key. Then he grabbed my wrist and gave it a savage jerk. "Come on," he insisted.

With the gun pressed against my neck, I had no choice but to let him force me back into the boiler room.

NAT

I slipped inside the main cabin, trying not to look as self-conscious as I felt. The room was in two sections. This smaller section contained a group of kids and a clown who was juggling with a determined look on his face. The clown didn't appear to notice me, though several of the kids pointed at my bare feet and damp pants and giggled. I hurried through to the bigger section of the room. I kept my head down but, even so, I was aware of the security cameras fixed to the walls. Any second I expected to be challenged by one of Riley's guards, but no one appeared.

The room was crowded with people standing, drinks in hand, and noisy with chatter. No one paid me any attention as I slid silently around the walls, searching for Charlie. From the conversations I caught snatches of as I passed, I gathered Riley had just been speaking.

". . . That man is *such* an inspiration."

". . . He plays so well with the voters, of course . . ."

". . . A natural leader . . . So charismatic . . ."

I shook my head. If these people only knew what the man

was really like, they would think very differently. I kept an eye open for security guards, but I couldn't see anyone who looked remotely official. I reached the far wall and looked around again. No sign of Charlie or Taylor, though there were several people in the room whose faces I vaguely recognized from the news. Politicians, presumably. Then, with a jolt, I spotted Latimer. He was talking with Riley and Riley's blond girlfriend. Aaron wasn't with him; he must still be trying to find me some clothes.

I watched Latimer talking. He was trying to appear relaxed, but I could see the tension that filled his body. I shifted sideways, behind a high table set with a vase of huge lilac and white flowers, then peered around. Riley was speaking now, a big smile on his face. Latimer was trying to smile too.

He looked up. Our eyes met. For a split second, Latimer's expression registered shock, then concern. Then he looked back at Riley, a mask of keen interest on his face. He nodded vigorously at whatever point had just been made.

I hesitated. It was obvious that Charlie was no longer in the room. Latimer, as Aaron had said, had clearly been right under Riley's nose since coming on board. And now he had seen I was here and was making no move to expose me.

My doubts vanished. Latimer was loyal to the resistance, and if I could only get him on his own, maybe he would have some idea of where Charlie had been taken.

Latimer was making his excuses, saying he needed to go to the bathroom. He glanced at me as he left the group, and I knew he wanted me to follow him. Keeping carefully out of sight, I watched as he strolled across the room. As he reached the nearest door, he turned and met my eyes again. Then he walked out.

I let a couple of seconds pass. Riley was deep in conversation with the rest of his group. No one was looking in my direction. Keeping close to the wall, I squeezed past more party guests until I reached the door Latimer had just gone through.

I slipped out into the hallway. Latimer was waiting just along the wall. He looked up, saw me, and shook his head.

Not now, he mouthed.

What was he saying? That it was too risky to talk? Screw that. I *had* to find Charlie, and Latimer was in the best position to know where she might have been taken.

I turned toward him, but before I could take a step, a hand grabbed my shoulder and pulled me roughly back.

CHARLIE

Leaving Aaron locked inside the storeroom across the hall, Spider tugged me back into the boiler room. My heart pounded as he slammed the door shut.

"*What* is your problem?" he hissed.

Furious, I squared up to him. Never mind he was at least a head taller than me and armed with a gun. He was an arrogant bully.

"Aaron could be seriously hurt."

"He was in my way." Spider snarled. "Anyway, he's irrelevant. We have work to do."

"How dare you say he's irrelevant?" I demanded. "He's a *person*. His life *matters*. All these lives matter."

Spider's black eyes pierced through me. "We're here to set off a bomb. *That's* all that matters."

"No. I'm not letting you do it." I made a grab for Spider's backpack.

Quick as a flash, he shoved my arm away and pressed his gun against my neck. "Move." He pushed me to the end of the room where a metal locker stood against the wall.

My pulse quickened. Spider was better trained in combat

than I'd expected. "Over there. Face the wall," he ordered.

I did as I was told. Behind me I could hear Spider fitting a key into a lock and turning it, then his backpack rustling.

I risked a quick look. He was positioning a phone inside the metal locker. I caught sight of numbers flashing on the screen:

06:39

06:38

06:37

"What's that?" I said, my voice hoarse. "Is that counting down to the bomb?"

"I told you to face the wall," Spider snapped.

I turned back, then sneaked a glance at my watch. It was totally in line with the countdown, even to the digital second hand. The bomb was due to go off in just over six minutes.

06:09

06:08

06:07

My heart beat hard as I stared at the wall. A moment later I heard Spider slam the locker shut.

"*Move!*" he ordered.

I stumbled out of the boiler room and back into the hallway. As we passed the storeroom, I could hear Aaron thumping on the door. Terror rose inside me as we headed up the steps and back to the main deck. In the distance I could hear people talking in the main cabin. Nat was here somewhere. I needed to warn everyone about the bomb. But how on earth would I do it?

"Turn left."

I followed Spider's command. As I walked, he put his arm around my waist. His jacket hung over his arm, concealing his gun.

"Don't think I won't use it," he hissed.

I glanced at him. His mouth was set in a determined line, but he wasn't meeting my eyes. Would he really shoot?

I couldn't be sure anymore.

Together we headed through the door at the end of the hallway and onto the deck. Spider took me over to the railings at the back of the boat. A security guard was standing there, arms folded. He watched as we approached, but said nothing.

A long minute passed. The boat slowed and did a U-turn in the water.

"What's happening?" I asked. "What are we waiting for?"

Spider said nothing.

As the boat finished its U-turn and began chugging back the way it had come, the security guard strode along the deck. I stared out across the water. The marina we'd left earlier was just visible up ahead on the right, but at the speed we were going, we'd never make it back before the bomb went off.

"Are we waiting for someone to pick us up?" I demanded.

Silence. I glanced at my watch.

03:44

03:43

03:42

"We *have* to go back belowdeck, Spider," I said, feeling desperate. "Stop the bomb. There's still time."

"I can't, Charlie," Spider muttered, his gun still pressed against my ribs. "I'm sorry, but my dad said you would do this. I told him you wouldn't. *Please*. It's not too late. I won't say you tried to run off." He stared at me helplessly.

Along the deck, the security guard was now looking out to sea. Four lifeboats hung over the deck to his right. There was no way I'd be able to stop the bomb on my own, which meant I had just over three minutes to get everyone onto the lifeboats and away from the boat.

I felt sick. How on earth was I going to achieve that?

"Hey!" the security guard called out in a loud whisper. "Rescue boat is nearly here."

So we *were* getting off the boat.

The guard disappeared from view, leaving just Spider and me at the back of the boat. Spider fidgeted beside me. I thought about what he had just said. I was pretty sure he was going along with this mission in order to prove himself to his dad and almost as certain that he didn't really want to hurt me.

Whatever. I had to take the risk. Otherwise Spider and I would escape and all the people left on board—including Nat and Aaron and Latimer—would die.

I reached for Spider's hand. Surprised, he looked around.

"Would you really shoot me?" I asked.

Spider's cheeks flushed, and I saw the answer to my question in his eyes.

"Thank you." I darted forward and pecked him on the cheek. Then, before he could say anything, I turned and ran across the deck, along the right-hand side of the main cabin.

A second later I came to a door and dived inside. I was in the short hallway that led to the main cabin. I could hear the chatter and the clink of glasses just up ahead. I ran toward the sound.

"Bomb!" I yelled. "There's a bomb on the boat!"

NAT

The security guard loomed over me, his hands pinning me down. He was clearly one of Riley's men, though he didn't move with the muscular fluidity of an EFA soldier.

"Hello, Nat," he snarled.

My heart skipped a beat—how did he know my name?

"What's going on?" Latimer demanded. He sounded furious, but I could see he was terrified.

The guard ignored him. "Where d'you think you're going?" he asked me.

I struggled, but the guard held me down.

"Let that boy go," Latimer insisted. "He's not doing anything wrong."

"He's trespassing," the guard said. "Back away, sir."

"Get off me," I growled. My EFA training kicked in, and I raised my knee between the man's legs. As he doubled over, releasing his hold on my arms, I punched his gut. One fist, then another. I spun him around, pushing him away from me. I raced to the end of the hallway and propelled myself outside. I was on the right-hand side of the deck. On the other side of the main cabin I could hear shouting, though not what was being shouted. Was that Charlie's voice? Another security guard was heading toward me.

"Come here!" he yelled.

I turned and fled, away from him, toward the back of the boat. But Riley's son was there, running in my direction. To avoid him, I skipped sideways, into the path of a lone male guest. Ducking under his arm, I reached the railings on the left-hand side of the boat and glanced across the water. We were still out on the river, but I could see the marina up ahead. I turned around. Riley's son and the security guard I'd attacked were charging toward me.

I was cornered. Desperate, I scrambled up onto the railings. Instinct took over. I couldn't help Charlie if I let myself be captured. I *had* to get away. I stood, poised for a fraction of a moment on the outer edge of the boat.

I felt a large hand swipe at me as I dived. "Aah!"

I hit the cold water. Down, into the murky silence. I pulled myself through, straining to see through the gloomy depths. I swam in the direction of the marina, surfacing only when I could no longer breathe. No one had dived in after me. I was safe. I swam hard, heading for the marina. My arms pulled me mechanically through the water, but all I could think was that Charlie was still on the boat.

I had failed to save her.

CHARLIE

I ran along the hallway, shrieking: "Bomb! Bomb!" The main cabin was just up ahead. The noisy chatter coming from the room was masking my yells. I glanced down at my watch.

02:31

02:30

02:29

Wham! I ran slap bang into a tall man in a suit. He staggered back. Winded, I reeled. Looked up. It was Latimer. I gasped.

Latimer stared down at me, wide-eyed with surprise. *"Charlie?"* He clutched at his forehead. "You need to hide. You're in danger. Riley found out that—"

"Bomb," I panted, my voice jagged. "Bomb . . . There's a bomb. . . . You have to get everyone off the boat, *now!*"

NAT

I broke through the surface, blinking the water out of my eyes. I had reached the boat at the end of the marina. I ducked behind its hull, then treaded water as I peered back toward the *Kimberley Jack*. It was chugging, very slowly, toward the marina.

Shame filled me. Logically, I knew I'd had no choice but to run. If I'd let the guard capture me, I would still be on board, a prisoner, of no use to Charlie. At least this way I could try to help her when the boat docked.

Filled with a new determination, I swam over to the jetty.

CHARLIE

There was a moment when I thought everything was going to be all right. Latimer was frowning as he clocked what I'd said. He was on our side. Nat had said so. He would help.

And then a man in a suit emerged from the main cabin and ran over.

"Are you all right, sir?" He stared at me with suspicion.

Latimer's face masked with indifference. "I'm fine," he said. "Go back to the party."

The man frowned.

"No!" I was almost screaming now. Latimer's aide had left the main cabin door open. I took a deep breath. "Bomb!" I yelled. "There's a bomb on the boat!"

"Stop it!" Latimer hissed.

The aide's frown deepened.

"Bomb!" I yelled again. I glanced at my watch.

01:48

01:47

01:46

"Bomb! Less than two minutes! Get off the boat!"

At last people had heard me. They were pouring out of the main cabin. In seconds a small crowd had gathered.

"Don't do this," Latimer muttered in my ear. "There isn't a bomb. There *can't* be. Riley's on the boat."

I tore away from him. "I've seen the bomb," I yelled at the crowd. "It's in a metal locker in the boiler room belowdeck. The timer is a phone. There's a countdown." I checked my watch. "It's going off in exactly ninety seconds."

A panicked muttering rose around us. Latimer shook his head. "No need for alarm," he said, turning to face the crowd. "I'm sure this is a hoax."

I stared at him. What on earth was he playing at?

"It's not a hoax. I—"

"Just a silly game," Latimer went on. "A prank."

"*What?*"

The aide who had asked if Latimer was all right cleared his throat. "Uh, shouldn't we at least take a look, sir?"

"Take a *look?*" I shrieked. "We need to get off the boat."

Latimer hesitated. "Very well," he said, ignoring me. "But just me and the girl." He gripped my arm and marched me past the crowd. I shouted out again, desperate to get them to stay back, to get off the boat, but several were following us, including Latimer's aide.

Still protesting, I broke into a run. Maybe if these people saw the bomb, they'd believe me. Maybe there'd still be time to get to the boiler room and back before the bomb went off. As we headed down the stairs to the lower deck, I twisted my wrist in his hand so I could see my watch again.

01:20

01:19

01:18

It wasn't enough time. "What are you *doing?*" I yelled. "You need to make them evacuate the boat."

Latimer bent his head to whisper in my ear. "I'm trying to help you. You need to run, to hide. There's no way there's a bomb. Riley's on board. So is his son and lots of his colleagues and EFA people. He changed the venue to a boat, for goodness' sake. There *can't* be a bomb."

"There *is*," I insisted as we sped along the hallway. We passed the store cupboard where Spider had shoved Aaron. I pointed wildly at the door. "Listen, *Aaron's* in there. Your *son*. Spider attacked him; he's going to die in the bomb too."

"Aaron's hurt?" Alarm shot onto Latimer's face. He disappeared from my side.

I raced on, into the boiler room. The aide followed me inside. Five or six people crowded in after him.

"So where's this bomb?" the aide said.

00:57

00:56

00:55

Panic whirled inside my head. I pointed to the metal locker. "It's locked," I said.

"Let's see." The aide ran over. He yanked at the locker door. To my amazement, it opened easily. The man stepped back.

"Unlocked and empty," he said. "No sign of a phone or anything that looks like a bomb."

I gasped, moving closer so I could see inside the locker myself. It was true. It was totally bare.

"It . . . it must be there," I protested. "I saw the timer."

The people behind us started to mutter.

The aide who had opened the locker door snorted. "You're saying a bomb is about to go off in an empty locker?"

My head spun. Then one of the people in the crowd swore. "I knew I recognized her," he said. "She's in that terrorist group behind the House of Commons bomb. She's wanted by the police."

Latimer's aide gripped my arm. As he did so, one of Riley's security guards emerged from the crowd. I suddenly caught sight of Taylor behind him. He was watching me. As our eyes met, he turned and walked away.

I glanced down at my watch. Less than thirty seconds to go till the explosion. I didn't understand. What was Taylor still doing on board? Where was the bomb Spider had planted?

The people around me broke into conversation, debating what should be done with me. The security guard was now on my other side, taking charge. I took a final look at the countdown on my watch. We were down to the last twenty seconds.

00:19

00:18

00:17

What was going on? The entire world seemed to spin around me. I closed my eyes. Wherever the bomb was, I had failed to get everyone off the boat. They were going to die.

So was I.

The voices around me grew louder. I thought of Nat and hoped that somehow he would survive. Then I glanced at my watch a final time.

This was it.

00:03

00:02

00:01

Nothing happened. The chatter in the room continued. My mouth fell open.

For reasons I couldn't begin to explain or understand, there had been no bomb. Riley, Uchi, Taylor, and Spider had all tricked me.

The whole thing had been a con.

As the security guard marched me to the door, the people watching parted to let us through. Out in the hallway people stared at me, horror—and in some cases contempt—on their faces. There was no sign of Taylor. Outside the storeroom, Latimer was crouching down. I could just make out Aaron's white shirt through people's legs. Latimer's hand was on his arm. I registered all this dully, in a state of total shock.

"Where are you taking her?" Latimer's aide asked.

"Police," the guard answered.

NAT

The *Kimberley Jack* was docking halfway along the marina as I hauled myself out of the water and gathered up my jacket, phone, and shoes. I crept along the jetty, getting as close as I dared and then crouched behind another boat so I wouldn't be seen.

I caught my breath as the *Kimberley Jack* disembarked. Soon the marina was swarming with men in suits, women in flowery print dresses, and children skipping toward the exit. Shivering with cold, I kept out of sight, watching everyone leave as I wrung the worst of the wet out of my pants, then took off Aaron's now-sopping sweater and put my jacket and shoes on. Where was Charlie?

Did I still have a chance to save her?

I moved closer still, straining my eyes for a glimpse of her. I caught sight of Roman Riley and his blond girlfriend on the far side of the deck and jumped back behind a nearby boat. As I did so, a small commotion started up on deck. People were bustling, making way for something. And then I saw Charlie being led along the deck between two of Riley's guards. Two more men followed directly behind them.

I hugged my arms around my chest, shivering as much from fear as from cold. No way could I rescue her from all those guards. I glanced back at Riley. He was keeping his distance from Charlie, but I could see him watching from the other side of the boat as she was frog-marched down onto the jetty. I vaguely noticed two paramedics rushing in the opposite direction, toward the boat, but I kept my eyes fixed on Charlie. Her head was down as she was led along the marina.

The guards were taking her to the exit. They were going to pass within yards of my hiding place. I held my breath as Charlie looked up. The sight of her face—of how strained and frightened she looked—cut me like a knife.

I shifted slightly so that if she turned very slightly she would see me. It was a risk, as the guards could easily see me too, but I *had* to let her know I was here. That I wasn't giving up on her.

I stared at her beautiful face, willing her to see me. Seconds passed; they were about to turn onto the ramp up to the exit. Another moment and it would be too late.

Charlie's gaze shifted slightly. Her eyes were dazed. Almost blank.

And then she saw me. Her face lit up with joy.

I stared back, transfixed.

I will find you. I mouthed the words.

And then she was gone. I took a deep breath, a storm of emotions raging inside me, ready to race across the jetty and follow Charlie and the guards through the exit. I was certain

I could get close enough to hear where they were taking her without being seen myself. But as I inched forward, the two paramedics I'd glimpsed earlier rushed past. They were pushing a hospital gurney. To my horror, Aaron was lying on top of it, his head in a neck brace. Latimer, white-faced, was striding along beside him, with Riley and his girlfriend on the other side of the gurney.

I ducked back into my hiding place, frozen with fear, praying Riley hadn't seen me, then took another peek. The whole group was heading swiftly toward the marina exit. I hadn't been spotted. I strained my ears, trying to hear what was being said.

"Which hospital will you take him to?" Latimer was demanding.

"Saint Matthew's," one of the paramedics answered. "He's conscious, so it's just a precaution, but we need to do a full assessment."

Saint Matthew's was Lucas's hospital. I'd been there only this morning. It seemed like years ago. I shrank into the shadows as they passed. Impatiently, I waited until they were through the marina exit, then rushed after them.

Where was Charlie?

I peered around the doorway that led out of the marina. Aaron was being loaded onto an ambulance. Just beyond, a group of black cars was pulling away. Presumably Charlie was in one of them, but I had no idea which one—or where it was going.

I sank to my knees. What the hell had happened? Charlie

had been captured and was now being taken goodness knows where, while Aaron looked badly injured and was on his way to Saint Matthew's, where Lucas had been lying in a coma since last year.

I tried to focus. Latimer had tried to protect me earlier and was my best source of information on Charlie. Which meant I needed to get to Saint Matthew's Hospital and talk to him. Fast.

CHARLIE

I sat in a room at the police station, waiting. Every so often I could hear footsteps hurrying along the hallway outside, then the large door at the end clanging shut. Each time I tensed myself, waiting for someone to come inside my tiny room. But nobody did. I was alone, with nothing but a table, two chairs, and a bottle of water to keep me company. There was no window in the room and no clock. As my EFA watch had been taken away from me, it was hard to keep track of how much time was actually passing.

In the end, a woman police officer brought me a sandwich. She chucked it on the table and turned to leave. She hadn't even looked at me.

"Wait," I said. "You can't keep me here like this. I'm entitled to a lawyer—to an adult from my family. There's my aunt Karen—she's my mum's sister. She . . ."

But the woman had already left.

I paced up and down. The situation I was in was bad. *Really* bad. Clearly I had been completely set up and there hadn't been a bomb at all. It kind of made sense. After all, it had always seemed odd that Riley and Taylor were so suspicious of me yet still trusted that I'd help plant the bomb. Riley had obviously decided that the best way to get me out of the way was to frame me yet again—this time as a hoaxer—and have me dealt with by the authorities. I had already been identified as the girl who'd kidnapped Aaron Latimer all those weeks ago; now I would be charged and tried and imprisoned. I wondered how much Uchi had known about it all. Had he realized I was undercover, working for the resistance from the start? Had he known all along that Riley was just using me? Or had he thought that I was actually persuaded by his arguments and that Riley was genuinely making me part of a mission?

An hour or so passed. I ate the sandwich—dry bread and flavorless cheese—and I drank the water. And I waited. I held on tight to that glimpse of Nat, to his handsome face as he'd stood, soaked and hidden, on the jetty and mouthed that he would find me.

It had been so amazing; for the split second that I'd seen him, I'd felt whole again. But it had left me missing him with a physical pain. And while the knowledge he was out there, somewhere nearby, filled me with hope, I knew, realistically, there wasn't a huge amount Nat could do as long as I was stuck in this police station. Nat was strong and brave, but he had no backup. I'd seen with my own eyes how limited the resistance's resources were. As for Mayor Latimer, he was so determined to stay undercover with Riley he'd let everyone in the resistance be captured rather than make an open stand.

I sat back down and put my head in my hands.

The door across the room opened. I looked up, expecting to

see the officer bringing me more food or water, but it was Riley. I sprang to my feet as he shut the door behind him.

"Why am I here? What's going on?"

A slow smile curled about Riley's lips. "Calm down, Charlie," he said. "You're going to be absolutely fine. Uchi has insisted that despite your persistent attempts at rebellion, we shouldn't hurt you—and I intend to respect his wishes."

"Why did you send me and Spider on a mission to bomb a party when there was no bomb? What was the point of that?" My breath caught in my throat. "And . . . and what about Aaron? Spider *punched* him. And Parveen? I saw the film of her all tied up. Is she all right?"

"Parveen is being held by my soldiers. She's fine. Aaron's at the hospital. I'm on my way there now. He's going to be fine too. They're just checking him over." He grinned. "Clearly my son doesn't know his own strength. He wasn't meant to knock Aaron down. Ironic"—he chuckled—"seeing as the hospital isn't the best place for *anyone* to be right now."

"What are you talking about?" I frowned.

Riley sighed. "I'm sorry that you were tricked. If it's any consolation, neither Uchi nor Spider wanted you involved in that hoax, but I overruled them. You were the best bait I could think of."

"Bait?" My head spun. "I don't understand. Bait for what? For who?"

"For Nat, of course," Riley said simply.

I stared at him. What was he talking about? I'd just seen Nat. He was free, back at the marina.

"Nat?" I said, feeling bewildered.

"Yes." Riley smiled, and I was reminded forcefully of Spider. "You see, Charlie, there was no conventional bomb of the kind you thought you were planting, but there *was* a weapon on that boat. A very powerful one."

"What's that got to do with Nat?" I demanded.

Riley shook his head. "Brave, Charlie, but not the brightest. Don't you get it now? He doesn't know it, of course, but Nat was—Nat *is*—the weapon."

NAT

It was ten p.m. and I had just arrived at the hospital. After trying various resistance members by phone and getting no reply, I'd headed for the safe house, skirting around it to see if anyone had made it back there in one piece and could help me. But if anybody had gotten away, they must have fled hours ago, as the place was swarming with police. This meant that at least some of the Resistance Pairs had surely been arrested. *And* that they'd talked.

Which meant the resistance itself had fallen apart just as it was set to get going. And that I was on my own.

I thought back to how I'd felt this afternoon—positive that there was a way to stand up to Riley at last. I had been wrong. *So* wrong. No one could stop Riley. I saw it now. Latimer and the resistance had tried—and failed. Charlie and I had tried—and failed. Riley was just too clever.

All that mattered now was rescuing Charlie, then finding Mum and Dad and Jas and going into hiding with them. Maybe we'd go abroad. I didn't mind where. I just wanted the people I cared about to be safe.

I pulled the hood of my jacket low over my head as I strolled through the hospital's main entrance. I had stopped at a public bathroom to dry out Aaron's sweater and my pants. They were still slightly damp, but not enough that anyone would notice. I was warm anyway, zipped up inside my jacket.

At the information desk I asked for Aaron Latimer. I wanted to make sure Aaron himself was okay, of course, but mostly I was hoping that his dad would still be with him—and would know what had happened to Charlie.

"Aaron's my best friend from school," I said to the woman in what I hoped was a convincing voice. It was hard to sound like I meant it. Apart from anything else, the whole concept of school felt like it belonged to another world, a different time.

The woman gave me Aaron's room number. I knew the way. It was on the floor below Lucas's.

Aaron was in a room by himself, lying under crisp white sheets. There was no sign of Latimer, but Aaron's mum—I recognized her from last year's memorial service—was sitting beside him, her head bowed as she held her son's hand. It was dark outside, though a bright light from the parking lot shone in through the window. Aaron himself was asleep, the covers rising and falling steadily as he breathed. The scene reminded me so forcefully of Mum with Lucas that I had to look away.

The last time I'd seen Mum had been in this very hospital, just this morning, when I'd told her and Dad to look after Jas, to take her away and hide. Jas would want to know about Aaron—and I would have to tell her he was in the hospital when she called. I was keeping my phone switched off in case Riley was trying to track me. I would turn it on later, somewhere busy, just for a minute, to see if Jas had called to say where they were.

Mum was probably fretting about having left Lucas. He had been on his own since then. It didn't matter much, I told myself. It was only a few hours, and Lucas was in a coma; he had no idea who was here and who wasn't. But as I stared at Aaron and his mother, guilt filled me to my fingertips.

Mrs. Latimer patted Aaron's hand. "Rest now, my darling. They're saying you're fine, that you won't even have to stay overnight."

That was a relief, on both counts. I shrank away, into the hallway. Guilt still pricked at my mind. I decided to go and visit Lucas. I needn't stay long, and perhaps when I came back, Latimer would have returned to pick up his family

Keeping my face carefully turned away from the hospital's CCTV, I slipped away to see my brother.

CHARLIE

I stood up. Riley stayed where he was, across the table. Outside, a man was yelling, a police officer telling him to calm down.

"What do you mean, Nat is a 'weapon'?" I demanded.

Riley studied me, his bright, sharp eyes fixed on mine.

"Spider did well, don't you think?" Riley paused, a proud smile on his face. "Considering that was his first real mission."

"Tell me about Nat," I persisted.

Riley sighed. "Nat is carrying an airborne virus called Qilota, which we implanted in him when he came to rescue Jas. The virus is in her, too."

"A virus?" I frowned. "Are they sick, then?"

"Oh, yes." Riley smiled. "Though they don't know it yet. That's the beauty of Qilota. It's been developed as a bioweapon. It takes two to three days to gestate before symptoms start to show, but the carrier is still highly infectious all that time. Anyone they come into contact with—anyone within a yard or so—is potentially at risk too."

My head spun. "So . . . so . . . whoever Nat and Jas have met since you infected them will get the virus too?"

Riley nodded. "Exactly. We used Jas to make sure the symptoms wouldn't show during the first forty-eight hours after infection, but today she should have started to feel sick."

"And . . . and Nat is one day behind?"

"Yes. He'll start to get symptoms soon, by tomorrow morning at the latest. Just blurred vision at first and a general feeling of weakness, then fever, blindness . . ." Riley trailed off, smiling at my horrified expression. "And the day after that, so will all the politicians on the boat he infected who, by then, will have gone on to infect others in their turn."

I stared at him.

"*That's* why you wanted Nat on the boat?" A terrible thought struck me. "That's why *I* was on the boat."

"Yes," Riley said matter-of-factly. "As I explained before, you were bait. It was our best option. You are associated with Nat already. Both of you are known terrorists. It fits with the public perception of you that you would bring a biological weapon to a political event, and the *Kimberley Jack* was an ideal venue because the cabin is small, so Nat would infect more people. It also makes sense that once Nat had been spotted, you would have started a panic over a fake bomb to give him a chance to get away. Getting him onto the boat was the only challenge, but"—Riley chuckled—"I knew that the harder I made it for him to rescue you, the more determined he would become. We were watching him the entire time."

My chest tightened. "So what happens after the first two to three days, after the weakness and . . . and blindness?" I asked. "How sick do you get?"

"Once symptoms show, the infected person has less than twenty-four hours to live."

I stared at him. His words were icy daggers in my heart.

"Nat and Jas are going to die?" I gasped.

"Yes," Riley said. "As will much of London, unless they receive the antidote in time."

So this was what he'd meant by "extreme casualties." "Why? How?" I clenched my fists. "What's the point of all of this?"

"There are two points," Riley said smoothly. "First, to discredit the government. When Nat and Jas pass away, no one will notice, but as soon as half the people at last night's party become sick, then we will step in to say we have just discovered that Nat—a known terrorist—was exposed to the deadly virus by government agents, working for the prime minister, that he was a government pawn, working for them—not the League of Iron—all along. You were assisting him and have now disappeared, also presumed dead."

"You mean you're going to frame us, like you did before?"

"It's not really about you," Riley said. "The important aspect to this is that once people become sick and the prime minister is denying all knowledge of the virus, we'll be able to 'expose' the fact that he and his government were responsible for illegally developing Qilota as a bioweapon."

"They'll deny it."

Riley nodded. "Of course, but we'll provide what looks like proof. *And* we'll be the first to locate and provide an antidote.

Symptoms will start to clear, people will be saved, and the next day the election will bring us a huge landslide victory as mistrust of the government reaches its height and the Future Party at last is seen for what it is: the savior of England."

"But . . . but you were on that boat too. You could have been infected. And Spider. And all the EFA people." *And me.* I thought those last words, but I didn't say them. I didn't want to give Riley the satisfaction of knowing how terrified I felt.

"We've already taken the antidote. So has everyone at the EFA, including Taylor and Uchi. And I've made sure selected political allies will be all right too."

What about me? Again, I didn't say this out loud. Instead I looked up. "You mean like Aaron's dad?"

"Yes, and his son."

I fell silent. Did that mean Latimer's cover with Riley was still intact? What did it really matter? I no longer held out any hope that Latimer or anyone else could make a real stand against Riley.

"You're wondering about yourself, Charlie?" Riley asked.

I held his gaze, my heart suddenly pounding.

"There's no need to worry," Riley said. "We slipped the antidote into your drink earlier today. Uchi insisted."

I stared into his eyes. His reassurance meant nothing. What good was my life to me if those I loved most lost theirs?

"But Nat and Jas will die?" I said flatly.

Riley smiled, and I remembered that moment, a month ago,

when I'd faced him with a gun in my hand. Then I'd been unable to shoot him. Now I was sure I would have no problem doing so. I didn't care if it was right or wrong.

"Yes." Riley paused. "Jas has another twelve hours or so . . . Nat about a day and a half. After that they—and anyone they come into contact with who doesn't receive the antidote in time—will be dead."

NAT

I kept my head down as I approached Lucas's room. Much to my relief, the hallway was empty, though there was a buzz coming from the waiting area at the end, where several nurses had congregated and were talking excitedly about something.

I turned into Lucas's room, bracing myself for the sight of his body hooked up to its usual tubes and wires. But his bed was empty. I stared at the white sheets, neatly folded back on themselves. I couldn't process what I was seeing. Where was Lucas?

Is he dead? Guilt surged up inside me, trapping all the air in my chest. Had Lucas died because I'd sent Mum away?

My legs threatened to give way beneath me. I reached for the doorframe, consumed with shock and fear.

"You all right there?" A nurse bustled past me, into the room.

I pointed to the bed, unable to speak.

The nurse frowned. I didn't recognize her from any of my previous visits. "Goodness, you look pale. Are you feeling all right?"

"What?" I gasped, still pointing to the bed and completely forgetting my need to maintain a low profile. "Lucas. Where . . . ? What happened?"

The nurse's eyes widened. "You know Lucas Holloway? Are you family?"

"Yes." I just got the word out. As I spoke, I remembered that I was still a wanted person—a fugitive. I needed to keep my true identity a secret. "I'm Lucas's cousin," I lied. "And his best friend."

To my surprise, the nurse grinned. "That's excellent to hear. We've been trying to track down Lucas's family since he woke up."

"*Woke up?*" The room spun around me. Mum had always said Lucas would regain consciousness, but the doctors had held out little hope, and for most of the past year I had thought Mum was deluding herself.

"Yes." The nurse was clearly enjoying herself now. "There'd been signs of partial consciousness for a couple of weeks, and we'd stepped up the physical therapy we were doing to help build Lucas's muscle strength. Then this morning he opened his eyes. Two hours later he was speaking and moving his limbs. We've been working with him all afternoon. He's even taken a few steps." She hesitated. "You should speak to the doctor. They can fill you in. And perhaps you could let us know where his parents might be."

"Speaking? *Walking?*" I said the words in a daze, too shocked to think straight.

"Yes." The nurse touched my arm. "Would you like me to take you to see Lucas right now?"

I nodded, still unable to process what she was saying. The nurse steered me along the hallway. The waiting area had emptied from a few minutes ago. Just two doctors were there now, conferring in a corner. One of the armchairs had been turned to face the window. A thin, pale arm lay across the armrest. I could just see the edge of the hand-shaped EFA logo that was tattooed on the inside of the wrist.

I hesitated, feeling dazed. The nurse gave me a little push. "Go on," she said encouragingly. "He's not as fragile as he looks."

I stumbled forward, past the row of plastic chairs and the coffee machine. I stood by the armchair, staring down at the shrunken figure—so familiar and yet so strange.

He was staring out the window at the rooftops of London.

"Lucas?" I said, my voice hoarse.

He turned, and his face lit up with the lopsided grin that had dominated my childhood.

"Hey, little brother," said Lucas. "So what's new?"

PART FOUR

EXECUTION

(n. [1] carrying out an action; [2] putting someone
to death)

CHARLIE

I paced around the cell, my fury at being imprisoned building with each step. Hours had passed, and just one thought consumed me: I had to save Nat. Of course I wanted to save Jas, too, not to mention all the other people who had been— or were going to be—infected with the deadly virus. And I still burned with desire to expose Riley for being prepared to sacrifice human beings to achieve power.

But mostly I wanted the boy I loved to stay alive.

It didn't look hopeful. It was surely late evening by now, and I was still stuck inside this police station. Apart from the officer who brought me food and water and accompanied me to the bathroom, Riley was the only person I'd seen or spoken to in hours. For all I knew, he was planning on keeping me here for days. But I didn't have days. Nat would be dead by the end of tomorrow, Jas even sooner.

The first thing I needed to do was get out of the police station. Then I needed—somehow—to track down the antidote Riley had spoken about and get it to Nat and his sister.

I was exhausted, my mind running over the options for escape on an endless loop. Each one seemed as hopeless as the next. There were no windows, and the only door was firmly locked. I had nothing I could use either as a weapon or to get past the lock. Apart from my clothes, the only item in the room that wasn't nailed to the floor was my plastic water cup.

The door creaked open. I scrambled to my feet as the bright electric light from the hallway outside streamed into the room. A man stood in the doorway. I squinted, trying to make out who it was. I was expecting Riley again. Or maybe Uchi.

But as the man stepped toward me, a furious scowl on his face, I saw that instead it was Aaron's father, Mayor Latimer.

NAT

The clock in the hospital cafeteria ticked loudly. The room itself was shut down, all the food-display counters empty and covered. A kind porter had let Lucas and me sit here, in the shadow of a soda dispenser, after Lucas had insisted on taking his first trip away from his ward. He had refused the offer of a wheelchair and was, instead, hobbling around on some kind of walking frame.

At least the cafeteria was empty. The nurses had swallowed my story about being Lucas's cousin and—thanks to the fact that I'd visited him only a few times in the past year—no one so far had recognized who I really was. Still, there was a strong chance that sooner or later someone would do so, and, as I was still wanted for terrorism, I was sure that their next step would be to call the police. In fact, the police could easily already be searching the hospital for me.

I needed to leave. But before I could get away, I had to explain everything to Lucas. And he wasn't making it easy.

"I want to speak to Taylor myself," he demanded. "I don't believe he set me up."

"Listen to me," I persisted. "He's working for Riley. They're terrorists themselves. They sent you into that market, knowing the bomb would go off once you left it there, not caring if you lived or died. Just like they did with me."

Lucas shook his head. There were gray rings of exhaustion under his eyes. "I was carrying a bag full of disposal gear. My job was to leave it in the market, then get away. It was just bad luck I was caught up in the bomb."

"No. You were *carrying* the bomb," I explained. "You left it and it went off and you hadn't gotten far enough away to be safe."

Lucas shook his head again. I went on, explaining how after his injury our family had fallen apart, how I'd thought he'd been one of the terrorists.

"You thought I was capable of *that?*" Lucas put his head in his hands.

I hurried on, feeling worse and worse as I told my brother how I'd tried to find out more about the terrorists I thought he'd been involved with and ended up being recruited and used by Riley's secret English Freedom Army myself.

"They took *you?*" Lucas raised his eyebrows. It was weird to see his expressive face moving after more than a year of pale, still silence. "But you're just a kid."

I felt the old irritation rise inside me. When was Lucas going to see that I'd grown up since he'd gone into his coma? Why was it so hard to accept what I was telling him?

I told the rest of my story as quickly as I could: how, like him, I and the rest of my cell had been set up and betrayed, how I had almost died, and how—most recently—Jas had been captured by Riley.

"But I got her out," I explained. "She's safe with Mum and Dad."

"Right." I couldn't tell if Lucas believed me now or not, but his hands trembled as he tried to push a straw through the top of his juice carton.

Was that from weakness? Or emotion? Either way, it was hard to accept. Before the coma, Lucas had always been the happy-go-lucky brother, a charismatic charmer with a new girl every five minutes, always popular with his friends, always in the middle of everything, universally loved.

"Well, if I can't speak to Taylor, let me speak to Jas," Lucas insisted. "At least switch your phone on to see if there's a message from her yet."

Reluctantly, I did so. As I'd expected, there was nothing yet. "I don't want to keep the phone on," I said, turning it off again. "It might be brand-new, but Riley's hacked things before."

"Right," Lucas said again.

I glanced at the time. With a jolt I realized I'd been with Lucas for nearly thirty minutes. I had to get back to Aaron's ward, find Latimer, and see if he knew where Charlie was.

I stood up abruptly. "I have to go."

"Yes." Lucas struggled to his feet, leaning heavily against the chair he'd been sitting in. "Have you got any money for a cab? We need to get to Mum and Dad, and I'm not sure I'll make it on public transportation."

I stared at him. "You can't leave," I said. "Not for a couple of days at least. Look at you. You can barely stand up."

"But we have to find Mum and Dad, show them I'm okay. They were here every day, sitting with me. Well, Mum was. The nurses told me she came all the time. I can't let her worry about me a second longer."

"I know," I said. "But if Mum and Dad know you're okay, they're going to want to see you, which puts everyone at risk."

"Not this again." Lucas stared at me as if I were crazy. "Of course they'll want to see me. I want to see them. Jesus, Nat. I'm sure I can find a way to do it without Riley luring us into a trap."

I bridled. That was so typical of the old, impulsive Lucas, brimming with a confidence that bordered on arrogance.

"Riley didn't have much trouble luring you into a trap before," I snapped.

"So you say." Lucas sighed. "Man, you've changed. Before I 'went away,' you were all geeky and shy. Now you've grown muscles *and* an attitude." He paused. "Look, we need to go now. Both of us. You can help me."

Silence fell. In the distance someone clanked a door open. We heard voices on the other side, and then the door shut again.

I *had* to leave. "No," I said firmly. "I need to find Charlie first."

"But it's too dangerous for you to go off on your own," Lucas insisted. He straightened up. "I can't let you do it."

A hot wave of anger washed over me. This was how it had always been with me and Lucas, I suddenly realized. Lucas in charge, dominating family life; me looking up to him, eager to please and to follow his lead in everything.

But not anymore.

"You can't stop me." I glared at my brother. I was as tall as him now. Well, almost. "You can't tell me what to do anymore."

I don't need your approval.

The thought rushed through my head, the truth of it—and its implications—startling me to my core. I suddenly realized why Mum and Dad had seemed so different earlier. It wasn't them who had changed.

It was me.

I took a step back from Lucas. "I'm leaving to speak to Latimer, and then to find Charlie. Go back to your ward. When I hear from Jas and Mum and Dad, I'll let them know you're okay."

Lucas's mouth gaped. For a moment I thought he was going to argue, but instead he held his hands up in a gesture of surrender.

"Fine," he said. "You win, little brother. But there's no way I'm staying in this hospital a second longer. I'm okay now. I just need to build up my strength—and I'm certainly not going back to that room or letting a bunch of doctors poke around doing tests on me."

"But—"

"No 'buts.'" Lucas pointed across the room to where one of the cafeteria workers had left a pair of orange overalls. "Fetch me those. You can go and find whoever you like, but I'm getting out of here."

CHARLIE

I shrank away as Latimer strode toward me, his fist raised.

"My son is unconscious, thanks to you," he roared.

I caught a glimpse of the female police officer in the hallway. She looked horrified. Out of the corner of my eye I could see her turning, hear her calling to someone, and then Latimer's hands were around my throat, spit flecking at the corners of his mouth. He looked insane.

I tried to pull away, but he was holding me too tightly, yelling terrible names at the top of his voice. Panicking, I punched at his stomach. He grabbed my wrist with one hand. Let go of my neck. As I reared away from him, he slid a piece of plastic into my palm. "Play along," he whispered.

I stopped struggling instantly. What was he doing?

The mayor's eyes narrowed. "You little bitch!" he roared.

Then, for a split second, he leaned in close and whispered in my ear. "Riley's plans . . . virus . . . Operation Silvercross," he hissed. "I just found out. Get away. . . . Warn Nat."

The piece of plastic he'd given me dug into my palm. Latimer's hands clamped around my throat again, but though he was holding me tightly still, he wasn't exerting any pressure.

His fury was a front; he was trying to help me.

I slid the piece of plastic into the pocket of my dress as he resumed his yelling. Hands free, I punched out again.

A second later two officers rushed in and dragged him off me. Still yelling and cursing, he was hauled out of the room. I rubbed my throat as Riley came in.

"Are you all right?" His voice oozed concern.

"Like you care." I glared at him.

Riley shook his head. "Actually, I do care," he said. "And so does your father. You'll be with him again in a couple of days, when all this is over."

I resisted the temptation to check that the plastic card, whatever it was, was still safe in my pocket. So the plan was to keep me here while Nat and Jas died and Riley made out like some hero, supposedly saving London from a bioweapon he had himself created and deployed.

The female police officer appeared with a blanket and a pillow. As she laid them on the floor, Riley spoke again.

"Get some rest, Charlie. This will pass."

I glared at him. Did he seriously think I would ever forgive either him or Uchi for what they were doing—what they *had* done? But I said nothing. I wanted to get rid of Riley as soon as possible, then see what Latimer had left me. His words echoed in my head.

Operation Silvercross.

Was that what this terrible plan with the bioweapon was called?

With a final concerned look, Riley said good night and swept out of the room, closely followed by the female officer. I sat down on the pillow and carefully retrieved the piece of plastic. It was Latimer's bank card—with the numbers 3299 written in black marker above his name. Was that the pin? Had Latimer given me a way of getting money? I glanced up at the door. Perhaps he had, but he had also given me my best chance of getting out of here. I had always been good at opening locks using the edge of a card or a knife; of all the "exit strategies" Taylor had taught us, this was the one I had truly excelled at. Did Latimer know that?

There was no time to think about it. Nat was under a death sentence. Jas, too. I hurried over to the door and pressed my ear against the wood. I couldn't hear anyone.

Taking a deep breath, I slid the bank card down the gap between the side of the door and the frame, feeling for the edge of the lock.

NAT

Lucas was in trouble before we reached the end of the parking lot. He was able to move only in a slow shuffle and was breathing heavily, every step clearly a terrible effort for him.

"This isn't going to work," I said as Lucas steadied himself against his metal walker. I stared beyond the wall, past the small patch of trees and bushes, all shadowy in the darkness, then glanced back toward the hospital. I had hoped I could get my brother temporarily settled in a nearby café, then go back to Aaron's ward and find his dad, but considering the state Lucas was in, I didn't think I should leave him alone.

"I'm fine," Lucas muttered. "Just need a bit of a breather. Get my legs used to moving again."

I chewed on my lip. Even if we made it out of the parking lot and into a café, I had no idea where I could take Lucas after that. Our house was out of the question—Riley would almost certainly be watching out for me there—and I couldn't simply show up at a friend's house and expect them to take us in, with all the risk and danger we brought with us. I should never have let Lucas talk me into helping him leave the hospital.

"I'm not going back inside," Lucas said, as if reading my mind.

"But—"

"No, Nat," he went on. "You've got no idea. I nearly went crazy when everyone around me started talking and I couldn't speak or move or even let them know I could hear."

I stared at him, shocked. "You could *hear*? But the doctors—"

"Doctors don't know everything," Lucas said darkly. "Look, I was only conscious or whatever for the last few days or so before my body started working again, but believe me, that was enough."

My thoughts sped back to early this morning, when I'd stood at Lucas's bedside and shouted at Mum and Dad to look after Jas. Had Lucas heard that?

"Why don't you rest there for a bit?" I said, pointing to the bushes to our right.

Lucas nodded and, leaning on my shoulder, he hobbled over and sank down, onto the grass.

"We were all here this morning . . . ," I started.

"Yeah, I heard you. Talk about tough love." He grimaced. "Poor Mum—and poor me. You told her I wasn't 'truly alive,' remember? Told her and Dad to get a grip and do their job as parents, or something like that."

So he *had* heard me. "I was just trying to look out for Jas," I said, feeling awkward.

Lucas chuckled, and I saw a glimpse of his old self: charming and laid-back and everyone's favorite.

"You were right, man. Everything you said. It's just hard getting my head around everything that's happened since last year."

"I know." I hesitated. "You do believe me about Riley and Taylor, don't you?'"

"I believe you *think* they're the bad guys," Lucas said.

What the hell did that mean?

"They took *Jas*," I said, my anger rising again. "They nearly killed us both."

"Okay. Okay." Lucas held up his hands in surrender, then propped himself up against a tree. He was hidden from the parking lot by a large bush. I glanced back at the hospital. My only hope of locating Charlie was through Latimer. And I had to talk to him immediately. I'd wasted enough time. The thought of what Riley might do to Charlie now that he knew she had tricked him made me feel sick to my stomach.

"Go on," Lucas said. "Get back inside. Stop thinking about it and *do* it."

I looked at him. "I won't be long."

"I'm not going anywhere."

I hesitated.

"Go." A shadow of his old grin flickered across Lucas's face. "I just hope she's worth it."

Embarrassed, I spun on my heel and headed back to the hospital. When I reached the entrance, I stood back, keeping my head down, as a burly man in a suit pushed his way out.

He looked around, then called to the people behind him. "Let's go. Quick as you can."

I glanced up to see who was emerging from the hospital.

To my surprise, it was Aaron. He hurried outside, his mother fussing over him, tugging a jacket around his shoulders. Aside from the bandage across his head, Aaron looked completely fine. As they passed me, Aaron glanced over.

"Nat!" he said.

I walked toward him. Immediately, the bodyguard stood between us. The wind whipped across my face as he drew back his jacket to reveal a gun in its holster.

"Stop," he said. "Stop or I'll shoot."

CHARLIE

It took three attempts before I managed to make the bank card Latimer had given me open the interview-room door. My palms were sweating as I slid it down the final time and, with a telltale click, the lock gave way. I pulled, very gently, on the handle and peered out through the crack between the door and the frame.

There was no one outside. I crept into the dimly lit hallway, closed the door quietly behind me, then tiptoed away. I reached a corner. Voices—loud and male—echoed toward me. I turned and sped in the other direction. I had no idea where I was—I'd been led through a maze of hallways to get here—but I was on the first floor, which meant sooner or later I would surely come to a door or a window.

Footsteps sounded ahead of me. They were getting closer. I ducked around the nearest corner and flattened myself against the wall. I peered back along the hallway as two men passed. They were just inches away, but so intent on their conversation that neither noticed me.

My heart thumped as they reached the room where I'd been

held. Were they going to check on me? No. I sighed with relief as the two men walked past the door. I crept along, hoping I was heading for an exit. I passed more doors, all closed. Voices drifted out from several of the rooms. At last I came to a fire exit. I hesitated. I'd managed to move silently so far, but opening a big door like this would make noise. Plus, I had no idea where it would lead. Still, there wasn't a choice. The longer I stayed inside the police station, the more likely I was to be found and imprisoned again.

I pressed slowly on the metal bar. With a clunk and a screech, the door opened. I peered outside. It was dark, but the light from the building revealed that I was in a parking lot, with squad vehicles on one side and unmarked cars on the other. Again I could hear voices in the distance, but nobody was in sight. Apart from the cars and a few bushes, there wasn't much to see. High walls surrounded the asphalt on all sides, the only exit from the parking lot being a solid metal gate. My heart sank. There was no way of getting a purchase on the gate to climb up it. Still, if I stood on top of one of the cars, I might just be able to get my leg over the brick wall.

An alarm sounded behind me, its sudden screech making me jump. Was that because of me?

Gritting my teeth, I raced over to the largest car, a station wagon with a roof a few inches higher than the other cars. As I clambered on top of it, the car alarm sent a deafening whistle into the air. Now both alarms screeched in my ears. I bent my knees and jumped, clawing onto the top of the wall. My muscles burned as I hauled myself up. My arms and legs scraped along the rough brick. I barely noticed the pain. The alarms were joined by shouting voices. I crouched on top of the wall, legs trembling. It was a long, long way down to the alley below. The shouts were getting louder. Closer. There was no time to look back.

I scrambled sideways along the wall about a yard. I was immediately above a pile of garbage bags.

"Hey! She's out here!" The yell was just yards away.

No time to lose.

I took a deep breath and jumped.

NAT

I put my hands in the air. Aaron's mother uttered a terrified squeak. The bodyguard narrowed his eyes and let his jacket cover his gun again.

"I'm not going to hurt anyone," I said.

"Shut it," the bodyguard snarled. "I've seen your face on the news. You're wanted for that bomb at the Houses of Parliament. I'm going to call the cops."

"Wait." That was Aaron. "It's okay. He's okay."

"What's going on?" his mum asked.

"I need to find Charlie," I said to Aaron. "If your dad is really on our side, he'll want to help."

"Who are you?" Aaron's mother demanded. She turned to her son. "What's he talking about?"

"I should call the police," the bodyguard threatened.

"No. Everything's fine." Aaron motioned them both to calm down. "This is Jas's brother. He's a friend. My dad knows him. He's cool."

The bodyguard gave a reluctant nod.

"Jas's brother?" Aaron's mum frowned. "I thought her brother was in a coma?"

"I'm her *twin* brother," I said, deciding now wasn't the time to confuse matters by explaining that Lucas was in fact conscious and hiding just yards away in the bushes by the parking lot.

"Have you heard from her?" Aaron asked anxiously. "I've been so worried."

I shook my head. "I'm sure she'll call later. Or Mum and Dad will. I'm only turning my phone on every now and then. I don't want anyone tracing me."

"Why would anyone—?" Aaron's mum started, but before she could finish, Aaron interrupted.

"Do you promise you'll call me if you know where she is?" Aaron pleaded. He pulled a phone out of his pocket. "This is brand-new," he said. "Definitely no bugs. I told her it was okay to call me on it, but she hasn't yet."

I hesitated. I was certain Aaron and his dad were genuinely on our side, but I still didn't trust their phones: Riley was capable of tracing anything.

"Please, Nat. Promise you'll let me know if you hear from her," Aaron repeated.

"Tell me where your dad is first," I said.

"What's going on?" Aaron's mum frowned at me. "Why do you want to speak to my husband?"

"It's fine, Mum." Aaron leaned close to my ear, so the others couldn't hear. "As far as I know, Dad's with Riley at his house.

Riley still thinks Dad's on his side. Mum doesn't know what's really going on. She'd freak out if she had any idea what a risk he was taking." He stepped back. "Now do you promise you'll let me know if you hear from Jas?"

"What did you just say, Aaron?" his mum asked.

"I promise," I said. "Thank you." I turned away from Aaron. I needed to make my way to Riley's house as fast as possible and wait for Latimer to emerge.

And then I remembered Lucas.

"Aaron?" his mum persisted.

"It's nothing, Mum."

I stopped. What on earth was I going to do with my brother while I traveled across London?

"What is it?" Aaron asked me. "Why have you stopped?"

"Aaron, we really need to get you home," his mum said.

I turned around. I'd had an idea.

CHARLIE

I landed with a thud, the ground hard even through the trash bags. One burst and a foul smell of rotting meat filled my nostrils. Flies swarmed into my face.

Spluttering, I pushed myself up and ran along the narrow road. Arms pumping hard, I turned on to what looked like a main street and raced past stores and a bus stop where people stood, waiting. Every one of them stared at me as I pelted past.

I swerved to the left, across a patch of wasteland. Over a fence into a backyard. A dog barked in the darkness. I had no idea where I was or where to head. I ran on, over another fence. Out into an alley. This time I heard my dress rip as I jumped down. I darted right, toward the lights, out onto another road—or was it the other end of the main street from earlier? More people stared at me.

"Good party, was it, love?" one man asked as I ran past.

I glanced down at my dress. It was ripped right across from halfway down the thigh. The loose strip of material dangled and flapped around my shin. I took it in both hands and tore it off, then tore a little more off the front in a hopeless attempt to even out both sides. Now it was ridiculously short. I reached a bank with an A.T.M. I stopped, determined to try out the bank card Latimer had given me. I could just make out a train station farther down the street, about forty yards away. I was too far away to see which one, but it didn't matter.

I punched in Latimer's PIN number. It worked, much to my relief. I examined my arms and legs as I waited for the machine to dispense its cash. They all were grazed and sore, but otherwise I was fine. I ran my fingers through my hair and rubbed at my face, hoping that I was removing the worst of the dirt. In the distance, sirens sounded. I needed to hurry.

I collected my money and took off at a run.

NAT

"What is it?" Aaron tightened his grip.

"Come on, Aaron," his mother said, an edge of worry to her voice. "We need to get you home. You were assaulted a few hours ago."

"I'm fine, Mum."

"Are you really okay?" I asked.

Aaron nodded. "What were you going to say?"

"It's just . . . It's Lucas—he woke up from his coma. . . ."

Aaron's eyes lit up. "That's amazing. Jas will be thrilled."

"Yes." I paused. "The thing is, he refused to stay in the hospital, but he's not well enough for me to take him with me to—to find out where Charlie is. . . ."

"We'll take him," Aaron said without hesitation.

"We'll *what?*" His mum stared at him.

"Where is he?" Aaron turned, ready to go back inside the hospital. "Which room?"

"Aaron, wait." His mum exchanged an impatient look with the bodyguard. "We can't just take him."

"He's Jas's brother," Aaron said firmly. "We have to help him."

"He won't go back inside the hospital," I said. "He's basically fine, just a bit weak. I don't have anywhere to take him, so, if you don't help, he'll spend the night outside."

"Oh, goodness." I could see Aaron's mum wavering.

"Where is he?" Aaron repeated.

"Uh, he's actually waiting for me over there. . . ." I pointed to the patch of bushes where I'd left Lucas. "He's really okay, considering, just needs to, um, rest a bit—"

"Please bring the car over there, Mum." Aaron cut through me, suddenly full of authority.

His mother hesitated, then shrugged. "Okay, if he's really well enough." She issued a long-suffering sigh. "I suppose we could look after him until Jas's parents can take him."

She took off to get the car while I led Aaron and the bodyguard across the parking lot. Lucas was still slumped where I'd left him. He attempted a smile when he saw me, which turned to a look of alarm as he noticed Aaron and the bodyguard.

"Who are they?" he asked.

I indicated Aaron. "This is Aaron." I paused. "He's Jas's boyfriend."

"*What?*" Lucas's eyes widened. "Jas has a *boyfriend?* When the hell did that happen?"

"Aaron can tell you all about it," I said. "He's going to take you somewhere safe."

"Somewhere where Riley and the EFA won't think to look for you," Aaron added.

Lucas gazed from me to Aaron, then back to me again. He looked dazed. "He's against Riley as well?"

I nodded. Perhaps sending Lucas off with Aaron—and giving them a chance to talk—would convince him at last about Riley's real nature.

"Let me help you up." Aaron hurried to Lucas's other side. Between us we lifted him off the ground. I was shocked again by how slight he felt. With the bodyguard's help, we got him onto the asphalt just as Aaron's mum pulled up.

Aaron opened the back door and Lucas collapsed onto the seat.

"Are you sure we shouldn't take him back into the hospital?" Mrs. Latimer asked, leaning out her window.

"No way." Lucas sat up, opening his eyes. "If everything Nat's told me is true, then Riley will want me out of the way as soon as he realizes I've come out of the coma."

Aaron's mum looked anxious.

"He'll be fine, Mrs. Latimer. He just needs food and rest," I said, hoping that this was true and that Lucas wasn't about to relapse into another coma because of all the stress of being moved about.

"Remember you promised to call me if you hear from Jas before I do, okay?" Aaron said, walking around the car to the other side.

"I will," I said.

From inside the car, Lucas gave me an exhausted nod. My chest tightened as he was driven away. Had I done the right thing, letting Aaron take him? I gave myself a shake as I hurried away from the hospital, onto the street. There wasn't a choice. I *had* to find Charlie. According to my phone, it was eleven fifteen. I should be able to get to Riley's house within the hour.

CHARLIE

I hurried up the road toward the underground station. I was shivering with cold now, and people were still staring at my bare legs and at the torn skirt of my dress. I had to find a way to cover up. It wasn't just my legs; I also needed to find a way to hide my face from the CCTV cameras in the station.

I passed a tourist shop selling badges and teddy bears. A shelf of scarves and sweaters met my eyes. I darted inside, quickly glancing over a rack of sweatshirts. They were all hideous—pale pink with an embroidered rainbow or neon yellow with a rag doll—but at least they had hoods and came with a pair of shorts. Gritting my teeth, I snatched a pink set off the rack, shoved some money at the guy behind the counter, and left.

I tugged the sweatshirt on as I walked, then stopped to hike the shorts up over my dress. I looked hideous, I was sure, but at least with the hood pulled up, it would be harder for the police and Riley's men to spot me.

I reached the station and quickly bought a ticket. I had two objectives: first, to find Nat and warn him that he and Jas were sick, and second, to find out where Riley was keeping the antidote and steal enough to cure them both.

I would start by breaking into Riley's house. Even if he didn't have any antidote on the premises, he would almost certainly have information about Operation Silvercross—including, I was hoping, where the antidote was being stored.

As I headed down to the platform, I couldn't stop thinking that in less than two days Nat would be dead. It filled me with terror. This wasn't the same as the adrenaline-fueled nervousness before a mission that was almost enjoyable for the sharp focus it gave me—the anticipation of triumph after dread. No, this was a dark, pitiless horror that if Nat died I wouldn't be able to bear it. That I had already lost Mum, that Uchi was useless as a father, that without Nat I had nothing and no one who truly mattered in my life.

The thought of it made me feel sick. I shook myself. I had to concentrate on my mission.

Half an hour later I arrived at Riley's house. I crept the last few yards, peering around the trees through the bars of the gate at the end of Riley's drive. Two cars and a van were parked in the drive, and an EFA soldier stood outside the front door. After ten minutes he took off on a patrol around the house. It took about ninety seconds. Ten minutes after he reappeared, he took off again. I stored the information: the grounds of the house formed a perimeter and the soldier was sweeping it every ten minutes.

As I watched from the dark shadows of the trees, a light came on in the downstairs window. For a few moments I could see Riley talking animatedly with Taylor, Uchi, and Martina. A figure was shoved in through the door. I gasped with horror. It was Latimer, his arms tied and his face bruised.

Had he just been punished for helping me escape?

A moment later a soldier I didn't recognize brought Latimer out of the house. I watched, feeling helpless, as he shoved the mayor across the gravel.

"This won't work," Latimer was muttering. "It will get out of control. Riley won't be able to control the spread of the virus. Too many people will die."

"You'll be dead too if you don't shut up," the soldier snarled.

I shrank into the shadows as the man bundled Latimer into a van and drove off. I peered back at the house in time to see Martina drawing the curtains at the dining room window.

I took a deep breath. If Latimer had been taken, then the resistance had lost its only political ally. Nat was in trouble. Operation Silvercross was under way. It was up to me to turn things around.

And then a hand touched my shoulder. I jumped, started to turn, but the hand pulled me back as the best, most familiar voice in the world whispered in my ear.

"Charlie, shh. . . ."

Nat released me and I spun around.

He was standing right in front of me, his finger to his lips. His dark hair was ruffled, falling over his face, his bright blue eyes full of emotion.

We stared at each other. I couldn't speak. Was he all right? He didn't look sick, but then Riley had said the symptoms didn't really show until the final day.

"Charlie?" He frowned. "Are you okay?"

"Just—just surprised. I didn't hear you creeping up on me," I whispered.

Nat's face broke into a grin, and my heart cracked into a million pieces. I loved him so, so much. It was terrifying but amazing, all in one.

"You're not the only one with stealth and combat training," he whispered, moving nearer.

His face was so close to mine, our lips almost touching.

"I thought you were in prison," he went on.

"I got out," I whispered, feeling my knees wobble. "Oh, Nat, I'm so sorry I didn't listen to you before. You were right, Riley was really hard to lie to, and he didn't believe me any—"

"Shh." He took my arms. "None of that matters. It's just so good to—" He stopped as I winced at the light pressure of his fingers against my sore skin. Nat's face clouded over.

"What's the matter?" he said.

"It's nothing. I—"

But Nat was already rolling up my right sleeve. He let out a low, angry hiss as he looked at the red, raw skin on my arm.

"Who did this to you?" he demanded.

"I did it myself, escaping." I reached up and took his face in my hands. "I'm okay. Really." I looked into his eyes. He had no idea he was infected, no clue that he was under a death sentence right now and that he was a walking weapon—fatal to anyone he came in contact with who hadn't been given the antidote. "It's so good to see you."

Nat smiled again, then lowered his face to mine.

NAT

For a minute I actually forgot where I was. Then the reality of the situation flooded back and I pulled away from Charlie. I had come to find her—and she was here. All that mattered now was getting away, picking up Lucas, and finding Jas and Mum and Dad.

Riley would go on, and the resistance would crumble. If Parveen and the others had been captured, they were probably already dead. If they'd gotten away, then they could hide out too.

None of that mattered anymore. All I cared about was making sure Charlie and the rest of my family were together. Together we could be safe.

Charlie was smiling up at me, but there were tears in her eyes. I'd never seen her so close to crying before. I hugged her, unable to find words to express how I felt. She let me hold her for a moment, then disentangled herself.

"We have to get inside," she whispered.

What on earth was she talking about? "Inside what?"

"Riley's house," she said, pointing toward the gates. "He's in there; so are Uchi—that's, uh, my biological dad—and Taylor. So was Mr. Latimer until a couple of minutes ago. They're holding him prisoner. I just saw them take him away in a van."

I swore. "Latimer's a prisoner? I need to let Aaron know." I took out my phone.

"So I'm thinking we enter via the backyard. I know the layout."

I stared at her. "But you just said they'd taken Latimer away." Was she crazy? "Besides, we don't have any weapons and there's a guard on the front door."

Charlie bit her lip. What wasn't she saying?

A thought struck me. "Okay, so *I* came here for *you*," I said hesitantly. "But—but why on earth are *you* here?"

"I came for details about Riley's next operation," Charlie said briskly. The tears were gone from her eyes now. She folded her arms. I suddenly realized she was wearing a pale pink sweatshirt with a rainbow on the front. I had never seen her in anything remotely so girly before.

"Don't say anything." Charlie had followed my gaze to the sweatshirt. "I know it's hideous. I needed a hood."

I took a deep breath. "Never mind Riley's next operation. Let's just leave here, right now, and forget Riley," I said. "Mum and Dad and Jas are in hiding. And Lucas . . ." I stopped, remembering that Charlie would have no idea about him coming out of his coma.

"We *have* to find out about it," she said stubbornly. "It's called Operation Silvercross. Mr. Latimer told me the name. He helped me escape so I could help stop it from happening."

"Okay, but there's nothing we can do unarmed and alone. The resistance is gone. Latimer's a prisoner. Riley's won. At least for now."

"I won't accept that." Charlie hesitated, as if there was something else she wanted to say but couldn't bring herself to. "We need to know about Operation Silvercross. We're here. There *must* be information inside Riley's house. It's up to us to find it."

"That doesn't make any sense," I insisted. "If we try to break into Riley's house, we'll just end up being captured ourselves."

Charlie looked away. What was going on?

"Charlie?"

"What were you going to say about Lucas?" she asked, still not meeting my eyes.

I explained quickly, then took Charlie's hand. I was still sure there was something she wasn't telling me.

"Please, Charlie," I said. "What's going on?"

"We need to find out about Operation Silvercross," she repeated stubbornly. "You have to trust me on that."

"Tell me *why*."

Charlie pressed her lips together and stared up at me. Her dark, slanting eyes looked haunted.

"What is this?" I demanded. "Why won't you trust me?" She said nothing. I moved closer again. "You can keep pushing me away if you like," I said, "but I'm not going anywhere. So you might as well tell me whatever it is."

Her lips trembled.

I racked my brains. "Is this something to do with your dad?

Or that boy I saw you with on the video? Riley's son?"

"No." Charlie's voice shook. "This has nothing to do with Spider. Or anyone else. We have to break into Riley's house and find out about Operation Silvercross because of *you*."

And then she told me.

CHARLIE

Nat listened in stunned silence, speaking only once I'd finished.

"What about you? Are you sure you're all right?" he asked.

I nodded. "Riley said my father insisted I was given the antidote to the virus. Aaron's had it too. But anyone who *hasn't* had it will be infected if you or Jas get within a yard of them."

"So Jas will die too," he breathed. "And Mum and Dad. And Lucas."

"I'm so sorry, Nat."

"And everyone that any of us have been anywhere near . . ." He went on, clearly in shock. "People at the hospital . . . Aaron's mother . . . the bodyguard . . . everyone I brushed past on the way here, everyone Mum and Dad and Jas have been near."

"That's right, unless they've had the antidote. Riley's planning on pretending to uncover the whole thing and finding the antidote in time to save almost everyone, but . . ."

"But not me and Jas—and quite possibly not Mum and Dad and Lucas . . . And, anyway, there'll be people who won't know they're sick until it's too late and—" Nat groaned. "Oh my God,

Charlie. This is . . ." He looked at me, unable to find the words to express the pain that was etched in his face.

"I know." As I spoke, I felt a stab of guilt that I'd already been given the antidote. I wanted to apologize. But that wasn't going to help Nat. Instead, I took his hand. "Do you see now why we need to get inside Riley's house and find out about Operation Silvercross?"

"I do, but—but surely there are other people we could tell about this. It's so extreme, even Riley's supporters will think he's gone too far if they know what—"

"No one will believe us; we're still wanted, remember? And even if they do, by the time they've gotten it together to raid Riley's house, his spies will have told him they're coming. Either way, it'll be too late to get you or Jas the antidote."

Nat stayed silent for a long time. His face was pale and strained. I wanted to put my arms around him, to hold him and share with him how terrible I felt about him being infected. But he seemed too lost in his own thoughts, and I didn't know how to break through them—or even if he'd want me to.

At last he looked up, a new determination in his eyes.

"Okay. Let's break in," he said. "The information is most likely to be in Riley's office on the second floor at the back of the house. We can get in through the backyard, like you said."

"Yes," I said. "There's a gate to the yard at the end of the path beside the house. We have to time it between the soldiers doing their sweep of the house every ten minutes."

"We can do that." Nat grimaced. "Hey, d'you remember

when we broke in here before? That stupid test Taylor made us do?"

"Yeah, when we thought it was a League of Iron house." I made a face too. "Riley's made fools of us too often."

Nat gave a curt nod. "Believe me," he said, "Riley's made fools of us for the last time."

NAT

My head reeled as we waited for the soldier to disappear from the front of the house on his next patrol. I was sick, infected with a deadly virus. It was surreal, especially because I felt fine. And yet if everything Charlie had found out was true, I had only a day or so to live. Jas, who had been captured and infected with the virus before me, must have even less time, our parents and Lucas maybe a little more.

I shook myself, trying to focus on the task in front of me. Charlie had counted that it took approximately ninety seconds for the EFA solider at the front door to walk around the building, which gave us a window of approximately twenty seconds—while he was on the far side of the house—to get into the backyard.

Still trying to push all thoughts of the virus out of my head, I busied myself with my phone. I had two messages. One was from Jas and one from Aaron. They had been in touch with each other. Jas was safe with Mum and Dad. They were all overjoyed that Lucas had come out of his coma. Lucas himself was asleep. Mum, Dad, and Jas were traveling to Aaron's house now. This was risky, of course, but I could just imagine how my family would react if I told them to stay away from Lucas.

Anyway, what did it matter? We were all going to die within the next day or two. *All going to die.* I said the words in my head, but they didn't feel real. And yet now that I thought about it, knowing I had been deliberately infected with Qilota made sense of everything that happened the day I went to rescue Jas. Riley had lured me to the ops base, exposed me to the virus during those first few hours, when I'd been unconscious, then let me escape. It had all seemed too easy at the time. And now I knew why. The whole thing had been a trap. A setup.

And Jas and I were the fall guys.

A new fury rose inside me. I was going to defeat Riley now, whatever it took. Not just to save my life and Jas's, but in order to show the world what an evil man he really was. I thought back to how I'd told Charlie that not killing him was the right thing to do. Maybe it was. But in that moment, for the first time in my life, I was certain that if I'd had a gun in my hand, I would have used it.

"I reckon we've got about a minute, and then the soldier will do his next sweep," Charlie whispered. She was standing next to me in the trees, peering through the gate toward Riley's house. "Are you ready?"

"Yes." I wrote Aaron a quick text telling him his father was Riley's prisoner and to be on his guard. I didn't say anything about the virus. There would be time enough for that later. Maybe—if we were lucky—we wouldn't have to explain until we'd gotten ahold of the antidote.

I sent the text, then switched off the phone. As I put it in my pocket, the soldier at the front of the house took off along the side path. As soon as he disappeared from view, Charlie beckoned me to the gate. Together we put our feet on the first rung and clawed up for a handhold. I reached the top first, being taller, then swung my legs over and jumped. I landed with the lightest of thuds on the gravel and held out my arms to help Charlie down. As we hurried along the side path, it struck me that we had climbed the gate far more quickly and quietly than we could have when we'd broken into this house all those months ago. And yet back then I'd felt like a superhero. Now, after being betrayed by those I trusted and more than a month on the run, I knew I was far stronger and tougher than I had been before. But I was also much more aware of how vulnerable I was. A few months ago I'd belonged at home and at school; I'd wanted to be part of the EFA and to stop all the extremist violence that was taking over the country. Now I belonged nowhere and to no one—except the girl beside me.

We stopped at the door into the backyard.

"Let me check it out," I whispered. I reached up to the top of the door with my hands, then hauled myself up until I could peek over. There was no sign of the soldier in the backyard. "Clear," I whispered.

Seconds later I was over the door. I landed silently on the path on the other side, then waited as Charlie sprang down beside me. Together we inched along the brick wall and peered around the back of the house.

Riley's office window was on the second floor, but which room?

"That one," Charlie whispered, pointing up at the window on the far right. Moonlight glinted off the glass. I had vaguely hoped that there might be a drainpipe we could use to get a purchase. There wasn't. On the other hand, part of the wall was covered in ivy. It didn't look strong enough to hold both of us, but it was all there was.

"Let me go first," I said. "Follow once you see I'm in." I took off across the garden path, ducking under the first-floor windows until I reached the ivy on the other side. I tugged at the leaves above my head. A few tore, but the plant was well rooted to the wall. I hauled myself up. Hand over hand, I clambered up the wall like a monkey. I would never have been able to climb like this last year. In spite of the situation, it felt good to really push my muscles to work hard and to have to keep balance as I did so. Charlie had said an early symptom of the virus would be physical weakness. How much more time before that kicked in?

I reached the window ledge, took the knife from my pocket, and levered up the sill until I'd made a gap wide enough to hook my arm over. It gave way with a groan. I froze. How loud had that sounded? I knew how far noise carried in the night air. I needed to hurry in case the guard came back early to investigate. More ivy tore away from the wall as I scrabbled to get my knee over the ledge. I slid into the room as quietly as I could, then tiptoed to the door. I could hear two men arguing downstairs. One of them was Riley. I curled my lip at the sound of his voice. I didn't recognize the other man speaking, but he was clearly angry about something.

I hurried across the room to the desk, experiencing a strong sense of déjà vu. Last time we'd been here, Charlie had been given instructions in her earpiece from Taylor about how to break through the computer's password and encryption codes. It had been a complicated process, and I was certain Charlie wouldn't be able to remember half of the data needed.

I stared down at the computer, my heart sinking.

How on earth were we going to get into Riley's computer and find out about Operation Silvercross?

CHARLIE

I clambered into the room and sped over to Nat. He was standing in front of Riley's computer.

"I have no idea how to get past the encryption on this," he whispered.

"It's not a problem," I whispered back.

Nat's face lit up. "You mean you can remember how to get through it?"

"No," I whispered. "There's no need. There'll be info in paper files too. Uchi keeps notebooks—I've seen them before."

Nat shook his head. "I don't see any notebooks in here."

I hurried over to the desk and turned over the keyboard. I had expected to find a key, just as there had been in Uchi's office. But nothing was there.

I looked up, feeling the blood drain from my face. I glanced around the room. Nat was watching me, a puzzled expression on his face.

I stood in the silence. Riley's voice rose from downstairs. He was shouting.

"I don't *know*, Uchi," he said.

"And why wasn't she locked in a cell?" Uchi yelled.

"She *was*."

I'd never heard either of them raise their voices before.

"They're talking about you," Nat said. "Any chance we can hurry this along?"

"The files must be here somewhere. Let's look through as much as we can. Any locked drawers or cupboards, that's the best place to start."

"Right." Nat sped across the room to the bookshelves and started examining the cupboards below. I turned my attention to the desk drawers. I'd imagined these would be locked, but they all opened easily, revealing nothing but clean pads of paper, pens, and other stationery.

My heart thumped painfully against my ribs. We *had* to find something about Operation Silvercross. And we had to do it in the next few minutes.

NAT

It looked hopeless. Despite Charlie's insistence that there would be a file on Operation Silvercross, as far as I could see, there was very little paper-based information in Riley's office at all.

I looked up from the cupboards under the bookcase I'd been examining. Apart from a box of ancient phones and two old-style cameras, all I'd found were some slim folders marked TAX and ACCOUNTS. I pulled out another, smaller file and flipped it open. It was full of photos of Riley when he was younger. I glanced through a few pages. In the dim light I couldn't see the finer detail, but one photo caught my eye, of Riley beside an older man with a serious expression. There was something in the shape and glare of his eyes that reminded me of Charlie.

"Is this your dad?" I asked.

Charlie scooted over. "Yeah," she said.

A door slammed shut downstairs. We both started.

"Hurry," she hissed, going back to the desk.

I shoved the photo album back and pulled out the next file. Maybe Operation Silvercross was just too secret for anything to be written down about it at all. The next file contained invoices. So did the one after. I scanned them, my heart sinking. There was nothing here that looked like a top-secret file. I flipped through the pages. There wasn't anything even remotely incriminating. It was mostly invoices for one of Riley's companies involving car rentals, business supplies, and research services. They were all dated at least three or four months ago. I had just put the file back when a floorboard creaked outside. I spun around. Charlie looked up.

Across the room, the office door started to open.

CHARLIE

I froze, paralyzed with fear as the door opened. A split second later Spider walked in. His jaw dropped as he saw us. In a flash, Nat was across the room, his hand over Spider's mouth. I ran over as Nat spun Spider around, hoisting his arm up behind his back.

Spider winced with pain, but he kept struggling, his eyes glinting dark and furious.

"Shh," I hissed, shutting the door softly. "Spider, *please*. Calm down."

He met my gaze and stood still. Nat lessened his hold on Spider's arm, though he kept his hand over Spider's mouth.

"Spider," I whispered, "do you promise you won't yell if Nat lets go?"

His eyes flared above Nat's hand, but he gave a quick, sharp nod.

"Let him go," I said.

"Are you crazy?" Nat whispered. "One shout and the whole house will come running."

"Spider's not going to shout." I fixed my gaze on Spider's hard, dark eyes. "Let him go," I repeated.

With an angry grunt, Nat released him.

"What the hell are you doing?" Spider demanded in a low voice, his eyes flickering over the hideous rainbow on the front of my pink sweatshirt.

"Trying to find out where the antidote to the Qilota virus is," I whispered. "Nat and his sister have been infected. Riley's going to let them die unless—"

"Whoa, what are you talking about?"

I stared at him. "You don't know about Operation Silvercross?" I said.

"Sure," Spider said. "But no one's going to die. Dad's going to bring out the antidote and save the day. It's like a shortcut to help people vote for him. I've already had it. It's just a few teaspoons of liquid. Really easy to drink. And there are loads of stocks of it, I heard Dad say."

I exchanged a glance with Nat. He rolled his eyes as he turned back to Spider.

"Man, Riley's totally brainwashed you, hasn't he?" he spat.

"*Nat*," I hissed. "*Not* helpful."

"You're Nat?" Spider looked him up and down scornfully.

"Yeah, I am." Nat squared up to him. He was broader than Spider, though Spider was slightly taller. "Why?"

"I thought you'd look tougher," Spider said with a sneer.

"I'm tougher than you are." Nat shoved him in the chest.

"Nat!" I gasped. What was he playing at? "Nat didn't mean to do that," I said.

"Oh, yes, I did," Nat said. He clenched his fists.

Spider raised his hands, ready to punch him.

I stared at them both, bewildered by how aggressive they were being. "Stop it, both of you," I hissed. I turned to Spider. "Listen to me. You need to help us find some antidote." I quickly explained how Nat and Jas were to be sacrificed.

Spider's face remained impassive as I spoke. Only a momentary flicker of emotion in his eyes gave any indication that he was shocked by what I was telling him.

"So do you know where the antidote is?" I pleaded. "Or have any idea where it might be stored? *Please?*"

Spider curved his lips into a sneer, but I sensed that underneath his bravado he was upset. "Help save *him?*" He glanced at Nat, then back at me.

"And my friend Jas," I said pointedly. "And probably me, if your dad catches me. Whatever Uchi says, your dad's not going to want me around now."

A voice shouted up from the hall. "Spider? Where are you?" It was Martina.

Nat darted close to Spider, hands raised again in case Spider tried to shout out, but Spider was still looking at me. I got the impression he wasn't wildly keen on Martina. Hadn't she said she didn't get along with Gracie, Spider's mum?

"Please, Spider." I moved closer, fixing him with what I hoped was a beseeching gaze. "We can't do this without your help."

I could feel Nat staring at me, but I kept my gaze on Spider. Heavy footsteps sounded on the stairs.

"That'll be Taylor." Spider hesitated. "You two should go."

"Thank you." I raced to the window, Nat at my side.

"Will you—?"

"Yes," Spider hissed. "I'll find out what I can. Meet me later. Green Park, by the Artillery Memorial."

The footsteps were crossing the landing.

"Thank you," I said.

"Come on." Nat tugged me toward the window. "Hurry."

I hooked my leg over the ledge and climbed. I glanced down into the yard. No sign of the patrolling soldier, thank goodness.

Above me Nat was clambering down the ivy too. A few moments later Taylor's voice drifted out over our heads.

"What are you doing, Spider?" he was demanding. "Martina told you to come straight back down."

I landed on the earth, flattening myself against the wall. Nat leaped down beside me. Seconds later we were racing across the yard again, over the door, then the gate, and away.

NAT

I leaned against the cool stone of the memorial. I was exhausted, but I couldn't relax. I had barely slept even in the early hours, when Charlie had insisted we took turns to rest under some bushes in the park, and I was far too wound up to do so now. It was late morning and the sun was high in the sky. Green Park was scattered with office workers on benches enjoying early lunch breaks and groups of tourists making their way across the grass toward the Mall and Buckingham Palace.

Hours had passed since Spider had vowed to help us. I had told Charlie repeatedly that we shouldn't trust him, that coming here and waiting for him was at best a waste of time and at worst a trap, but Charlie had insisted it was our only chance to get our hands on the antidote in time to save me and Jas.

She was taking a turn to rest while I watched out for him. I squinted across the park. The grass grew suddenly blurry. Charlie had said the virus could affect your vision—but maybe I was just tired. I blinked and my vision cleared. I walked around the memorial again. At least this part of the park was relatively empty. We had taken back streets the whole way here, and I'd made sure I kept as far away as possible from everyone we passed. I'd wound a scarf around my nose and mouth too, for extra protection. I'd gotten some funny looks over that, but I didn't care. The days when I remotely cared about what anyone thought of me were long past.

Anyone other than Charlie, that is. I gazed down at her, outstretched on the nearby grass. My blurry vision cleared as jealous thoughts crowded my head. I'd seen the way Spider had looked at Charlie. If he was going to help us, it was because he liked her. *Really* liked her. And I'd seen the soft, pleading way she'd looked at him. Did she like him back?

Anger like acid swirled in my guts. Soon, I knew, I would become weak and sick, too frail to help get the antidote. Was that what Spider was planning? Act like he wanted to help, but really leave things so late that I died anyway? I wondered how Jas was. The last time I'd switched my phone on—several hours ago—there'd been another text saying that she and Mum and Dad had arrived at Aaron's house and been reunited with Lucas. She'd sounded so happy, making no mention of any symptoms, that I hadn't had the heart to tell her about the virus and the death sentence that hung over her and all of them.

I knew I should; after all, though everyone she was with right now was either infected already—or, in Aaron's case, immune—once Jas left the house, she would infect everyone she met.

My vision suddenly blurred again. I blinked and, again, it cleared. A woman pushing a buggy walked past as Charlie got up and came over. Her pale pink sweatshirt was grimy and earth-stained, but her eyes sparkled with determination.

"Are you feeling okay?" she asked.

I nodded. I was sure the blurred vision was just exhaustion. "No symptoms yet," I said.

"Good." Charlie paused.

A soft, warm breeze rustled the leaves in the trees across the grass. Chatter and laughter filled the air. Under other circumstances this would have been a great place to have pulled Charlie into my arms, to have kissed her, to . . .

"No sign of Spider?"

Charlie's question shook me out of my reverie.

"No," I said curtly.

"Wait." Charlie peered across the park. "Is that him?"

It was. He was pelting toward us, his long limbs at full stretch. A few moments later he ran up, panting.

"Hi." He looked at Charlie as he spoke.

"Hi." She smiled. Man, she looked so pretty when she smiled.

Spider gazed at her, transfixed.

"What did you find out?" I asked.

Spider turned to me as if he was only just registering I was present.

"The antidote is being stored in a few secret locations around London," he said. "I've got the address of the main place, the Silvercross Institute. It's what the operation was named after. It's a scientific research center not far from here. I think it's where they developed the virus."

"That's great." Charlie flung her arms around him. Hugged him hard.

Spider's face colored a deep red as he hugged her back. I looked away. It was great news that we had this lead—but could we really trust it?

"Did anyone see you snooping about?" I demanded.

Charlie disentangled herself from Spider's arms. "You were careful, weren't you?"

"'Course I was." Spider drew himself up. He glanced at me. "I'm not an idiot." He said the words in such a way as to imply that I probably was one.

I gritted my teeth.

"What's the address?" Charlie asked.

As Spider gave her the information, I felt my phone buzz in my pocket. Had I left it on? I thought I'd turned it off last time I'd checked for messages. Was getting forgetful a sign of the virus taking hold? No, that was surely just tiredness too. I turned away and took out the cell phone.

It was Aaron.

"Hello?"

"Nat?" Aaron sounded desperate. "Listen, it's Jas. She's *really* sick."

CHARLIE

I glanced at Nat. He was hunched over his phone, muttering in a low, intense voice. Was he really all right? His face seemed very pale and his eyes looked strained. Still, that could just as easily be because of our situation as because of the virus inside him.

"Charlie?" Spider's voice was sharp.

I looked back at him. Spider, on the other hand, was glowing with health. His cheeks were flushed from running and his hair, swept back from his face, emphasized those amazing cheekbones of his.

If I were judging objectively, I would have to say that Spider was more conventionally good-looking than Nat. His wild dark hair and dark eyes made him look like a teenage model, as did his designer clothes. As for that white-toothed smile of his . . .

But to me Nat was ten times more attractive.

I tore my eyes away from him, back to Spider.

"Thank you for telling us all this," I said. "We're going to have to move fast. Nat doesn't have much time. Jas even less."

Spider reached for my hand. I glanced at Nat again, but he was deep in his conversation, an agonized frown on his forehead. He was probably talking to Jas, telling her she was infected. My heart went out to him.

"I don't want a thank-you." Spider tugged at my hand, pulling me toward him. I looked up into his dark eyes. Brown instead of Nat's ice-chip blue, but every bit as intense. "I want to see you again."

I hesitated. Part of me felt I owed Spider, that I should say yes. After all, he'd just risked his neck to bring us information. But Spider and I were, in the end, on opposite sides of the battle. Quite apart from how complicated it would make things with Nat or that Spider might even think I was into him if I agreed to meet him again, it just wasn't possible for me to be friends with someone who thought it was okay to murder and lie to get into power.

"Do you still support your dad?" I asked.

"Of course." Spider frowned. "I mean, it's like he's always saying. You have to be ruthless to make a difference." He looked up at the memorial behind us. "Dad brought me here a lot when I was little, told me about the soldiers and how they gave up their lives. He's always talking about how you have to keep remembering the big picture, that a noble goal justifies all the sacrifices that have to be made to achieve it."

"Like the sacrifice of Nat and his sister?" I shook my head. "How do you justify that? And what about Aaron's dad, Mayor Latimer? Riley's just taken him prisoner. What noble goal did *that* achieve exactly?"

Spider shrugged. "I get they're your friends. And, look, I've helped you with Nat. I'd feel bad if he died—if *anyone* dies—but it doesn't change the fact that you belong with me and Dad and Uchi and all the other senior EFA people." He pulled me closer still, his hand now on my waist. "You're special, Charlie. You're beautiful. You're—"

"No," I said, pulling away.

"Come on. We're made for each other." Spider tugged me back toward him.

"She said no," Nat snarled, appearing suddenly beside us.

Spider spun around. Seconds later the two of them were squaring up again, foreheads locked, fists clenched.

"Enough." I pushed my way between them and stood in front of Nat, facing Spider. "I'm really grateful you've given us a location for the antidote, Spider. But I'm with Nat. And . . . and anyway, your dad organized the bomb that killed my mother. If you can't see how terrible what he did was, if you insist on standing by him, I can't support that."

Spider's face flushed. "Fine," he said, backing away. "That's just fine." He ran off.

I turned to face Nat, expecting him to smile or hug me, but he just stared at me, his expression unreadable.

"What is it?" I said.

I wanted him to hold me and to talk to me, but instead he pulled away.

"Nothing," he said.

"Right."

There was an awkward pause.

"So who was that on the phone?" I asked, trying to hide my hurt.

"Aaron." Nat's face creased in another frown. "Jas is really sick, apparently. They didn't understand why. . . ." His voice wobbled. "Her vision had gotten a bit blurry, but that was all. . . . Then she collapsed. I—I just had to explain why."

"Oh, God . . . Nat, that's awful." I forgot my own hurt feelings and squeezed his hand.

He squeezed my hand back, his mouth trembling with emotion. "What did Spider say?"

I explained what I'd just learned.

"Spider says the institute is big but that it should be empty right now. Just a security guard at the desk."

"Right," Nat said. "I'll call Aaron and tell him. He can meet us there."

After he'd given Aaron the institute's address near Trafalgar Square, I took the phone and told Aaron in detail how I'd seen his dad being taken away from Riley's house in a van. Aaron sounded distraught but determined to help find the antidote.

"Once we've got that, it should be easier to expose Riley—and to get help for Dad," he said.

We arranged to meet within the hour. Then Nat and I took off. Nat kept his nose and mouth well covered with his scarf again. As we hurried through the side streets, toward the institute, all thoughts of how Nat and Spider had almost come to blows faded from my mind. What mattered now was getting that antidote. If Riley had been telling me the truth about the virus, Jas wouldn't survive beyond the night and Nat would be dead by the end of tomorrow.

I wasn't going to let that happen.

NAT

The sun was still shining as Charlie and I waited in the doorway of a boarded-up store for Aaron to arrive. Almost an hour had passed since Spider had brought us the address of the Silvercross Institute. Charlie had already scouted around the building and was confident that—as Spider had claimed—it was empty. So far so good, though I still didn't trust that he hadn't gone straight back to Riley and given us away.

My vision wasn't any worse. That is, it still grew blurry every now and then but not so that it was a problem—and not so bad that Charlie had noticed. At least I was sure I hadn't infected anyone on the way over here. I'd crossed the road to avoid the few people we had passed and kept my scarf over my nose and mouth.

Charlie was keeping a lookout for Aaron while I checked my phone for any last-minute messages. There had been a distance between us since Spider had left. I knew I should have said something to her after she'd said all those things about being with me. . . . I should have told her that I chose her too. But somehow the moment was gone and I didn't know how to get it back. I was useless at stuff like that.

"There he is."

I followed Charlie's pointing finger. Aaron had turned off the main road and was hurrying along the alley toward us. I stared, aghast. Lucas was beside him. What on earth was he doing here? He certainly looked a lot better than he had last night, though still very pale and thin. But surely he wasn't well enough to be out on a mission like this? Plus, he was infected with the Qilota virus, just like I was, which meant he was spreading it just by walking around.

Lucas strode straight up to me. "Nat, I'm so, so sorry," he said. And then he flung his arms around me.

Startled, I let him hug me.

"Are you feeling all right?" Lucas pulled away, an anxious frown creasing his brow.

"Yeah, not bad, considering," I mumbled. "Um, what are you doing here?"

"I came to help," Lucas said. "Listen, Aaron, here, and Jas have told me everything. About Riley, the EFA, the truth about what's really going on. I'm sorry I didn't get it earlier."

I nodded, feeling relieved. Despite how sick I was feeling, it was good to see Lucas looking more like his old self and it was great that he understood the terrible situation we were in. Out of the corner of my eye I could see Aaron and Charlie watching us. Charlie had changed—she was now wearing a black sweater that Aaron had, presumably, brought her from his house. Her sharp eyes were fixed on Lucas, an expression of curiosity on her face.

"You do realize you're infected too, Lucas?" I stammered.

Lucas nodded. "I know. I've tried to keep my distance from everyone we've passed. Anyway, if we can find this antidote, it won't be a problem soon." He gave my back a firm pat. "Never mind me. I've been infected for only a few hours. I've got no symptoms yet. It's you and Jas I'm worried about."

"How is she?"

Lucas shook his head.

"Really bad," Aaron said miserably. "She can't see; she's so weak she's had to go to bed. Your parents have taken her home; they're sending us updates every thirty minutes."

Something shriveled inside me; I couldn't bear the thought of Jas suffering.

"Oh, that's awful," Charlie said.

At this Lucas turned toward her, as if noticing her for the first time. Feeling a little awkward, I introduced them, then watched Lucas's frown transform into a smile.

"Hi," he said. "Good to meet you."

"Hi." Charlie smiled back. "We should get going."

We took off toward the institute entrance.

"I'm really worried about my dad," Aaron confided as we walked. "Riley could be doing anything to him. I called a couple of his colleagues and they said they knew people in the police they think they can trust, but . . ." He trailed off, not needing to finish the sentence we were only too aware of: that it was virtually impossible to know who in the police could be trusted at all.

"I'm sorry about your father, Charlie," Lucas said. "I mean, I'm sorry that he's behind so much of what Riley has done. That must be difficult."

Charlie flushed, then threw me a hard stare. "Nat? You *told* him?"

"*I* told him," Aaron said quickly.

"How did *you* know?" Charlie demanded.

"Uh, my dad told me," Aaron stammered.

"And how did *he* know?"

Aaron glanced at me, then looked away. Charlie raised her eyebrows.

"I told Mr. Latimer at the resistance meeting," I said, feeling uncomfortable.

"Right." Charlie rolled her eyes. "So basically now everyone knows."

"Sorry." I met her gaze. "It just came out."

Charlie opened her mouth as if to say more, then shook herself. "It doesn't matter now," she said. She pointed across the road to the Silvercross Institute, a large brick building built over several floors. "I took a look around earlier," she explained. "It's mostly offices, as far as I can see—though it says online that they do chemical research here, that there are labs in the basement. The best way in is going to be through the front door, and then to overpower the security guard before he has a chance to call for backup."

"I'll go in first and pretend to be a courier," I said, explaining the plan we had discussed. "I'll leave the front door open so you can rush in while I'm distracting him. Then we search the building. You two as one team, me and Charlie as the other. Okay?"

Aaron nodded.

"Sure," Lucas said, "except I should pretend to be the courier. I'm older, it'll be more convincing."

"Good idea," Charlie said.

"Fine," I said, feeling rattled. It was stupid. Of course Lucas was right. But I didn't like being told what to do. Especially by him.

A few moments later we were all in position. Lucas rang the doorbell while the rest of us hid out of sight of the security camera.

"Hello?"

"Delivery," Lucas said into the intercom.

The door buzzed. With a final glance at us, Lucas disappeared inside. I held the door.

"Will he be okay?" Aaron whispered.

I nodded. "Lucas was trained by the EFA, just like me and Charlie. Come on. Let's go."

We burst through the door. The security guard sprang to his feet as I ran in, but Lucas was already behind the desk. Charlie and I raced over. In seconds, the security guard's hands and feet were tied. Lucas wound a gag around the man's mouth. Charlie took the bunch of keys that hung from his belt.

"Wow." Aaron's eyes were wide with awe. "That was *fast*."

"We need to search the place," Lucas said, brushing back the hair that had fallen over his face in the struggle with the guard. Apart from his rather gaunt appearance, there was no trace of the pale, sick victim I had helped from the hospital just a few hours earlier. His eyes were clear and bright, and he wasn't even panting that much more than the rest of us.

"Charlie and I will take this floor and the basement," I said, pointing to the stairs behind the guard's desk. "You two try upstairs."

We took off. As the others disappeared up the stairs, Charlie and I explored the first-floor rooms. We moved in silence, passing through four or five meeting rooms, each one set with a semi-circle of tables and chairs.

As we headed down to the basement, Charlie asked again if I was all right.

"Seriously, I'm fine," I said.

We reached the basement and turned onto the main hallway.

"Lucas seems really nice," she went on.

"Yeah, he is," I said. "Everyone loves Lucas."

Charlie fell silent. I shivered. Was it cooler down here? Or was I cold because of the virus? I pushed the thought out of my head and glanced at Charlie. The black sweater Aaron had brought her was slightly too big for her, and she had rolled up the sleeves. In the dim light, her eyes shone, huge and brown. She looked unbearably beautiful.

I turned away. Even if we found the antidote and I somehow managed to survive the Qilota virus, there was no way I'd hang on to Charlie.

"What the hell is your problem, Nat?" she demanded suddenly.

I stopped in my tracks, shocked.

"Why won't you talk to me?" she said, stamping her foot. "I know you're upset about Jas *and* about getting sick yourself *and* about Spider hitting on me, but you won't talk to me about any of it—though you didn't seem to have any problem telling the entire world about my biological dad, even though I specifically asked you not to."

"I don't . . . I didn't . . ." My voice fell away. I didn't know what to say. Which was, of course, part of the problem. Guys like Spider and Lucas and Aaron, they *always* knew what to say and when to say it.

Charlie's eyes flared with exasperation. "You didn't *what?*"

I latched on to the easiest thing to explain.

"I didn't like the way Spider acted like you owed him something," I muttered. "I didn't mean to upset you."

Charlie looked me in the eyes, her expression as hard and as bright as I'd ever seen it. "You didn't upset me, not over that. But you see, if you don't talk, I don't know how you feel, or how to tell you how *I* feel."

"How *you* feel?" I stammered, feeling uncomfortable. How had we gotten on to the subject of emotions so quickly?

"Yes." There was a long pause, and then Charlie jutted out her chin. "You see, I love you," she said defiantly. The way she spoke the words made them sound like a challenge.

My mouth gaped. My head spun. I had no idea what to say.

"Now, come on," she said, suddenly grabbing my hand. "We need to find this antidote."

I felt bewildered as we raced along the hallway, opening each door in turn. There were three labs, all fitted with gleaming metal pipes and bottles of chemicals, plus a kitchen with an old-fashioned dresser and a dumbwaiter in the corner. We scoured these thoroughly, using the keys Charlie had taken from the security guard upstairs to open the various cupboards we came across, but could find no reference to the Qilota virus.

I kept hearing Charlie's words in my head.

I love you.

I had never said those words to anyone. Now that I thought about it, I wanted to say them back to Charlie, but how? I'd already let the moment pass. Again. My vision blurred and, for a few seconds, I was completely blind. Then the floor came back into view. I didn't have many more moments to tell Charlie anything. I didn't have many more moments at all.

"There's nothing here," I said, pushing my thoughts away along with an empty packing crate. "Shall we go back upstairs?"

"I want to take another look in the kitchen first," Charlie said. "It looked like it was all just catering stuff, but maybe there's some info in the dresser, behind the pots and pans."

I shrugged. I couldn't believe information about an antidote to a deadly virus would be stored in a basement kitchen, but I didn't have a better suggestion. Charlie left the office. I heard her padding into the kitchen and opening and closing a cupboard door.

I rifled through the papers stashed in the corner of the biggest lab. Again, there was nothing that obviously related to the development and weaponizing of the Qilota virus, though that was surely what had gone on in these very rooms. Most of the paperwork consisted of academic research documents—not a million miles away from the essays I used to write for school. Everyone there would be gearing up for finals. I should have been taking plenty of them myself. I was expected to achieve a whole bunch of top grades. How pointless did that seem now?

I wondered how things were going upstairs for Aaron and Lucas. It was time to find them. I hurried along the hallway. There was no sign of Charlie in any of the rooms we'd examined. She must still be in the kitchen.

I peered around the door. The room was empty.

"Charlie?" I hissed.

No reply. I raced up and down the basement hallway. Charlie was nowhere to be seen. Heart beating fast, I rushed up the stairs to the first floor. Lucas and Aaron were walking toward me, expressions of disappointment on their faces. So they hadn't found anything useful either.

I stared up at them, my vision smudging again, my pulse throbbing.

"Where's Charlie?" Lucas asked, looking around.

"I don't know," I said as the full horror of the situation sank into me. "She's gone."

CHARLIE

My second search of the kitchen revealed a low door behind the dresser, which neither Nat nor I had noticed before. It was locked, but one of the keys from the security guard's bunch fit.

I crept through and found myself able to stand upright. The room I was in was pitch-black and utterly silent. I felt for a light switch with trembling fingers. *There.* With huge relief, I flipped it on. The two naked bulbs hanging from the low ceiling cast a dim and shadowy glow around what I realized right away was a narrow hallway. There was a fire exit at one end, with an alarm set above it and a door halfway down the hallway that led into a room on the left. No sounds came from the room, so I scurried inside. It was some kind of storeroom, with boxes stacked against three of the four walls.

I hurried over to the nearest box. What was inside? The docket on the top of the seal made me gasp.

Serum 3489 for use in treatment of Qilota virus

It was the antidote. *Yes.*

I tore open the box. Inside were eight or ten smaller boxes. I lifted one out and opened it up. The box contained twenty or so tiny plastic vials, each filled with a pale yellow liquid. The label on the box read:

Serum 3489. 5ml vial—one adult dose. Half for children under twelve.

This was it. At last I had a cure for Nat and his family in my hands. For the first time in days, hope surged through me. I grabbed a box, tucked it under my arm, and headed back to the low door that led into the basement kitchen.

The door had shut. I pulled and twisted on the handle, but it wouldn't open. It must have self-locked when it closed behind me. Panic rising, I fished Latimer's bank card out of my pocket and slid it along the gap, trying to find the edge of the lock. But unlike most of the other doors I'd used this trick on, the little basement door was crooked, its wood warped. I tried again and again, but it was no good.

I was trapped.

NAT

I checked the security guard. He was still tied up, exactly where we'd left him.

"Maybe she went outside?" Aaron suggested.

"She wouldn't have gone anywhere without telling me," I insisted.

"You're sure she isn't still downstairs?" Lucas asked.

"Definitely. I went into every room."

"Let me check," Lucas said. "You and Aaron take a look outside, just in case." He hesitated. "Charlie's great, Nat." He winked. "I'm impressed."

I nodded. A year ago Lucas's approval would have meant everything. Now all I could think about was how much danger Charlie might be in.

As Lucas disappeared down the stairs to the basement, I hurried over to Aaron. He was already at the front door, his hand pressing against the wood. With a sudden shove, it opened against him. Aaron stumbled back. A second later, two masked soldiers forced their way past him.

"No!" I yelled. I turned, ready to run. A huge hand gripped my shoulder.

"Let me go!" I shouted, as the soldier wrenched me around to face him. In seconds he wound a length of rope around my wrists and yanked on it, hard. Across the room, Aaron was being similarly trussed up. A moment later Lucas was shoved into the room, his hands also tied.

"Roman Riley wants a word, Nat," the soldier hissed.

And, leaving Charlie goodness knows where, we were forced out of the building and into the car that had pulled up outside.

CHARLIE

I tried—and failed—to break through the lock on the low door again.

"Nat!" I yelled. "*Nat!*"

There was no reply. Had he gone to look for me upstairs?

I couldn't help but think how weird it had been seeing Nat with his brother. Of course, it had been weird seeing Lucas at all. He didn't look like Nat. Well, maybe around the eyes. But Nat was all I really saw in any room. He hadn't said anything when I'd told him I loved him. I hadn't expected to say it, but the words had just come out. At least I'd told him how I felt. But how did Nat feel?

I tried the lock of the low door one last time. It still wasn't opening. With an exasperated sigh, I gave up on it, picked up the box of antidote serum, and ran along the hallway to the alarmed fire exit at the other end. It was marked EMERGENCY EXIT. A key sat in a tiny glass box on the wall, along with a notice explaining that the exit was set with an alarm and to be opened only in an emergency or with prior permission from the security desk.

I hesitated. I had no idea what was on the other side, but I had to find out. Staying here any longer simply wasn't an option. Gritting my teeth, I broke the glass and took the key. As I pushed open the door, an alarm screeched into the air. Cursing under my breath, I raced outside. The door opened on to a small basement yard. Stairs led up to the pavement. I didn't recognize the street, but I was clearly at the back of the building. Gripping the box of antidote vials, I ran up to ground level, the alarm still ringing in my ears. I crept to the end of the road and peered around the corner. I waited a few seconds, my heart pounding, then raced over to the institute's main entrance. The front door was open wide. I went inside, blood thundering in my ears. The place was utterly silent. Where had Nat, Lucas, and Aaron gone?

And then I saw the two EFA guards—I recognized them both from Riley's house. They were by the reception desk, untying the security guard.

Horrified, I spun around.

Only to find Taylor blocking my way. Before I could make a move or a sound, he had grabbed my wrist and wrenched the box of antidote vials out of my hand.

"We've got her," he said into his mouthpiece. Terror spiraled in my head. I struggled, but Taylor held me tight. "We've got them all."

NAT

I paced up and down past the window. Even if it hadn't been locked, with concertina bars fastened over the glass, the rope around my wrists would have made it impossible to open. I peered out. The sun was low over the horizon outside, glinting off the fishpond.

Lucas and I were prisoners in Riley's house. We had been here for roughly an hour, and the only person we'd seen so far had been Taylor. He had marched us up the stairs into this bedroom without speaking.

I had no idea what had happened to Aaron. He had been trussed up with me and Lucas and shoved into the back of a van, but taken out when the van first stopped, ten minutes or so before Lucas and I had arrived at Riley's house. As for Charlie, I had no idea if she had gotten away or was a prisoner too. I didn't want to think about Parveen or the other members of the resistance who had been trying to stop Operation Neptune. Were they being held captive somewhere? Or had they already been killed? As for me and Lucas, I could only assume that Riley was just waiting for it to get dark before he disposed of us.

I wandered over to the bed. Lucas, his hands tied like mine, was nudging open the top drawer of the bedside table. He peered inside.

"Nat," he whispered. "Look."

He indicated something in the drawer. As I bent over to see what it was, my vision blurred again and a wave of nausea rolled through me. I stopped moving, closing my eyes for a second, fighting off the feeling of sickness. How much time did I have left? Another whole day? Until midnight? Whatever. Jas had even less time. Not wanting to think about it, I looked up.

Lucas hadn't noticed. He was still staring down at the drawer. I leaned closer, my vision clearing. A pair of nail scissors met my eyes. The points looked sharp, but the blades were short.

"If you hold them, you can cut through my ropes," Lucas said. "Then I'll do yours."

I thought it was unlikely the scissors would cut through any-thing tougher than our hair, but it was better than doing nothing.

"Okay." I scrambled off the bed, turned around so my back was to the drawer, and felt for the scissors. I opened them and, holding one blade between my fingers, I started sawing at Lucas's binding.

Even if we managed to cut through the rope around our wrists, there was nothing here—other than the wooden lamp by the bed—that could conceivably be used as any kind of weapon.

Still, Lucas was not yet showing any effects from the virus, and he had once been trained as an EFA agent. If we could get the ropes off, we stood a chance of overpowering whoever next came into the room.

It was hard work, sawing at the rope without being able to really get my body weight behind what I was doing. I frowned, trying to press harder. I couldn't tell if the scissors were making any difference or not.

As we worked, Riley's voice rose from the floor below. "You little idiot. What were you thinking?" he shouted.

Another voice, younger and male, shouted back. It was Spider. "You said no one would die. You said it was controllable."

"I said *containable*." Riley's voice was like ice. "You know sometimes sacrifices have to—"

"They're not *your* sacrifices, though, are they?" Charlie's voice sounded above the others.

I froze, the scissor blade still in my hand. She was here, just downstairs.

"Get her *out* of here." Riley sounded furious. "As for you, Spider, I'm sending you back to your mother."

Silence fell.

"Nat." Lucas moved his wrists impatiently. "*Nat*, keep going."

I redoubled my efforts with the blade.

CHARLIE

Taylor shoved me into the living room. I sank onto the sofa, my head in my hands. Where were Nat, Lucas, and Aaron? And what about Parveen and Mayor Latimer and the rest of the resistance? Where was Riley keeping them? Were they prisoners somewhere in the house? Or were they already dead?

At first I had thought it was Spider who had betrayed us. After all, he was the one who had told us about the Silvercross Institute. But as soon as we'd gotten back to Riley's home, Uchi had explained that he had been suspicious of Spider and forced the truth out of him earlier today.

"I told him I didn't want anything to happen to you," he had said.

"So Spider thought he could trust you?" I shook my head, despair filling me to my fingertips. I couldn't believe after all my efforts I was back here, a prisoner, and that Taylor had taken the vials of antidote I'd found.

At least I knew Spider had genuinely tried to help us. Not

that it mattered now. Riley had everyone exactly where he wanted them. And even if Nat *was* still alive, he would *stay* alive for only a matter of hours without the antidote. Jas, who'd been infected first, had even less time.

Outside in the hall, Riley was barking out orders. He sounded more stressed than I'd ever heard him. Taylor was in the doorway, arms folded, watching me. I stood up, all my frustrations and fears turning to fury at this man who had done so much to train us, to give us a sense of identity and purpose—and then had ripped it all away with his betrayal. I stormed over to him. He looked down at me, his eyes hard and clear as emeralds.

"I suppose you've been given the antidote?" I asked.

Taylor nodded.

"You're a coward and a liar and a murderer, *sir*," I spat.

Taylor's expression didn't waver.

"I hate you."

There was a long pause. For a second I thought I saw just the faintest tinge of regret in Taylor's eyes. "I know you do," he said, and then he left the room.

I heard him a moment later in the hallway. He was on his phone, talking about arrangements for tonight's rally. I shook my head, my fury now morphing into despair. How could Taylor and Riley continue campaigning with all this upheaval going on in the house? It was a sign of how powerful they were, of how easily they had controlled Nat and me—and everyone else—right from the moment I'd arrived here.

Suddenly distant voices were raised. Who was arguing? Taylor was still on his phone call just outside the door. Was that *Uchi* yelling at Riley? I strained to hear what they were saying.

"For the last time, it's the cleanest option," Riley shouted. "It deals with Nat *and* Charlie. It's the only way."

Deals with Nat. My heart skipped a beat. That meant Nat must still be alive. Was he somewhere here, in the house? Were the others?

"Not Charlie." Uchi sounded emphatic. "You went against my wishes using her as bait in the first place. And I didn't force the truth out of Spider earlier only to—"

"Will you *shut up!*" Riley roared.

Silence. I opened the living room door a crack. Taylor was still on his phone. He stood by the coat stand next to the front door, his back turned to me. He was ordering a car for Riley. There was no sign of Riley himself—or of Uchi—but I could just make out their voices, now lowered to the point where I couldn't hear what they were saying, coming from the dining room. A moment later, Taylor finished his call and bounded up the stairs. He was calling out to one of the men. His voice faded away as he went into a room on the second floor.

I walked into the empty hall determined to look around upstairs, to see if I could find out where Nat and the others were being held. I tiptoed toward the stairs.

"Charlie?"

I spun around. It was Spider, whispering at me from the kitchen doorway.

"Go away," I hissed, still mad at him for telling Uchi where we were. "You *talked*."

"I know. I'm sorry." He hurried over. "I need to speak to you. In private. It's about Nat. About the antidote. *Please*."

I hesitated for a second, then followed him into the kitchen.

NAT

With a final, ragged cut, I sliced through Lucas's ropes. He spun around and grabbed the scissors from my hands.

"My turn," he muttered. He began carving through my rope as my vision blurred again. "We need to be ready. Are you sure you're up to this?"

"Definitely," I said, ignoring the weakness in my limbs and the sick feeling in my stomach. There was no point worrying Lucas by admitting how horrible I felt.

It took Lucas just a few minutes to free my wrists. As my vision cleared again, a tumult of thoughts raced through my head. Where was Charlie? Had she found the antidote? Might there be some in the house? How much time did Jas and I have? And what about Lucas and our parents? Soon they, too, would be showing symptoms.

Lucas sawed at my wrists for a couple of minutes, his movements fast and hard. "There." He stood back, triumphant. The rope fell from my hands, and I rubbed my wrists. I should have felt glad we were free, but all I could think was that my hands, like my feet, were numb. And that I felt weak and achy—all signs of the virus taking hold. I couldn't ignore them anymore.

Metal on metal. The sound of a key turning in the lock made me spin around. Lucas was already at the door, fists raised.

I tried to focus, praying my eyes weren't going to blur at just the wrong moment.

The door opened softly. A masked soldier walked in. Quick as a flash, Lucas jumped forward, landing two swift punches to the man's sides.

Except it wasn't a man. It was a woman, and quite a slender one. She staggered sideways, clawing at her mask as Lucas loomed over her, reaching for her arm.

"Wait." It was Parveen. She ripped the mask off her face and glared at Lucas. "Stop it. I'm freakin' trying to help you."

Lucas's mouth fell open. He glanced from her to me.

"Par?" I gasped.

She rolled her mask down over her face again. "Come on," she said, beckoning us to the door.

I hurried over. Lucas was still staring at Parveen.

She peered out along the hallway.

"How did . . . ?" I started.

"I was being held outside," she whispered. "I heard you were up here. I just got away, took down the girl on guard at the front door. If we hurry, we can get out that way too."

I grabbed her arm. "What about Charlie? And Latimer and Aaron? We have to help them."

"Latimer and his men are somewhere else. Aaron's with them," Parveen said, her chocolate-colored eyes narrowing with impatience. "And Charlie's okay here for now. Her dad's protecting her. Come on. We need to go."

I opened my mouth to protest, but Lucas spoke before I had a chance.

"Whoever this is, she's right," he said, flashing Par a quick grin. "Um, who *are* you?"

"Parveen, from Nat's cell. We trained together." She flushed slightly as she spoke, and then she peered outside again. "It's clear," she said.

We crept outside, over to the stairs. The hall was still empty, the front door ajar. I could just make out the splayed figure of the soldier Parveen had knocked out on the doorstep.

I held my breath as we tiptoed down the stairs. There, by the front door, was the coatrack I remembered from my first visit here all those months ago. Except that now the scarf I'd seen was gone. I glanced at the row of coats belonging to Riley and his girlfriend. Taylor's leather jacket hung from the rack beside them. I shivered. Riley's other men were bad enough, but Taylor was a ruthless soldier. Him being here made it even more important that we tried to rescue Charlie.

"I think we should look for Charlie," I whispered.

"Later," Parveen insisted.

"Come on, Nat. It's too big a risk," Lucas added.

Parveen slid out through the front door. She held up her hand, indicating we should wait for her signal. Lucas glanced around, checking that I was all right. I gave him a swift nod. I could feel the adrenaline coursing through my body, the weakness and numbness lifting.

Seconds ticked away.

Riley's voice drifted toward us across the hall. I was pretty certain it was coming from the room across from us.

"I've told you I can't talk about this now," he was saying, his voice loud and tense. "I have to speak at a rally in less than an hour."

"You need to keep your sights on the big picture." That was Charlie's father, Uchi. "And Charlie is part of the big picture. I won't let you hurt her."

"It's going to happen, old man," Riley said curtly. "Get your head around it. She's got to go."

Got to go?

"Now!" Lucas urged. He took off through the front door, immediately behind Parveen.

I didn't follow. I had to know what Riley was planning to do to Charlie. She was right here, at Riley's mercy. I'd left her behind once before. I wasn't going to do it again. I sped silently across the room and peered through the crack in the door.

Riley and Uchi were alone in a formal dining room, on either side of a polished wooden table.

"I *am* seeing the big picture," Riley was insisting. "We've already gotten reports that half the boat party are affected, the early signs. Everything else has gone completely to plan, but Charlie hasn't worked out. As I predicted she wouldn't. You have to accept it."

"I can still convince her," Uchi said stubbornly.

"No," Riley said, his voice suddenly low and venomous. "Time's up. Charlie's going to die," he said. "Tonight."

I gulped. Across the room, the front door was still open a fraction. Lucas and Parveen must have made it out to the road. No one had seen us. My eyes fell again on Taylor's jacket hanging from the coat stand. His phone was peeking out from the pocket.

As soon as I saw it, I knew what I had to do.

CHARLIE

Spider led me through the kitchen and into the yard. The sun was no longer shining on this side of the house, and the air felt chilly on my face.

"We'll have a few minutes before the next patrol interrupts us," he said.

"What for? Do you know where the antidote is?" I whispered. "Do you know where I can get some?"

"Let's talk over here." Spider took my wrist and led me over to the fishpond.

I stared into the dark water. I was suddenly certain that he didn't know anything about the antidote. He just wanted to get me on my own. I was going to have to find some other way to help Nat.

"Charlie?"

I looked up. Spider was standing close to me. Too close. His dark, curly hair fell over his forehead as he gazed down at me. I wanted to step back, but the only thing behind me was the fishpond.

"I'm so sorry Uchi went to my dad and told him that I'd

warned you," Spider said, letting go of my wrist and pushing his hair absently out of his face. "I thought Uchi wanted to help you, not bring you back here."

"Never mind that," I said. "You said you knew something about the antidote?"

Spider nodded. "Before I tell you, I want you to know that I feel really torn. I mean, I totally get where my dad's coming from with all the ruthless, need-to-take-risks stuff he's always talking about, but—"

"Taylor took away the antidote I'd found," I interrupted, looking him steadily in the eye. I didn't need to hear all this garbage. "If Nat and his family don't get some in the next few hours . . ."

"I know." Spider groaned. "I know and I'm sorry, okay?"

I nodded. The wind was whipping up, the hint of rain in the air.

"Okay, so this is what I'm thinking," Spider went on in a low voice. "If we can get some antidote to Nat, then he can take it and pass it to the rest of his family."

"Yes," I said, my heartbeat quickening. "Do you know where?"

"I do," Spider said, pulling me toward him again. "But first there's something I need to ask you."

NAT

I snatched the phone out of Taylor's pocket and raced back across the hall.

"You know sometimes this is the way it goes," Riley was saying.

I peered down, fighting to clear the blurred edges of my vision. The phone was on. I squinted at the screen, searching for the camera app.

Uchi shook his head. "I won't accept that. Charlie is different."

I raised the phone, positioning the lens to take in both Riley and Uchi across the room. They were so intent on each other that neither saw me—but anyone coming into the hall would have spotted me instantly.

"For God's sake, you stubborn old idiot," Riley said. "I can't discuss this any more. I have to go in two minutes. Taylor's finding someone to drive me to the rally. I'm running late as it is. This is *not* the priority."

I pressed the record button on the phone.

"I won't let you hurt Charlie," Uchi said stubbornly. "She's my *child*."

"Oh, so being ruthless only applies to other people's families?"

Riley said, his voice rising. "Listen to me. Charlie is going to die. Just like her mother died. It's all set." He checked his watch. "Two hours from now, she'll be gone."

What the hell did that mean? *How* was Charlie going to be killed? What was Riley planning?

"I won't let you do it," Uchi said.

"Is that right?" Riley snarled, raising his right arm. He was holding a gun.

CHARLIE

Spider was so close I could feel his heart beating through his top.

"I want you to come with me down to Mum's," he said. "Will you, please?"

I stared at him. How on earth could he think I would go anywhere with him?

"It's the only way I can see you'll be safe until the election's out of the way," he said urgently. "Dad will agree if I ask. I know he's angry now, but it gets us both out of the way and he has to put you somewhere. You can't stay here. And Uchi won't let him hurt you. It's a good solution. You just have to agree, please?"

"What about the antidote?" I asked, playing for time. "Tell me where it is first and how on earth you think we're going to manage to get it to Nat."

"Nat's upstairs, locked in with his brother. The key is in the door. I've seen it. If I distract Taylor, you could let him out."

My heart leaped. So Nat was here and alive. I nodded, a plan already forming in my head. Spider shoved his hands into his pockets, then drew out four small plastic vials of antidote. My eyes widened.

"I took these from the box you found," he said. He held them out to me. "One vial contains enough antidote for one person."

I shoved the vials into my pockets, the blood thundering in my ears. Now I could save Nat. There was no time to lose.

"Thank you," I said. "I have to go."

"Wait." Spider's hand caught my arm. "What about coming with me to Mum's?"

I sucked in my breath. I itched to lie to Spider, to pretend that I liked him so that he would help me rescue Nat, but the words stuck in my throat. There had already been too much lying, too much deception.

"I'm going with Nat," I said, trying to keep my voice steady. "I belong with Nat."

Spider's eyes filled with pain.

And then, before either of us could say or do anything else, a muffled shot echoed toward us from inside the house.

NAT

The shot fired. For a moment, time seemed to stand still. And then Uchi crumpled to the floor. Riley stood, his arm outstretched, the gun—its long silencer over the barrel—still in his hand.

I blinked. It had happened so suddenly.

Just seconds ago Uchi had seen the gun and gasped: "What are you doing?"

"I've come to the conclusion," Riley had spat, "that you have definitely outlived your usefulness, old man." And before Uchi had time to move, Riley had fired.

I watched, frozen to the spot. Riley stared at Uchi's body, unaware of me standing there outside the door. And then Taylor yelled from upstairs:

"What the hell was that?"

I jumped into action. My thumb pressed the screen, closing the app. Taylor thundered down the stairs as I raced across the hall. Gripping the phone, I reached the front door.

A fist grabbed me. Shoved me. I clattered into the coat stand. It toppled over. I fell on top of it, coats and jackets surrounding me.

The phone went flying out of my hand. Taylor loomed over me.

"No!" I roared. With a swift punch, I lifted the coat stand and whacked it across Taylor's head. He reeled back, then fell to his knees. Lucas appeared at the front door.

"What the hell are you doing?" He grabbed me. Hauled me outside.

"Wait," I said. I didn't have the phone.

But Lucas was dragging me to the gates, where Parveen was hiding. Together they pushed me up over the bars, then held me up between them—a hand on either arm—as we raced along the road.

"Stop!" I cried out, but they were too strong.

We didn't stop running until we reached the subway station. Lucas dived in, bundling me over the barrier. The ticket guard shouted after us, but his voice vanished as we sped down the steps and onto the platform. A train was just closing its doors. Lucas dragged me on board. The three of us stood, panting, as the train roared off.

At last Lucas let go of my arm and I sank into a seat. Lucas swore, then hugged Parveen.

"Yes!" he cried.

"We did it!" Parveen's eyes shone.

I looked down at the grimy floor between my feet. All I could think was that I'd just seen Riley murder Charlie's father in cold blood and make it clear he was about to murder Charlie herself. I had held the proof in my hands.

And now it was gone.

CHARLIE

Spider and I rushed through the kitchen and out into the hallway as Riley walked out of the dining room.

He saw us, and for a second, he faltered. I peered past him. Inside, Uchi lay on the floor, a pool of blood gathering around his head.

He was dead. I stared, numb with shock.

Riley shut the door behind him with a *click*.

"Get out of my sight," he ordered.

I didn't move, couldn't move. Beside me Spider was open-mouthed. Across the hall, Taylor was staggering to his feet, clutching his head. The front door was open, the coat stand was on its side and all the coats scattered across the floor.

"What happened?" Riley barked.

"The boys and Parveen got away," Taylor said, his voice hoarse.

My stomach flipped over. Nat had escaped. Riley let out a groan of irritation, and then he shook himself. "It doesn't matter. Nat will be dead soon. The others don't count."

A shiver ran down my spine. If Riley was really that

unconcerned, then Nat must have very little time left. I stared at the closed door in front of me. My father was on the other side of it. He was gone. I couldn't take it in.

"Where the hell is my car?" Riley snapped.

"They're bringing it now, sir," Taylor said, picking up his phone and his jacket from the ground, then righting the coat stand.

Had Nat or one of the others hit him in order to escape? If it had been Nat, then maybe he wasn't quite as sick as I'd feared.

Taylor put on his jacket, tucked the phone in his pocket, and winced. He rubbed the back of his head. Riley glanced at the dining room, where Uchi's body still lay behind the closed door. "We can clean that up later. Put a guard on the door and get Martina to take Spider to Cornwall," he ordered. "Then meet me at the rally."

"You killed Uchi," I said. "You *killed* him. In cold blood."

Riley ignored me. "I have to go," he said.

Taylor straightened up. His face was unnaturally pale. "What about Charlie?" he asked.

I held my breath, waiting for Riley to give Taylor the order to murder me. But instead Riley strode to the hall mirror. He smoothed back his hair and straightened his tie. Then he sighed out his breath and turned to the front door.

"Let her go," he said. "There's nothing she can do now anyway."

And he walked out without a backward glance at either me or Spider.

NAT

Half an hour later we jogged across Hyde Park to the rally. As we neared the stage, the crowd erupted in cheers. I was aware that all three of us were infected with the Qilota virus and liable to pass it on to anyone we came near, but we had to get to Riley. There was no other option.

"Riley's just coming onstage to speak," Parveen said.

"Look at how relaxed he is," Lucas marveled. "He just murdered someone. *Look.*"

"I know," Parveen said bitterly.

"Me too," I added. But the truth was, I couldn't see Riley right now. I could barely make out the stage or the huge screens positioned on either side of it that showed what was happening in detail. Everything on it was a collection of blurs. Over the past few minutes my vision had grown much worse, but I was worried that if I confided just how bad it was to Lucas and Parveen, they would insist on leaving me behind. And retrieving Taylor's phone was too important for me not to be involved.

Saving Charlie—and bringing down Riley—depended on it.

I wasn't sure, of course, if Taylor had realized I'd made a

recording, but I had switched off the camera app before I had dropped it and, thanks to the coat stand toppling over, it was highly possible that Taylor would simply think the phone had fallen out of his jacket pocket in the general chaos.

It hadn't been hard to persuade Lucas and Parveen to come here. We knew we were putting ourselves—and everyone around us—at risk to get so close to Riley and his men, but this felt like our last chance.

I followed Lucas and Parveen around the side of the stage. Guards were posted at every entrance. From the stage, Riley's voice boomed through the late-afternoon air.

"Friends," he said. "An illicit weapons project, inadequate safety procedures, a careless disregard for the rule of law. The government has shown that it is riddled with corruption and plainly unfit to govern. We are currently working on sourcing sufficient stocks of the only antidote to the virus, which we are confident should be available by the end of the day tomorrow."

Beside me, Lucas and Parveen glanced at each other. This news meant, surely, they would be saved and so, hopefully, would Mum and Dad. But the end of tomorrow would be too late for Jas and me.

". . . ensuring that election day may be overshadowed by scandal," Riley went on, "but that tragedy has been averted."

"I can't believe Riley's getting away with this," Lucas muttered.

"He's not going to," I said. My vision, thankfully, was starting to clear, but I knew it was only a matter of time before it clouded again.

"I will be issuing an update later this evening," Riley went on. He sounded tired but heroic.

I groaned inwardly. If we didn't make this work, on top of everything else, he was certain to win the election at the end of the week. He had played everything to perfection.

CHARLIE

I got out of the taxi and ran along the pavement to Nat's house, the four vials of antidote safely shoved deep in my pockets.

Would Nat be here? I knew that Jas and her parents were inside, so surely it was only a matter of time before Nat turned up too. I wouldn't have gotten here so quickly if it hadn't been for Spider. As soon as Riley had left for the rally, I had turned to him.

"Do you have any money?" I had asked.

Spider had stared at me, his forehead screwed up in a frown. "I don't get it. Dad's letting you go. Something's wrong."

"No. Everything's right, for the first time in a long time. If I'm free, I can get this antidote to Jas and Nat and the rest of their family."

"But it doesn't make sense. Dad knows you're against him. He knows you've seen that he killed Uchi. Why is he letting you leave?"

"Because he knows no one will believe anything I say. I'm still wanted for kidnapping and terrorism, remember?" I turned on my heel. If Spider wasn't going to help me get away, there was nothing left to talk about.

He ran up behind me, fishing in the pockets of his skinny jeans. "Here," he said, thrusting a bundle of notes at me. "Take this and—and look after yourself."

I stopped and gave him a quick hug. "Thanks, Spider."

His cheeks had pinked, but before he could speak again, I had rushed out of the house, running hard to find a taxi.

And now here I was at Nat's house. I pressed the doorbell. It felt completely surreal being back here. Although fewer than two months had passed since I'd been living a relatively normal life in this part of London, it felt like I'd been away from everything I knew for years, that the girl I was back then had been a different person.

I rang the doorbell again. A few moments later Nat's dad opened the door. I was shocked by how old he looked. Last time I'd seen him, he'd seemed gray and tired. But now exhaustion could be seen in every line of his face.

"Charlie?" His eyes widened. "Are you all right?"

"I'm fine," I said. "How's Jas?"

To my horror, his face crumpled. "She doesn't have long," he said, clearly trying not to cry. "We're desperately worried about the boys, too, of course, but Jas is close now. *Really* close."

"Show me," I said, reaching for the vials in my pocket.

I raced up the stairs after him, my heart pounding. Was I too late?

NAT

I steadied myself against the wall. My vision had, thankfully, cleared, but I still felt weaker than I'd ever felt in my life.

Beside me, Lucas peered through the gap in the curtains. We had snuck past one guard—thanks to Parveen causing a distraction—and were now close to the stage, where Riley was speaking.

"Taylor's right there," Lucas hissed in my ear. "I'll take him. You go for the phone."

I nodded, steeling myself. If my plan was going to work, the next few minutes were crucial.

CHARLIE

I raced across the landing, glancing at Nat's old bedroom door as I passed. I had a sudden flashback to the first time I'd gone inside his room and thought, mistakenly, that he was involved in the bomb that had killed Mum.

So much had happened since then. I hoped Nat was on his way here now. I had no way of contacting him, but surely he and his brother would get back here as quickly as they could. I had been fast because Spider's money had paid for a taxi. But Nat and Lucas couldn't be far behind. Whatever the risk, they would both want to see Jas before she died.

I stopped outside Jas's bedroom and knocked lightly on the door. There was no reply, so I pushed it open. The room was just as I remembered it, full of the pretty fabrics and soft, feminine design touches that Jas loved. Jas herself lay, eyes closed, on the bed. She had always been skinny and fragile-looking, but I was shocked by how ghostly she looked. Her mother, red-eyed, sat beside her. She looked up as I came in.

My heart in my mouth, I hurried over, a vial of antidote in my hand.

As I drew near, Jas opened her eyes. Her expression was glassy and her skin looked clammy. She breathed in—a rasping, shallow breath.

"Who is it?" She turned her face toward me, her eyes unseeing. "Who's there?"

She was looking straight at me, but she clearly couldn't see a thing. I gasped and looked at her mum.

"She's blind," her mother said with a sob.

The words hit me like a punch. Poor Jas. And poor Nat. This would be him soon. And then Jas's mum stood up and, leaning close so Jas couldn't hear, she whispered in my ear, "I wanted her to be in the hospital, but she insisted on staying here. She's not in any pain, but there's nothing anyone can do. It will take a miracle to save her."

I pulled away and held out the vial.

Please, I prayed, *please let this be that miracle.*

NAT

Lucas spoke under his breath: "There's another man with Taylor. We should wait till he goes."

I nodded, though I was itching to move. To get this done, once and for all.

"They're walking away, to the sound area. I can just see the mixing deck from here. Let's give it a minute."

I nodded again. There was a pause, and then Lucas cleared his throat.

"So, Parveen says she met you and Charlie when she was recruited to the EFA?"

"Yeah," I said. "Par's a friend." I paused. "Wouldn't want to get on the wrong side of her, though."

"Mmm," Lucas mused. "She's, like, *really* cool. You know she must have the virus too. She'll need the antidote just like us."

Obviously. Why was he going on about Par? A few moments later she appeared behind me.

"Riley's nearly finished," she said.

Lucas turned back to peer through the curtains. "Taylor's coming back now," he said. "He's alone. On my mark."

Parveen stiffened. I tensed, praying my vision—and my strength—would hold.

"Go." As Lucas rushed through the curtain, the audience beyond broke into a round of applause for Riley.

Rushing forward, Lucas and I bundled Taylor to the ground. I pressed my knee against the man's neck, as Taylor himself had shown me. Lucas made a fist and punched his stomach. Taylor let out a muffled groan. Then Lucas leaned forward. "That was for putting me in a coma last year." He punched Taylor again. "And that was for everything you've done to my family." Taylor looked up at him, winded. He glanced at me. For a moment I saw remorse in his eyes—a look of defeat. Then Lucas nodded at me, and I whipped my knee away, as Lucas landed a third punch smack on Taylor's chin. Taylor immediately went limp.

Parveen was already searching his jacket pocket. "Here," she said, holding up a gun.

Lucas snatched it off her.

"Phone!" I urged.

Parveen and I dived into the rest of his pockets.

"Got it!" I yanked the phone out. "Come on."

The three of us raced to the sound station farther backstage. The applause for Riley was still loud in our ears.

I quickly found the recording I'd made earlier, then thrust the phone at the terrified sound engineer.

"Play this," I ordered.

"But—but—" the man stammered.

Lucas drew Taylor's gun and pointed it at the man.

"Cut Riley's mike and the screen feed and play what's on this phone," Parveen insisted. "Or we'll shoot you."

The sound guy stared for a moment at the gun, then took the phone. He bent over his equipment. Seconds later the sound of white noise filled the air. The applause of the crowd died away. Uchi's voice could be heard, faint from the film.

"Turn it up!" I yelled.

Lucas pressed the gun against the sound guy's back. The volume levels shot up so that Uchi's voice was now distorted. The crowd fell silent. The engineer fiddled with the buttons on his desk.

I rushed to the edge of the stage.

Riley was still standing in front of the microphone. I followed his gaze to the screen at the side, where he and Uchi stood, as I'd filmed them, on opposite sides of the dining room table in Riley's house.

The on-screen Riley was speaking, his voice a vicious snarl, utterly different from the way he'd just spoken to the crowd, who were watching, rapt.

"Listen to me," he was saying, "Charlie is going to die. Just like her mother died. It's all set. Two hours from now, she'll be gone."

I glanced at the real Riley. He turned and saw me at the same time. Fury filled his face. He rushed toward me. I blocked his way. He thrust me aside.

And then Lucas was there, the gun still in his hand. The real Riley stopped just as the film showed the screen version raising his gun. And then the shot that had killed Uchi echoed across the park. The audience gasped, witnessing the murder on film, just as I had witnessed it in real life less than an hour ago.

Riley had seen it too. He stood at the edge of the stage. Lucas cocked his gun. I could see in Riley's eyes that he knew he had lost.

And then he turned to me.

"It's still too late to save them," he said quietly. "Too late for Charlie."

CHARLIE

I stared out of Nat's bedroom window. The street outside the house was empty and I was starting to feel uneasy. Where were Nat and Lucas? They should surely have been here by now.

Had something happened to Nat? Jas had been bedridden since early this morning. I knew that Nat had been given the virus after his sister, but how long after? What if he was too ill to travel?

At least Jas seemed slightly better since I'd given her the antidote. Her temperature was lower and she was sleeping peacefully. Her parents and I had no idea if she'd taken the drug in time to save her life, but the signs were promising. Anyway, there was nothing else we could do now. Mr. and Mrs. Holloway were both in there with her, sitting on either side of her bed, heads bowed. Her mum was praying.

At least I had enough antidote for them. In a minute I would go and explain that they each needed to take one of the three remaining vials. But I knew that as soon as I did, they would start worrying about their sons all over again, asking questions to which I had no answers. I wandered around Nat's bedroom. Everything was covered with a fine film of dust. The old computer on the desk in the corner reminded me again of those first few weeks after I'd met Nat. He had seemed to dislike me back then. But now I knew he had just felt awkward because he had thought Lucas was involved in the bombing that had killed Mum.

I hadn't thought much about Mum herself in the past few days. Not since I'd discovered how she had lied to me about my birth father. It hurt that she hadn't told me the truth about her affair with Uchi—or that I might be his daughter—but maybe she had just wanted to protect me from finding out about him. Was that really wrong? Maybe it wasn't all that different from me wishing I could protect Nat's parents right now.

The house was so still it was hard to imagine a busy, bustling world outside. In the silence, I couldn't avoid facing my feelings. I missed Mum, but she was already gone. And Uchi was dead, but I'd never really known him. Nat was different. I couldn't bear the thought of losing him.

I went back to the window. Where was he? Why didn't he come?

NAT

"What do you mean, it's 'too late' for Charlie? Or—or 'to save them'? Who are 'them'?" I demanded.

Riley narrowed his eyes. "Charlie is trying to save your sister. I gave my son access to the antidote to see what he would do. I'm afraid he handed the antidote straight over to Charlie and she has taken it to Jas, but she'll be too late." He held up one hand, slowly so that Lucas could see he wasn't reaching for a weapon. A thick black watch was around his wrist. "Take it," Riley said. "Then you'll see."

I unfastened the watch and examined it. The face was blank, as if all the power had gone from the device.

I glanced at Lucas. He shrugged.

"What is this?" I asked Riley.

But he shook his head. A moment later, people started pouring in through the curtains. They saw Lucas and the gun and Taylor unconscious on the floor. Soon we were surrounded, everyone talking at once, asking about the film they had just seen of Riley murdering Uchi.

Riley himself stayed completely silent, his head bowed.

Parveen was in the middle of the group, explaining how Riley had tricked and manipulated us. Out in the park, the crowd was going wild. Someone needed to talk to them, to explain what was happening.

Without thinking about what I was going to say, I hurried to the front of the stage.

"Roman Riley is a murderer!" I shouted. As one, the crowd fell silent. My voice carried on the wind. "Riley has lied and killed to gain power. He is a con man. He carries out terrorist attacks, then gets others to take the blame so he can look like a hero. I just saw him murder that man." I pointed to the screen, still showing Uchi's body lying on the floor, surrounded by a pool of blood.

The crowd surged forward, voices raised again. This time I could see they were frightened. Angry. My vision blurred again, and a wave of nausea rolled through me. I crept to the side of the stage. It was done. At last, it was done. All these people would never have taken accusations against Riley seriously before. But now that they had seen the film of him killing Uchi, everything was different.

Everything *had* to be different.

I leaned against the wall, a yard or so away from where Taylor lay unconscious on the ground. Two men were examining him, both bending over his face. After a few more minutes, the hubbub across the room grew louder. I looked over, straining to see what was going on. As my vision cleared, I caught sight of Riley being marched away between two policemen. Then, to my horror, I realized that Lucas, minus his gun, and Parveen were also being taken. Were they being arrested too?

I raced over, intending to protest, but just before I reached Lucas he glanced over his shoulder. His eyes flared as he saw me.

Get out of here, he mouthed. *Go home.*

I gulped. He was right. I needed to see Jas. Riley seemed to think Charlie was with her *and* that she had the antidote. If that was true, maybe there was a chance Jas was going to be okay and that I would be able to get my hands on some antidote too. If it wasn't true, at least I might be able to say good-bye to Jas and our parents before it was too late.

I was still holding Riley's watch. I shoved it in my pocket and crept around the stage. I kept hunched over, praying that if I kept my face hidden I would pass unnoticed in all the confusion. It worked. At last I made it off the stage. I sped across the grass to the park exit. I had only enough money for a subway ticket, so I made my way to the Hyde Park station and was soon on a train, traveling home. I kept my hood up and my mouth covered, praying I was infecting as few people as possible. Hopefully, it wouldn't matter now. Hopefully, if Riley was at last defeated, stocks of the antidote could be released in plenty of time to save everyone only recently infected.

Sitting still helped with both my vision and my nausea. And once the train emptied at King's Cross, I started to feel better.

Surely there would be time to save Jas now. And Mum and Dad and Lucas.

And then I felt my pocket vibrate. It was Riley's watch, whirring into life. I pulled the watch out and glanced down at the screen. It was showing a countdown.

9:56

9:55

9:54

I stared at the seconds as they passed. Was this countdown somehow connected to Riley's threat against Charlie? Was it somehow connected to a bomb? That was Riley's normal method of killing people. I examined the watch. In itself it was clearly no explosive, but perhaps it was a way to keep track of a bomb—a bomb that would detonate in just under ten minutes.

How did that fit with what Riley had told me before—that Charlie would die and Jas wouldn't make it either? Except he hadn't said Charlie and "her" as in, "and Jas." He'd said Charlie and "them." Who were "them"?

I frowned, my mind racing. Two long minutes passed. The countdown ticked away.

07:58

07:57

07:56

One more stop until I got off. Almost there.

Riley's voice flashed into my head again: *Too late to save them.*

I sat up straight, the terrible realization hitting home. This countdown *did* relate to a bomb. It was the way Riley was going to know when the bomb had exploded.

And the bomb—I gasped with the full horror of it—was going to go off in my own home.

07:05

07:04

07:03

CHARLIE

I lay down on the bed in Nat's room. The one remaining vial of antidote was beside me. I had just given a vial each to Jas's parents. Mrs. Holloway had drunk hers distractedly, but Mr. Holloway had asked, with something of Nat's sharp intelligence, if there was enough left for Nat. I reassured him there was.

The house was still so silent and there was something soothing about being here in Nat's old room. Where was he? Why wasn't he here? I closed my eyes, exhaustion overcoming me.

There was no way I could sleep.

I would just rest my eyes for a moment.

NAT

The train stopped. I could almost feel the adrenaline pumping through my veins, pushing back the weakness that threatened to creep through my limbs. My vision was still blurry, but I could see the door, then the platform, then the stairs. I raced up to street level. As I tore out of the station, I glanced at the countdown.

02:16

02:15

02:14

Only two minutes until the bomb went off. I had no phone, no way of warning them. All I could do was run.

I pounded along the street, fighting the weakness that dragged at my lungs and filled my bones with lead. I saw home in my mind's eye: Mum and Dad and Jas talking in the kitchen. And Charlie, smiling, her beautiful eyes intent on mine.

01:33

01:32

01:31

I pushed myself on. On to my own street. My house was just a few doors away. Another few steps and I saw the path. The door.

I ran up and hammered on the wood, pressing the doorbell at the same time.

"Hey!" I yelled. "Mum! Dad! Charlie!"

00:59

00:58

00:57

There was less than a minute. I yelled out again. Where *were* they?

And then the door opened. Charlie was standing there, dark shadows under her eyes. Her mouth rounded into a shocked O as she saw me.

"Get out of the house!" I shouted, pushing past her and into the hall. "There's a bomb in here. Out! All of you, out!"

CHARLIE

Nat stumbled along the hall, almost tripping over the shoes stacked by the living room door. His mother appeared at the top of the stairs.

"Nat? Is that you?" she said.

"Get out!" Nat spun around, waving his arms wildly. His eyes squinted up the stairs as if he was straining to see her.

"Nat, what is it?" His dad appeared next to his mum.

Nat held out a piece of black plastic. "There's a bomb. No time. *Hurry*. Get out!"

I raced up beside him. Over his shoulder I could see that the black plastic was a watch. It showed a countdown.

00:40

00:39

00:38

I gasped, the full horror hitting me. Nat sagged against the wall. He looked completely spent. I glanced up the stairs. Nat's mum was standing, frozen to the spot, his dad wide-eyed beside her.

"Get Jas," I ordered. "Bring her down. Outside."

Nat's parents stared down at me, shell-shocked.

"Move!" I yelled. I grabbed the watch from Nat's hand and raced up the stairs.

Nat's mum burst into tears. "I don't—"

I shoved her toward the stairs. "Get out of the house. Get Nat out." Without waiting to see if she moved, I gripped Nat's dad's arm and forced him toward Jas's room.

"Come on!" I ordered.

00:29

00:28

00:27

Nat's dad picked his daughter up from the bed and rushed to the stairs. Down in the hall, Nat looked barely conscious. His mum was steering him to the front door. Mr. Holloway was halfway down the stairs now. They were going to make it.

As I took a step toward the stairs, I glanced at the countdown again.

00:18

00:17

00:16

Then I remembered the last vial of antidote in Nat's bedroom, lying where I'd left it on the bed.

Nat needed that antidote. Needed it badly. He might die before we could get any more.

I turned and raced into his bedroom. Blood thundered in my ears. I grabbed the vial. Tore back to the stairs.

"Charlie!" Nat's cry came from outside the house. "Hurry!"

I pounded down the stairs.

00:09

00:08

00:07

I was going to make it.

00:05

00:04

00:03

Nat was waiting at the front door. I shoved the vial into his hand. Pushed him out, onto the path.

BOOM!

The ground shook underneath me. The roar filled my ears. Darkness and stone slammed me down. The world crashed around me.

And above the explosion, Nat's yell.

"Charlie!"

NAT

Debris fell everywhere. Charlie disappeared beneath falling brick. A hand reached out and pulled me back, away from the house. I turned. It was Dad, his face filled with horror.

I stumbled back to where Mum and Jas were waiting. Jas was awake and leaning against Mum, her hands over her mouth. The four of us watched through an eternity of seconds as our home collapsed in front of our eyes.

Dust settled onto the heap of rubble where the house had once stood. Our home was now just bricks and mortar and bits of twisted metal and burnt plastic. For a few seconds my eyesight seemed to return, the image of the house destroyed seared into my vision. Then darkness blurred the scene in front of me.

"Charlie!" I wrenched myself away from Dad, stumbling toward the spot where she had been standing.

"Nat!" I heard Mum's desperate shriek, but I barely registered it.

"Charlie!" I yelled. *"Charlie!"*

Dad rushed up beside me. "No." He grabbed my arm. "It's not safe, Nat."

"Get off me." I shook his arm away, fury and fear swirling in my guts. "We have to find her."

As I pulled at the pile of rubble in front of me, I registered that there was something in my hand. The thing Charlie had pushed at me before the house had fallen. I glanced down. It was a small plastic tube.

"It's the antidote," Dad said.

I stared at it in horror. Charlie must have wasted precious seconds to fetch this.

For me.

Numbly, I snapped off the top and drank the liquid. It was sour, with a sweet overlay. Like cough medicine I'd once had.

I reached again for the rubble.

"It's no good," Dad said. He put his hand on my arm. "Nat, I'm so sorry."

I looked at him blankly, then gazed over my shoulder. Mum and Jas were still huddled together on the pavement. Around them, our neighbors were emerging onto the street. Shouts filled the air.

I turned back to the fallen masonry.

"She could be alive." I shook Dad's hand off and tugged a large piece of brick from the pile. "She was right under the door-frame. It could have protected her."

I knew as I said the words that there was only the slimmest of chances that Charlie could have survived the house collapse, but it was enough. I pulled away another piece of stone. Then another.

"Nat, please." Dad sounded desperate.

"I have to find her," I insisted.

"She couldn't have survived that," Dad said softly. "No one could."

"People *do*. *Charlie* could," I persisted. "Charlie could survive anything."

I pulled at another piece of brick.

"Nat, for Pete's sake!" Mum was here now, Jas still beside her, pale and terrified.

Ignoring them all, I pulled at the stones. A wave of nausea washed over me. I bent over, breathing deeply, willing the sick feeling to pass. How much time had passed? If Charlie was under there, how much breathable air would she have left?

I straightened up and redoubled my efforts.

My parents stood helplessly on either side of me.

"Charlie!" I yelled. *"Charlie!"*

No reply. Tears filled my eyes. I tugged at another, larger piece of rubble. It fell, narrowly missing my feet. And suddenly Jas was beside me, pulling at bricks, her small hands grabbing and dragging stones off the pile.

"Jas?" Mum said weakly.

"Come on." Dad strode forward, put his arms around a huge piece of masonry and hurled it to the path beneath.

I moved another stone. "Charlie!" I yelled.

Now Mum joined in. The four of us worked together. Behind us, I could hear voices rising, shouts and demands to call the fire department. Gritting my teeth, I worked on.

"Charlie!" I yelled into the silence.

And then, through the dust and the stones, came a small, muffled cry.

"Nat?"

I gasped, hauled another brick out of the way just as Dad moved a large bit of concrete. A tiny gap appeared in the rubble.

I leaned in close. "Charlie, are you all right?"

No reply. My heart thudded.

I pulled at more bricks. Beside me Mum and Dad and Jas worked furiously.

After a few seconds, the hole in the stones was large enough for me fit my hand through. As sirens sounded, faint, in the background, I reached inside.

"Charlie?" I shouted. "Can you see my hand?"

Still silence.

"Charlie?" Fear filled me, a sick terror worse than any I had ever known.

"Charlie?"

And then I felt Charlie's warm fingers linking through my own. Her whisper was barely audible.

"Don't let go," she said softly.

I leaned in close, my mouth right over the hole in the rubble. "I'm not letting go," I said. "I love you. I'm not ever letting go."

CHARLIE

Two hours had passed since Nat, his family, and the fire department had pulled me out of the rubble. Apart from a few cuts and bruises, I was remarkably unharmed. It had been scary with the brick all around me, the dust in my nostrils, and the air close and hot, but the doorframe I'd been standing under had kept the weight of the fall from crushing me, and Nat had been there so quickly and I'd been rescued so fast that the whole thing now felt like a bad dream.

All except for the touch of Nat's fingers and his soft whisper.

I'm not ever letting go.

Those words slid deliciously around my brain. Nat and I hadn't spoken about them since we'd been brought by an ambulance to the hospital. But something had shifted between us. I knew we were tight now, that no one could separate us.

For the first time since we'd been together, I truly felt safe, which was kind of crazy, since it was pretty obvious that the hospital staff would soon realize we were fugitives and send for the police. And although Riley had been arrested, that didn't mean we were in the clear yet.

Nat—who had clearly spent the past few hours running on adrenaline—was in worse shape than I was, almost collapsing as we walked to the ambulance. However, now that the antidote he'd taken had started to take hold, both his sight and his strength were returning, and I was hoping that soon we would be able to leave.

For now we sat side by side on a hospital gurney. A doctor had examined us both and Nat's mum had just left. She was in a total state, flitting between us and Jas, who was being checked over in another cubicle. Nat's dad was at the police station, making sure that Lucas and Parveen were given the antidote too. The hospital had notices up, urging anyone experiencing symptoms of the virus to contact their doctor or come to the ER for the cure. At least they had access to plenty of stock now that I'd told the hospital staff about the boxes stored at the Silvercross Institute.

Through the curtains we could see the TV over the nurses' station. The words BREAKING NEWS flashed on the screen, then a picture of Roman Riley. The newscaster was explaining in a hushed, horrified tone that a film had been broadcast at this evening's rally allegedly showing Riley in the act of murdering an unknown man.

At this Nat and I glanced at each other.

The newscaster went on, explaining that police were now examining the evidence, that the body of a man had been found at Riley's house, identified as the figure in the video, and that Riley was under arrest for his murder. A moment later he added that politicians and others were coming forward to speak out against Riley and—most shocking of all—that Riley himself had organized the development and release of both the Qilota virus and its antidote, which was currently being administered to the scores of people already believed to be showing signs of infection.

"It's all out in the open," I said, a huge wave of relief washing over me. "We did it. We showed people what Riley was really like. Nobody will vote for him now. Lucas and Parveen will be released. And we'll be cleared of everything."

Nat looked skeptical. "Hopefully," he said. "It depends what Riley admits to. If he doesn't confess to everything, some people will see him as a martyr." He pointed at the screen. "Look. There's Mr. Latimer."

NAT

Charlie and I watched the screen as Latimer announced he had a statement he wanted to read. His face was badly bruised, but despite the pain and exhaustion riven into his face, relief shone from his eyes.

"Earlier today I was beaten and my son and I were held captive by Riley for hours," Latimer explained calmly. "Worse, Riley was prepared to murder scores and risk the deaths of thousands of people in order to gain power. If it weren't for the actions of a few brave people who risked their lives to expose him, many of those under threat would have died."

"They'll have to release Lucas and Parveen now," Charlie whispered.

"Too many people stood by while Riley committed crime after crime, for far too long," Latimer went on. "He was allowed to make contact with terrorists who had developed illegal bio-weapons and, through his own secret army of young recruits, set about staging bomb blasts around the capital and beyond."

"See?" Charlie nudged me. "The truth's coming out now."

"Some of it will," I said with a sigh. "And some things will never be known."

CHARLIE

I looked at Nat. "We'll be okay, won't we?" I hesitated, wondering what "being okay" would mean for me. Nat had his family, but I belonged nowhere. The thought of going back to live with Uncle Brian and Aunt Gail appealed to me as little as the prospect of leaving London to stay in Aunt Karen's spare room again.

Nat squeezed my hand. "We'll be okay," he said. "I won't let us not be."

Soon after that the police came, and we were taken away, separately, for questioning. I told the officer who interviewed me everything that had happened.

Aunt Karen came to London, and we moved into a B and B. I didn't see Nat for a couple of days, but we spoke every few hours.

NAT

Information slowly trickled through: Riley had already been charged with murder, and now he and other leading EFA members, including Taylor, were charged with a whole range of terrorist-related crimes. They were all likely to go to prison for a long time. I had expected to feel more satisfied about that, but when I heard the news, all I could think was that no punishment, however severe, would bring back the last year, or all the lives that had been destroyed. I knew Charlie felt the same. Her mum was gone. Nothing could ever change that.

I guess we had the answer to the question we'd been asking ourselves about killing Riley. However badly we wanted him gone, his death wouldn't have given us what the hospital psycho-therapist called "closure." Only time and going on with life would do that.

Spider and his mum were brought in for questioning, though released without charge. I suppose that was fair. After all, Spider was young, and there was never any evidence that either he or his mum had actually carried out any violent acts. Others who almost certainly had—such as Saxon66, WhiteRaven, and many of the low-ranking EFA soldiers—just vanished. At least Lucas and Parveen were released and, much to my amazement, immediately started dating each other.

At the end of the week, the general election took place. Riley's Future Party did badly, while the party Latimer belonged to won a surprise majority of seats. Latimer's term as mayor was soon going to be over, and he was already being tapped as a leader for the future.

He's not perfect, but he's basically honest and well meaning— and hopefully smart enough not to screw things up too badly.

Like democracy itself, he's the least worst option.

The best chance we have.

ONE YEAR LATER

CHARLIE

So, the new government, with Latimer already in a senior position, has made a few radical moves and, thanks partly to the stability that's come now that Riley isn't planting bombs and stirring up riots, the economic situation is slightly better than it was.

It's like Nat said: some things have changed for the better; some things will never be known; and some people see Riley as a martyr in spite of everything he did.

There's a new extremist party building up support. It's led by Saxon66, though he's using his real name now. He's been clever about his past, distancing himself from the League of Iron and claiming the entire organization was manipulated by Riley and his team. To me and Nat it's obvious that this new party is a cover and that Saxon66's ambitions are as ugly and as violent as they always were. He's still getting more popular every day.

Riley and Taylor are in prison. I'm glad about that, of course, but it hasn't made as much difference as I thought it would. Killing them wouldn't have changed anything either. Nat was right about that, too. At least there's no way Riley can dream of a political career again.

After agonizing about it for weeks, when Uchi's funeral was finally held, I went along. Nat came with me so I didn't have to go alone. It was weird, saying good-bye to him. I even cried, though mostly because the funeral reminded me of Mum's. I didn't really mourn Uchi himself, though I know I'm still grieving the father I never had.

But don't get me wrong. I'm happier now than I've been for a long time. Nat and Jas and I had a few months off, but now we are back at school, redoing last year and about to take our finals. I'm not sure how well I'll do, but Nat's going to get all A's. He's supersmart, you know. As well as kind and brave and funny and gorgeous. And in love with me. As I am with him.

Nat's family is back together and all moved into a new house—a big one, with a room each for Nat, Jas, and Lucas. Nat's mum is at home all the time now, baking and fussing and spoiling everyone. Lucas has a job—and is madly into Parveen—and Aaron and Jas spend all their spare time together too. I go there a lot; it's a real home now: sunny and happy, just like Nat says it used to be.

As for me, Aunt Karen asked if I wanted to go to live with her in Leeds. And Brian and Gail stepped up too—once they knew I was innocent of the crimes I'd been accused of. They offered me a home again as well, which was nice of them.

But I know the score now. I told Uncle Brian I'd rather have my own place, so he's helping me rent an apartment. I live here alone. Yes, I'm young to do it. And, yes, sometimes it gets lonely.

But it suits me.

I come home and I can be at peace. I need this space. And, gradually, with Nat's help, I am building myself up, coming closer to trusting the world again. Because though it's easy to shut out trust and love, in the end those things are all that really matter. And with Nat by my side, they seem possible at last.

One thing's for sure. After everything I've been through, I know that life can be taken away in the blink of an eye. So now I'm trying to live every day well, with openness and hope.

To make every second count.